RELIQUIÆ TROTCOSIENSES

OR

THE GABIONS OF
THE LATE JONATHAN OLDBUCK ESQ.
OF MONKBARNS

WALTER SCOTT

RELIQUIÆ TROTCOSIENSES
OR
THE GABIONS OF
THE LATE JONATHAN OLDBUCK ESQ.
OF MONKBARNS

Edited by
Gerard Carruthers and Alison Lumsden
with an Introduction by
David Hewitt

EDINBURGH UNIVERSITY PRESS
in association with
THE ABBOTSFORD LIBRARY PROJECT TRUST

© The Abbotsford Library Project Trust 2004

Typeset in Linotronic Ehrhardt
by Speedspools, Edinburgh and
printed and bound by CPI Group (UK) Ltd
Croydon, CR0 4YY

ISBN 978 0 7 486 2072 2

A CIP record for this book is available from the British Library

FOREWORD

Reliquiae Trotcosienses, or The Gabions of the Late Jonathan Oldbuck Esq. of Monkbarns is one of the two major unpublished Scott manuscripts in Walter Scott's library at Abbotsford. Two extracts were published in the late nineteenth century, but this is the first time that it has been published in full. Late in life Scott signed a contract with his publisher, Robert Cadell, for the publication of *Reliquiae*, but it never appeared, presumably because Cadell, with the support of J. G. Lockhart, Scott's son-in-law and biographer, suppressed it on the grounds of its apparent incoherence. But that incoherence is superficial, and when the Abbotsford Library Project Trust was established in 1996 it commissioned Dr Gerard Carruthers (University of Glasgow) and Dr Alison Lumsden (University of Aberdeen) to edit Scott's highly idiosyncratic, but most intriguing fictionalised account of Abbotsford and its library. In due course it will sponsor the publication of the second manuscript, *Sylvae Abbotsfordienses*, Scott's account of the woods of Abbotsford and the creation of his estate.

The Abbotsford Library Project Trust is a charitable foundation, set up in 1996 for the purpose of conserving the library at Abbotsford, which has been vested in the Dean and Faculty of Advocates since 1956. An Advisory Committee is charged by the Trustees with administering the Trust, is chaired by the Keeper of the Advocates Library, and is directed by the Honorary Librarian, Professor Douglas Gifford of the University of Glasgow.

The library at Abbotsford is the physical embodiment of the learning of Sir Walter Scott, and in that is its primary importance. But it is also a superb collection, and is extraordinarily rich in popular literature, and literature relating to the supernatural and the occult. The primary objective of the Trust is the conservation of this inheritance, and so one of the first activities of the Trust was to undertake a check of the library contents, identifying missing volumes, unrecorded manuscript material and problems of condition and maintenance. This was undertaken between 1998–2002 by a team of postgraduates from the University of Glasgow under the direction of Professor Gifford. In addition the Trust has recently decided to develop a revised and more user-friendly catalogue, updating that originally created by George Huntly Gordon and published under the name of J. G. Cochrane in 1837, and making it available on-line. Other longer-term activities include the identification and study of an area hitherto unexplored, Scott's astonishing collection of popular pamphlets, tracts and chapbooks.

Whilst the primary consideration is conservation, access by scholars to the Library is facilitated and research into the Library, with the publication of results, is encouraged. However as there are no research facilities at Abbotsford all enquiries about the Abbotsford Library should be directed to:

Andrea Longson
Senior Librarian
Advocates Library
Parliament House
Edinburgh EH1 1RF
Tel: 0131 260 5637
Email: andrea.longson@advocates.org.uk

CONTENTS

Acknowledgements   ix

Introduction   xi

RELIQUIÆ TROTCOSIENSES   1

Note on the Text   73

Emendation List   82

Explanatory Notes   96

Glossary   139

ACKNOWLEDGEMENTS

Editing Scott requires more knowledge than any individual scholar now possesses, and the editors acknowledge, with great gratitude, the help and advice they have received from many sources: Mr Angus Stewart Q.C. and Mr Edgar Prais Q.C., respectively former Keeper and current Keeper of the Advocates Library, together with Ms Andrea Longson, and Ms Catherine Smith; Professor Douglas Gifford of the University of Glasgow, and Honorary Librarian of the Abbotsford Library; Professor Michael Bath, Dr Kenneth Simpson, and Dr Alison Thorne of the University of Strathclyde; Professor Ted Cowan, Dr Colin Kidd, and Professor R. P. H. Green of the University of Glasgow; Dr J. H. Alexander, Professor David Hewitt, Mr J. Derrick McClure, Dr Wayne Price, and Ms Ainsley McIntosh of the University of Aberdeen; Professor R. D. S. Jack, Professor James Laidlaw, and Mr Roy Pinkerton of the University of Edinburgh; Professor Peter Ainsworth of the University of Sheffield; Professor Peter Garside of Cardiff University; Professor Jane Millgate of the University of Toronto; Mr Tony Inglis of the University of Sussex; Dr Iain Gordon Brown and Dr Brian Hillyard of the National Library of Scotland; Professor Thomas Craik of the University of Durham; Ms Eileen Dickson of New College Library, Edinburgh; Ms Karin Brown of the Shakespeare Centre Library; Mr Hugh Cheape, Mr Trevor Cowie, and Mr Colin Wallace of the Museum of Scotland; the staff of the Music and Scottish Rooms of Edinburgh Public Library.

Finally a guide to Abbotsford, even if it is a fictionalised guide, must thank the people of Abbotsford, Dame Jean Maxwell-Scott and the curator, Mr Larry Furlong, for their most courteous support and endless helpfulness.

GERARD CARRUTHERS
ALISON LUMSDEN

ix

INTRODUCTION

Scott called this work *Reliquiae Trotcosienses or the Gabions of the Late Jonathan Oldbuck Esq. of Monkbarns*. It is a challenging title, for the Latin provokes the question 'what does this mean?', while the term *gabions* raises the question 'what are they?'. Both are good questions. The very first paragraph purports to address the problems, explaining that a famous author thinks that there is an advantage in giving a book an 'intelligible' title that tells the readers nothing, for no false expectations will be raised. But this answer, which does not answer the questions is, of course, a bam, a tease, a deferment of intelligibility.

In *Memoirs of the Life of Sir Walter Scott, Bart.*, J. G. Lockhart writes of 'the quaint caricature of the founder of the Abbotsford Museum', to be found in 'the inimitable portraiture of the Laird of Monkbarns'. He continues:

> The Descriptive Catalogue of that collection, which he began towards the close of his life, but, alas! never finished, is entitled *"Reliquiæ Trottcosianæ—or the Gabions of the late Jonathan Oldbuck, Esq.."*[1]

Mary Monica Maxwell Scott (Scott's great-granddaughter) published *Abbotsford: the Personal Relics and Antiquarian Treasures of Sir Walter Scott* in 1893, quoting liberally from *Reliquiae*. She edited and published extracts in *Harper's Monthly Magazine* in 1898 and in *The Nineteenth Century* in 1905. That *Reliquiae* was a description of the collections at Abbotsford had been established, and so it is no surprise that in 1972 (to choose but one example) W. E. K. Anderson in his superb edition of Scott's *Journal* talked of *Reliquiae* as 'a descriptive catalogue of the curiosities he owned'.[2]

The manuscript of *Reliquiae Trotcosienses or the Gabions of the Late Jonathan Oldbuck Esq. of Monkbarns* was relocated at Abbotsford in 1996 by Douglas Gifford of the University of Glasgow in his role as Honorary Librarian of the Abbotsford Library. The contents of the library are owned by the Faculty of Advocates which after the appointment of Professor Gifford accepted its responsibility both to conserve the contents of the Abbotsford Library and Museum, and to open them up to scholarly and intellectual enquiry. As part of the latter endeavour it invited Gerard Carruthers also of Glasgow and Alison Lumsden of the University of Aberdeen first to transcribe, and then to edit the manuscript for publication. The results of their work totally transform our idea of what this work is. A large part of the manuscript has never before been published, and this unknown material fundamentally qualifies the status of what has previously appeared. This is no simple catalogue. The work includes a sort of a catalogue, which describes some of the museum objects and the books at Abbotsford, but the literary, fictionalised context implies that the catalogue is merely one form of literary representation. The reader will notice that Lockhart got the title a bit wrong. His habit of making small mistakes is known to all who read Scott but is always unsettling: do we know, can we know, the Great Unknown? That is a constant issue in Scott studies because it is a constant issue in Scott's works particularly those like *The Gabions of Jonathan Oldbuck* which seem to proffer an answer. The title involves a series of literary jokes, which emphasise fictionality. *Reliquiae Trotcosienses*, the relics, the antiquities, or the antiquarian collections of Trotcosey, links the work at once to Scott's third novel, *The Antiquary* (1816). The estate of Monkbarns once formed part of the lands of the Abbey of Trotcosey, and the house, so we are told, may have been built by an abbot.[3] But the connection between Monkbarns and the abbot-monk is fanciful: it is a Polonial identification—and we also remember that Scott's house was called Abbotsford. The name of the abbey makes a joke about a monk's habit, a *trotcosey* being a modern (late eighteenth and early nineteenth century) cloak with a hood, the etymology of which might combine *trot* (like a horse) and *cosy* (meaning warm and snug). Contemporaneity and antiquity are confounded in one, invented, Latin appellation.

The term *Gabions* similarly pulls our literary legs. We are soon told:

> The meaning of the word *Gabion*, as it is used in the poem, is not to be sought for in any dictionary. It was of the venerable old gentleman Mr Ruthven's own coining, and it was well enough understood among his select friends, to mean nothing else but the miscellaneous curiosities in his closet humorously described in the poem. (6)

We are given a further definition: *Gabions* 'may be generally described as curiosities of small intrinsic value, whether rare books, antiquities, objects of the fine or of the useful arts' (6). It therefore appears to be an invented term (in fact it is not as I shall argue below), an invention which raises a question as to whether antiquaries make antiquities. The Oldbuck of *The Antiquary* is imposed upon: he triumphantly identifies the praetorian gate in a Roman camp supposedly situated on his land, imagines 'Agricola to have looked forth on the immense army of Caledonians, occupying the declivities of yon opposite hill', only to be deflated by Edie Ochiltree coming behind and saying: 'Prætorian here, Prætorian there, I mind the bigging o't'.[4] The Oldbuck of *The Gabions* may also have cheated himself:

INTRODUCTION xiii

It chanced at a sale of household goods by auction, that the present
proprietor and a gentleman of rank in the neighbourhood were
contending with emulation for possession of what they well knew
was, especially from its size, a gabion of great merit, ... when an old
woman, after a long look at the countenance first of the one bidder
and then at the other, at length ejaculated with a sigh at the extremity of the contention, "Heigh Sirs! the foundery wark must be sair
up in Edinburgh to see the great folk bidding that gate about a kail
pot." (32–33)

The definitions of the term *gabions* make irresistible a connection with
Autolycus, a 'snapper-up of unconsidered trifles', and raise questions
about the ownership and authenticity of antiquarian objects: are they
stolen from the past, stolen from their owners, or are the antiquaries
themselves cheated as Oldbuck is? Finally there is Jonathan Oldbuck, a
fictional character, and yet one in whom all readers recognise a version
of Scott satirically and ironically represented by the artist himself.

If the title and the words to be found in the title raise questions about
whether meaning is intrinsic or imputed, the form of *The Gabions* continues the questioning, for even if there is a catalogue, it appears within a
kind of fiction that spoofs a Waverley Novel. There are three different
bits (Introduction, Proem, and Preface) before we get to the main
matter, much like the opening of the novels in Scott's Magnum Opus,
the collected edition of his fiction which had begun publication in 1829.
The introduction consists of a quotation from Burns, just as there is on
the title page of the three series of *Tales of My Landlord*. The Proem is
nominally the work of a friend of Oldbuck, and he writes an essay on the
business of antiquarian collecting. Jonathan Oldbuck supposedly con-
tributes a Preface, in which he says that in his will he has made arrangements which will require his executors to publish the pages that follow.
This makes the main narrative of *Reliquiae* the creation of Oldbuck, but
the narrative itself professes to be the work of Oldbuck's friend—in
other words it is a fiction in which Oldbuck borrows the identity of
another man. The aping of the Waverley Novel structure continues into
the main 'story', *Reliquiae Trotcosienses* proper, for it has three parts,
mimicking the three-volume structure of the novels. The work may not
have been finished, but it *is* sufficiently complete for the parody to be
wholly apparent.

The content of the prefatory materials satirises the world of the
antiquary. The quotation from Burns comes from his poem 'On the
Late Captain Grose's Peregrinations thro' Scotland, collecting the
Antiquities of that Kingdom':

He had a fouth of auld nick nackets:
Rousty airn caps and jingling jackets,

Wad hald the Lothians three in tackets,
A towmont good;
And parritch-pats, and auld sault-backets,
Before the Flood.[5]

The mockery is overt. The 'author' of the Proem refers to his material as: 'the sweepings of the study of Mr Jonathan Oldbuck' (18), and the friend who appears in the Proem asks: 'What could we learn from your *Reliquiæ Trotcosienses* as you are pleased to call them, except that you have been led into foolish bargains by interested individuals who, every way inferior to yourself, continued to impose upon you by a little flattery and an appeal to your ruling foible of giving hard names and detailed histories to bits of trumpery; which they continued to make you purchase at an exorbitant rate' (20). And to bear out these judgments the nominal author of the Proem quotes extensively from *The Muses Threnodie*, a long, and almost unknown, poem about Perth's antiquities and the Ruthven Conspiracy, by Henry Adamson, first published in 1638. Ostensibly he does so purely to explain the word 'gabions'[6] but he also offers lengthy descriptions of Henry Adamson and his antiquarian friends. This picture of the Perth antiquaries 'amusing themselves by remarks on the scenery or the antiquarian remains' (13) emerges as absurd, but is also curiously reminiscent of Scott's own activities with his friends of the 'Blair-Adam Club', William Adam, William Clerk and Sir Adam Ferguson. Indeed, when he came to write an account of their yearly antiquarian excursions in 1834 William Adam almost seems to quote from *Reliquiae*[7] as if Scott's description of Henry Adamson and his associates had in fact been about himself and his friends. The in-jokes, games and disguises of the novels, it would seem, continue in this late text.

If the Proem suggests endless fictionality, Jonathan Oldbuck's Preface denies the fiction and takes us to 'reality'. He tells us that it is not the imaginary mansion-house of Trotcosey, or Trotcossey as it appears here, which is described because 'that venerable house, founded for monastic mortification, is not so well adapted for the convenience of a scholar and student as I would wish to have the credit of living in'. He has, therefore, 'borrowed from a friend, who chooses to have his name concealed, the description of a house in the south of Scotland built as much on the system of free will as heart could desire' (24). The house is manifestly Abbotsford, but although we apparently see Abbotsford and its collections emerge from the fictions we must still be ware: Abbotsford is never mentioned by name and when the dimensions of the unnamed mansion are given, we can only conclude that Scott had an extremely poor spatial understanding of the house he himself helped design and build, or that he is, again, reprising those fictional sidesteps and man-oeuvres which so characterised the Waverley novels.

The learned buffoonery of the Introduction and Proem of *Reliquiae Trotcosienses* mocks antiquarianism, and mocks the kind of activity in which Scott engaged as writer and collector; it offers a disparaging perspective on the description of Abbotsford and its collections. The opening sections thus set up a context which proposes that the three main parts both are, and are not about Scott and his antiquarian activities, both are and are not about Abbotsford, and are or are not to be taken seriously. Thus *Reliquiae Trotcosienses*, as it emerges from the manuscript at Abbotsford, is a curious text that offers a quasi-fictional account of Scott's home and collections which both describes Abbotsford and the artefacts which it contains, and simultaneously satirises the impulses of antiquarian collection.

What then can this new version of *Reliquiae Trotcosienses* add to our understanding of Scott's antiquarian pursuits and their relationship to his fiction? Some hint of the nature of this relationship may be discovered in those sections of *Reliquiae* where the narrator begins to describe the house and its antiquarian collections. The narrator sets out a plan by which he will first describe the house, and then move on to describe the 'gabions' which it contains. As he writes, however, he is unable to stick to this plan but frequently stops to describe an object and a story attached to it. At one point, for example, while describing the hall, he discusses a suit of armour and suggests that it may have belonged to John Cheney, a warrior of the Battle of Bosworth Field. He reprimands himself, however, reflecting that he is 'gliding into the true musing style of an antiquarian disposed in sailors' phrase to "spin a tough yarn" ' (34). In spite of this reprimand, however, such observations run throughout *Reliquiae*, every object mentioned prompting the telling of some tale inspired by it, the impulse for 'story' frequently usurping that of mere description or categorisation.

In his famous preface to *The Fortunes of Nigel*, Scott's classic statement on the Romantic impulse, he describes the author as 'bewitched', incapable of writing to any set plan, but overtaken by a demon on the feather of his pen who inhabits him with a creative impulse which overtakes his original designs.[8] It is a similar impulse which emerges as being at the heart of the relationship between Scott's writing and his antiquarian collections in *Reliquiae*. Repeatedly, Scott's 'gabions' emerge as springboards for story, starting points from which whole fictional worlds may be created. The Rob Roy artefacts, for example, were intimately involved in the imagining of *Rob Roy*, while the door of the tolbooth, acquired just before the writing of *The Heart of Mid-Lothian*, acted as one of many catalysts for that great epic novel. The pattern is repeated as Scott describes his collections in *Reliquiae*, artefacts, books and their illustrations repeatedly recalling echoes of his fiction.

This is not, however, to propose a direct correlation between artefact and fiction. The evidence of the *Reliquiae* suggests a more oblique relationship and one that is essentially Romantic in conception. The impulse of antiquarianism, as it flourished in the eighteenth century, was to suggest that an empirical truth about the past could be located by piecing together the artefacts which represented its material culture. Many did, and still do, identify this impulse as being that which inspired Scott and the Abbotsford collections. But Scott's books and exhibits were not pieces of a jig-saw puzzle that could be collected together to give a coherent version of the past, but, rather, *bricolage*—fragments which invite the construction of narratives around them. For the Author of Waverley the past can never be finally located, but only approached via complex, multiplex and elusive acts of narration; via fictions which, just as they seem to offer us some fixed referent for the personal and national histories which they recount, repeatedly subvert their own conclusions, offering up a myriad of possibilities and opening spaces for further narratives. The satire is not aimed at correcting human folly, but seems rather to suggest that the objects of collecting have no meaning without a human memory to invest them with significance: that surely is the point of the self-disparaging story in which the nominal author of *Reliquiae* says that 'like the man in the Arabian tale who forgot the charm "open sesame," my treasures are useless to me because the spell is lost' (45–46).

This view of both personal and collective history as endlessly elusive, knowable only through narrative constructions and deconstructions, is, of course, essentially a Romantic one. The framed narratives, multiple narrators and shifting points of reference which shape the Waverley novels are also characteristically Romantic. That Scott should have reprised these self-reflexive tropes in *Reliquiae Trotcosienses* is profoundly interesting. Here, in one of his last works, and when writing about his own antiquarian collections, it would have been easy for Scott to view his home and its contents more sentimentally. That Scott's impulse was, rather, to create the playful, complex and ambiguous text which emerges in the manuscript of *Reliquiae* confirms the evidence of the Waverley Novels; that it is only via such subversive paradigms that we can hope to approach the past.

The self-deprecation, and the self-mockery to be found in *Reliquiae Trotcosienses* is characteristic of Walter Scott: he never would take himself seriously. Yet in spite of his continuous dodging behind fictional trees and hiding behind fictional masks, there is an underlying personal urgency which, at least at first, is easy to overlook. In spite of protestations, *Reliquiae* really *is* a guide to Abbotsford House itself, and to what

Scott wanted to achieve by Abbotsford. At the beginning of Chapter 1 Oldbuck's friend explains that he cannot invite all his readers to visit his new mansion to which they had greatly contributed, but argues that it shows 'a becoming sense of obligation to make the outside of his house so far different from the ordinary style as to call for a second and more attentive gaze' (27). The outside is indeed 'Conundrum Castle' (27), a 'whimsical building' (28), but he makes a just claim when he says that the inside is so designed that the inhabitant is 'completely provided for in point of domestic accommodation' (27). One of the pleasures of *Reliquiae* is being guided round Abbotsford by its only begetter, and seeing which of the decorations, which of the historical objects, and which of the books interested him most (at least at the moment of talking). The very lack of discrimination—he seems as proud of the old panelling from Dunfermline Abbey as the new stained glass decorated with the arms of the different families of Scott, with the armour from Bosworth Field as the cuirasses from Waterloo, with modern pictures of antiquarian subjects as the portrait of his son, with his ballads and popular poems as his magnificent gift from the King, *L'Antiquité Expliquée*—the very lack of discrimination is not an intellectual fault, as some might have argued in the past, but indicative of an inclusiveness about the past: all is interesting, all is relevant, nothing can be discarded. The sense of different pasts coexisting with each other that comes from a visit to Abbotsford is strongly realised in his own enthusiastic description of his house and its contents. He applies his critical intelligence to the 'evidences' around him. His set of D'Urfey's *Wit and Mirth: or Pills to Purge Melancholy* is a made-up copy (50); songs labelled 'Scotch' are not necessarily Scottish (51); he wonders whether he should praise Allan Ramsay for writing words to traditional tunes and so preserving the tunes, or to complain that in doing so he made the original words obsolete (53). He is fascinated by the strange mind of George Sinclair, author of *Satans Invisible World Discovered*, but also of *The Hydrostaticks*, a book which among other things deals with the best way to drain coal seams, but finishes with 'a cock-and-a-bull story of a demon or fiend which haunted the house of one Gilbert Campbell, a weaver of Glenluce' (58). This is a narrative by a man who is a brilliant reader and interpreter of literature, and who can 'sell' his enthusiasms by turns of phrase which simultaneously enlighten and amuse: Thomas D'Urfey, for instance, 'enjoyed a certain sort of half-reputation' (51), and indeed he is frequently mentioned but never discussed in the writings of his contemporaries.

In spite of the literary joking the preliminary materials are equally revealing. Scott got the word *gabion* from Henry Adamson's poem *The Muses Threnodie*. Although Scott apparently goes along with James Cant in his 1774 edition of the poem when that latter says that the 'meaning of the word *Gabion*, as it is used in the poem, is not to be sought for in any dictionary', he must have responded to the warning implicit in 'as it is used in the poem'—this is not an invented *word*, but an invented *use*. As it is possible that he had once read the first edition (see Note on the Text, 79–80), he may have been aware that Adamson explains that Dr Ruthven referred to the ornaments of his cabin 'by a Catachrestick name'.[9] In other words *gabions* as used in the poem, and so in *Reliquiae*, is a term misused. As a historian Scott would have met the word in John Knox's *Historie of the Reformatioun of Religioun in Scotland*, and Robert Lindsay of Pitscottie's *History of Scotland*, and even if he did not find it in any dictionary he might well have realised that its proper meaning is, in the words of *The Dictionary of the Older Scottish Tongue*, a 'wicker basket filled with earth used in fortification'. If gabions, in one catachrestic sense, are worthless nothings, in another sense they become fragments shored against his ruin. A threnody is a song of lamentation, and in *The Muses Threnodie* the objects in George Ruthven's antiquarian collection lament the passing of their owner. The parts of the poem quoted by Scott treat of the 'inconstant course of all things here below' (10). In fact it is the transitoriness of human beings that is lamented—the antiquarian objects live on to lament, while writings create permanence on earth. Why does God, the 'prime and supreme cause of all' (11), permit wicked men to have 'both wealth and dignity'? Because real wealth consists of 'written riches'.

Scott uses Adamson's poem because it is about antiquarianism: it provides an analogue and perspective on Scott's own activities as sociable collector. But antiquarianism in *The Muses Threnodie* is, inevitably, seen in a seventeenth-century context, where the attempt to recover the past is seen as a way of defeating the transitoriness of human life. Scott was capable of writing in an elegiac way about the passing of time. The introductions to the six cantos of *Marmion* contemplate the past and the role of memory in recovering the past, but do so in a 'Romantic', psychological way: there is pleasure in pain. But in 1830–31 Scott knew he was facing his end, and the fingering of his sensibilities and sensitivities was no longer a comfort: he needed a theological perspective which assured him that in his writings, in his house, and in his collections, in all the ways in which he tried to recover the past, there was a future.

*

Scott suffered a stroke in February 1830. His rehabilitation took time. His publisher Robert Cadell, visiting him in September, hoped to persuade him to restrict his activity to writing introductions and the notes for the Magnum Opus 'without straining at more difficult tasks'. But, says Lockhart, he found his friend

> by no means disposed to adopt such views; and suggested very kindly, and ingeniously too, by way of *mezzo-termine*, that before entering upon any new novel, he should draw up a sort of *catalogue raisonnée* of the most curious articles in his library and museum. Sir Walter grasped at this, and began next morning to dictate to Laidlaw what he designed to publish in the usual novel shape, under the title of "Reliquiæ Trottcosienes, or the Gabions of Jonathan Oldbuck."[10]

A contract dated 6 September 1830 was agreed.[11] However, even although Cadell paid Scott £750, *Reliquiae Trotcosienses or the Gabions of the Late Jonathan Oldbuck Esq. of Monkbarns* was suppressed. The friend in the Proem who tries to wriggle out of being appointed Oldbuck's literary executor explains (*inter alia*) that

> I would far rather forgo the honour of crowning a long life of friendship with acts of regard which should continue after death than I would, for the paltry consideration of a legacy, bind myself to lend my aid to diminish your fair fame by lending my hand to a publication which, to say the least, would multiply your follies and blaze them through the world instead of lapping them in the friendly mantle of oblivion. (20)

There is no doubt that Lockhart and Cadell took this view when savagely editing *Tales of My Landlord* (fourth series), and suppressing the fifth series of *Tales of a Grandfather*,[12] *Reliquiae Trotcosienses*, Scott's letters on income tax and reform,[13] and *The Siege of Malta*. They seem to have thought that oblivion was preferable to the exhibition of what they thought was the obvious diminution of Scott's powers.

In the twenty-first century we are much less concerned with maintaining appearances; that Scott's faculties were impaired by three strokes during 1830–31 is not shameful, and there is no need to hide the evidence. The manuscript of *Reliquiae Trotcosienses* is often muddled, and the work comes to us now through repeated acts of reconstruction by Gerard Carruthers and Alison Lumsden. That they have been able to do this is because the underlying literary structure is manifest, even although in local areas it may be obscured. In *Redgauntlet* Darsie Latimer, writing up his Journal in arrears, claims that in spite of his illness and false imprisonment 'The rage of narration, my dear Alan . . . has not forsaken me'.[14] Similarly in Scott 'the rage of narration', a phrase which resonates with theories of Romantic art, and which also has significant psychological and neurological implications, does not seem to leave him. The editors have seen that and using their detailed and intimate knowledge of Scott's writing habits have been able to discern the essential structure of the *Gabions*.

The acts of reconstruction involve interpreting local evidence, as can be seen from an examination of the first paragraph.

> We are told by an author of the present day whose freinds ⟨enemies⟩ ↑ as well as enemies if ⟨he⟩ his ⟨stei⟩ ↓ either will confess that he is a voluminous if a that thier is a certain advantage in giving a book to the publick⟨ick⟩ under a title which conveys an intelligible meaning ⟨or⟩ ↑ nor ↓ leads the reader to injure of inducing him to form an an exaggerated idea of the amusement which he is destind to receive from the contents (f. 2)[15]

Spellings such as 'freinds', 'publick', and 'destind' are normal in Scott, common to many writers educated in the eighteenth century, and need no further comment. The substitution of one homophone for another, 'his' for 'he has', and 'thier' for 'there', is found in all Scott's holograph writings, but in this manuscript is more pronounced. The omission of words (such as 'writer' after 'voluminous') and the duplication of words, letters and syllables is also a feature of Scott's writing before his strokes, as is the evidence of his changing the shape of an utterance even while he writes ('or' giving place to 'nor' and thus raising the possibility that 'intelligible' ought to have been changed to 'unintelligible' in grammatical sympathy, or writing 'if a', and then starting a new construction, 'that thier'). All these habits are characteristic of Scott, but are more frequent here than in earlier work. What is different is, firstly, the deterioration in Scott's motor skills noticed by the editors (see pages 73–74), and, secondly, Scott's inability to recognise what he has written—he would previously have caught many (although not all) of such mistakes. But the 'rage of narration' and the instinctual syntactic patterning do not seem to have suffered essential damage. Indeed, one might take this further and argue that the evidence of impairment actually tells us about the workings of Scott's brain, because it is more apparent in this context than in any of the earlier works that first and foremost Scott hears words, rather than sees them. The sounds are in his head, but the neurological connections which translate those sounds into written words seem to have been dislocated. In the manuscript it is 'Audley' who asks is this 'a true thing or no', but the question is that of Audrey in *As You Like It*.[16]

The first twelve folios of the manuscript are in Scott's hand, with William Laidlaw taking over as amanuensis half way down folio 13 (page 16 of the present text, 'Antiquaries, at least. . .'). Scott resumes on folio 35 on a fresh piece of paper (page 27), with Laidlaw returning on folio 39 (page 30, 'There is also. . .'). Scott again resumes on folio 126 (page 70, 'Although the collection. . .'). The composition of these *Gabions*, was, then, more complicated than Lockhart suggests, but the transition from Scott to Laidlaw does not produce heightened coherence in either narration or syntax. Laidlaw was not editing Scott in an intelligent way as he took down Scott's words. The striking difference in intellectual coherency between the Proem and the *Reliquiae* proper must therefore been intentional: creating the intellectual cloudiness that will shock every reader who begins this work may not have been sensible, but it looks as though it was a deliberate outperforming of Jedidiah, and not a simple consequence of the mental deterioration of the author.

In a way that is truly extraordinary, the textual evidence supports the literary interpretation of the *Gabions*. If the literary jokes persuade us that the past, truth, reality, whichever might be the 'something' that the scholar and the creative artist strive to articulate, cannot be captured simply, in particular artefacts or in specific literary kinds, the writing itself is repeatedly prompting the reader of the manuscript to recognise that there is something beyond the language system, to which written language only approximates. The narrative structure and the sounds of the words have a kind of pre-existence in Scott's head; he struggles to translate what is inside into the code of written language, and in so doing suggests, without this being a conscious intention, that even language approximates to something other, is not truth in itself but a medium that proposes, suggests, hints, without ever coinciding with the imagined idea.

Reliquiae Trotcosienses, or the Gabions of the Late Jonathan Oldbuck Esq. of Monkbarns is never going to be a 'good read', but it is a remarkable Romantic text.[17]

DAVID HEWITT
Aberdeen 2003

NOTES

All manuscripts referred to are in the National Library of Scotland.

1   J. G. Lockhart, *Memoirs of the Life of Sir Walter Scott, Bart.*, 7 vols (Edinburgh, 1837–38), 4.12; cited below as Lockhart.
2   *The Journal of Sir Walter Scott*, ed. W. E. K. Anderson (Oxford, 1972), 660.
3   Walter Scott, *The Antiquary*, ed. David Hewitt, EEWN 3 (Edinburgh and New York, 1995), 20.
4   *The Antiquary*, 29–30.
5   Robert Burns, 'On the Late Captain Grose's Peregrinations thro' Scotland, collecting the Antiquities of that Kingdom' (1789), lines 31–36.
6   See text 5–6, and Explanatory Note to 1.3.
7   William Adam, *Blair Adam from 1733 to 1834: Remarks on the Blair-Adam Estate* (Scotland, 1834).

8   Walter Scott, *The Fortunes of Nigel*, ed. Frank Jordan, EEWN 13 (Edinburgh, 2004), 10.

9   H[enry] Adamson, *The Muses Threnodie, or, Mirthfull Mournings, on the death of Master Gall* (Edinburgh, 1638), 6. See also note to 1.3.

10 Lockhart, 7.218.

11 MS 745, f. 211.

12 This work was recently published for the first time as: Sir Walter Scott, *Tales of a Grandfather: The History of France* (Second Series), ed. William Baker and J. H. Alexander (DeKalb, 1996).

13 MSS 876 and 1000; P. D. Garside, 'Scott's Essay on Reform, 1830: New Information', *The Scott Newsletter*, 6 (Spring 1985), 7–14; 'Scott's Second "Letter on Reform": A Transcript of the Canterbury Manuscript', *The Scott Newsletter*, 7 (Winter 1985), 4–15; 'Scott's First "Letter on Reform": an Edited Version', *The Scott Newsletter*, 6 (Spring 1986), 2–14.

14 Walter Scott, *Redgauntlet*, ed. G. A. M. Wood with David Hewitt, EEWN 17 (Edinburgh and New York, 1997), 152.

15 In this transcription angle brackets ⟨⟩ are used to indicate deleted material and arrows ↑ ↓ to indicate material inserted.

16 Text, 70.7–8; *As You Like It*, 3.3.15. It might be argued that, in editing the text, however conservatively, to remove 'errors', the editors have destroyed evidence that is of interest. However, manuscript readings can be reconstructed by using the Emendation List, and a full transcription of the manuscript is available from the author of this Introduction.

17 I wish to acknowledge and thank Alison Lumsden for the generous help she afforded me in writing this introduction.

RELIQUIÆ TROTCOSIENSES

OR

THE GABIONS OF
THE LATE JONATHAN OLDBUCK ESQ.
OF MONKBARNS

INTRODUCTION

He had a fouth of auld nick nackets:
Rousty airn-caps and jingling jackets,
Wad hald the Lothians three in tackets,
    A towmont good;
And parritch-pats, and auld sault-backets,
    Before the Flood.

BURNS' *Verses to Captain Grose*

PROEM

WE ARE TOLD by an author of the present day whose friends as well as enemies, if he has either, will confess that he is a voluminous writer, that there is a certain advantage in giving a book to the public under a title which conveys an intelligible meaning, yet which does not lead the reader to injury by inducing him to form an exaggerated idea of the amusement which he is destined to receive from the contents. Our late excellent friend Jonathan Oldbuck Esq. of Monkbarns, to whose library the public is now indebted for the amusement which these sheets may impart, seems to have followed his contemporary's receipt to the utmost by using a word in the title which not only conveys no distinct meaning of the contents but which never did so, and is not more intelligible now than it would have been a century ago in the year 1700, except perhaps by a few antiquaries about the town of Perth, who would have understood what was meant by "Gall's gabions." These words, or the single word "gabions" taken by itself has, in the neighbourhood of that ancient burgh, a distinguished and precise signification of its own, which has we believe been adopted by a few at least of the celebrated book club which sends forth its reprints on a scale only second to the Roxburghe itself.

Sterne, for example, has given a synonym in what he has called a man's hobby-horse, some humour or fancy namely proper to his own and of which, though privately delighting in dressing and exercizing the hobby-horse aforesaid, he is impelled in sober sadness to admit—*Nos hæc mirum esse nihil.* Such could be said of the old medals, coins and curiosities of an antiquarian collection of a certain humorist of the seventeenth century who resided at Perth, and inspired his own taste into one or two fantastic but amiable persons like himself, whom he taught to distinguish the objects of his whimsical curiosity by the name of "gabions," which became so far a correct phrase as with those at least among Dr Ruthven's friends who sympathized with him in his love of their curiosities, and agreed in the cant name by which they were distinguished.

6 RELIQUIÆ TROTCOSIENSES

These friends were, firstly, Dr Ruthven himself who was distinguished by his professional knowledge and particularly by his good humour and activity. The dark and bloody catastrophe called the Gowrie Conspiracy which extended far and wide involved the whole family or clan named Ruthven and the Doctor possessed no amulet which could avert his share of it. But his peace was made when the king's resentment grew more temperate than at first. The next of these friends was John Gall younger, merchant in Perth. He was a young man of great acuteness, gentle manners and high accomplishments who died early in life and by his decease broke up the knot of friends which pursued their antiquarian studies, and of which Dr George Ruthven was the Caiaphas and is the subject of the first poem respecting them and their gabions.

The third of these associates was Henry Adamson, upon whose poetical exertions must rest the fame of Dr Ruthven and his friends, for it is believed that both parts of *The Muses Threnodie*, though one is in the name of Gall, are to be ascribed to Henry Adamson. Henry Adamson was educated for the pulpit, a good classical scholar and a good historical antiquary.

The first poem in the collection, the earliest in point of date, was by Mr Henry Adamson being "The Inventory of the GABIONS of Mr George Ruthven's Closet or Cabinet," which word is thus explained:

The meaning of the word *Gabion*, as it is used in the poem, is not to be sought for in any dictionary. It was of the venerable old gentleman Mr Ruthven's own coining, and it was well enough understood among his select friends, to mean nothing else but the miscellaneous curiosities in his closet humorously described in the poem.*

The following is a part of the poetry of the first part, which has been popularly but inaccurately called *Gall's Gabions* which will give a more distinct idea of the subjects of collections called gabions which may be generally described as curiosities of small intrinsic value, whether rare books, antiquities, objects of the fine or of the useful arts.

The recommendation of the celebrated William Drummond of Hawthornden succeeded in inducing the author Henry Adamson to send his poems on both subjects to the press under the title of *The Muses Threnodie or the Mirthful Mournings on the Death of*

* Introduction to *The Muses Threnodie* by James Cant, 1774, p. vi.

Mr Gall whose decease seems in a great measure to have broken up Mr Ruthven's little society. The recommendation of Hawthornden, though marked strongly by the pedantry of his age, seems also strongly imbued with its love of historical learning which may be seen from glancing it over:

To my worthy friend Mr HENRY ADAMSON

SIR,

These papers of your mournings on *Mr Gall*, appear unto me as *Alcibiades Seleni*, which ridiculously look with the faces of *Sphinges*, Chimæras, Centaurs on their outsides; but inwardlie contain rare artifice, and rich jewels of all sorts, for the delight and weal of man. They deservedly bear the word, *non intus ut extra.*

Your two champions, noble zanys (Buffoons) discover to us many of the antiquities of this country, more of your ancient town of Perth, setting down her situation, founders, her huge colosse or bridge, walls, fowses, aqueducts, fortifications, temples, monasteries and many other singularities. Happy hath *Perth* been in such a citizen, not so other towns of this kingdom, by want of so diligent a searcher and preserver of their fame from oblivion. Some Muses, neither to themselves nor to others, do good, nor delighting nor instructing. Yours perform both, and longer to conceal these, will be, to wrong your *Perth* of her due honours, who deserveth no less of you than that she should be thus blazoned and registrate to posterity, and to defraud yourself of a monument, which, after you have left this transitory world, shall keep your name and memory to aftertimes. This shall be preserved by the town of *Perth*, for her own sake first, and afterwards for yours; for to her it hath been no little glory, that she hath brought forth such a citizen, so eminent in love to her, so dear to the Muses.

W. D.

Edinburgh 12 July 1637.

"The above letter," says the introduction, "was the strongest motive with our author for allowing the poems to be printed which were published the next year and the year after (1639), he (Mr Henry Adamson), died much lamented."

As several passages in the following pages lead us to recall this ancient Threnodie to recollection we therefore shall begin by giving an accurate idea of both the sections or parts which

between them constitute *The Muses Threnodie*. The First Part is
entitled:

The Inventory of the GABIONS of
Mr George Ruthven's Closet or Cabinet

OF uncouth forms, and wondrous shapes,
Like peacocks, and like INDIAN apes;
Like leopards, and beasts spotted,
Of clubs curiously knotted;
Of wondrous workmanship and rare,
Like eagles flying in the air;
Like *Centaurs* Mermaids in the seas;
Like dolphins, and like honey bees;
Some carved in timber, some in stone,
Of the wonder of *Albion*;
Which this close cabin doth include,
Some portends evil, some presage good.
Ye gods assist, I think ye wrought them;
Your influences did conspire,
The comely cabin to attire.
   Neptune gave first his awfull *Trident*
And *Pan* the horns gave of a *Bident*.
Triton, his trumpet of a Buckie,
Propined to him, was large and luckie.
Mars gave the glistering sword and dagger,
Wherewith with some time he wont to swagger.
Cyclopean armour of *Achilles*,
Fair *Venus*, purtrayed by *Apelles*.
The valiant *Hector*'s weighty spear;
With which he fought the *Trojan* war.
The fatal sword and seven-fold shield
Of *Ajax* who could never yield.
Yea more the great *Herculean* club,
Bruised *Hydra* in the *Lerne* dub.
Hot *Vulcan* with his crooked heel,
Bestow'd on him a temper'd steel:
Cyclophes were the brethren Allans,
Who swore they swat more than six gallons,
In framing it upon that forge,
And tempering it for Mr *George*.
But Esculapius taught the lesson,
How he should use't in goodly fashion,

And bade extinguish't in his ale,
When that he thought it pure and stale.

The author proceeds near a page farther in an enumeration of the
same kind including an immense variety of centurae and curiously carved walking-sticks presented by *Mercury*:

And more this cabin to decore,
Of curious staffs he gave fourscore:
Of clubs and cudgels contortized,
Some plain works, others crisp and frized,
Like satyrs, dragons, flying fowls,
Like fishes, serpents, cats and owls,
Like winged horses, strange chimæras,
Like unicorns and fierce pantheras.
So livelike, that a man would doubt,
If art or nature brought them out,
The monstrous branched great harthorn,
Which on *Acteon*'s front was born,
On which did hang his velvet knapsea,
A scimitar cut like a hacksaw,
Great buckies, partans, toes of lapsters,
Oyster shells, ensigns for tapsters,
Gaudie beads and chrystal glasses.
Stones, and ornaments for lasses;
Garlands made of summer flowers,
Propined him by his paramours;
With many other precious thing,
Which all upon its branches swing:
So that it doth excell, and scorn,
The wealthy *Amalthean* horn.

Further of the Cabinet

In one nook stand Lochabrian axes,
And in another nook the glaxe is.
Here lies a turkass, and a hammer,
Here lies a Greek and Latin grammar:
Here lies a book they call the Dennet
Here lies the head of old Broun Kennett:
Here hangs an ancient Mantua bannet,
There hangs a robin and a jannet.
Upon a cord that's strangular,
A buffet-stool sexangular:

Whatever matter come athorter
Touch not, I pray, the iron morter:
His cougs, his dishes, and his caups,
A totum, and some bairnes taps;
A gaurdareilly and a whistle,
A trump, an Abercorne mussel;
His hats, his hoods, his bells, his bones,
His alley bowles, his curling stones;
The sacred games to celebrate,
Which to the gods are consecrate;
And more, this cabin to adorn,
Diana gave her hunting horn.

The account of the gabions of which it may be now not easy to
trace the humour, which the contemporaries of the poet discern
therein, is concluded by a species of apology as to an address by
the mourning poet to the lovers of learning; and having given
an account of the first of *The Muses Threnodie*, we ought to hold it
our duty to continue. Scandal, it seems, had spread a rumour that
instead of a harmless and playful satire, the author was about to
take up the melancholy history of the Gowrie Conspiracy. To this
he replies in the apology aforesaid which connects both parts of
his threnody, and states his actual purpose in writing them:

An Apology of the AUTHOR

LET none offend, though in my age I sing
Swanlike, some lawful joys youthead did bring:
My songs are mournings, which may clearly show
The inconstant course of all things here below;
Yet guided by that stedfast hand always,
Which, mid confusions great, the balance stays.
Thus *Heraclitus*-like, sometimes I mourn
At giddy fortunes reeling: Thence I turn
Like to *Democritus* in laughter wholly,
To see the inconstant changes of this folly.
Thus do I mourn, and laugh oft-times by course,
As giddy fortune reels from bad to worse:
For neither is the battle to the strong,
Nor doth unto the swift the race belong;
Nor bread to these whose wit should have commanding,
Nor riches to the men of understanding;
Nor fame doth to men of knowledge fall,

But chance (as would appear) doth order all:
So if the second causes we do view,
We shall find out a paradise most true.
  But, O thou prime and supreme cause of all,
Nothing to *Thee* by fortune doth befall!
For *Thou*, in midst of all these great confusions,
Foresees and works most permanent conclusions;
Keeping most comely order in variety,
And making concord in all contrarieties:
Thus doth it come to pass of thy benignity,
That wicked men possess both wealth and dignity:
But as it's written riches are preserved,
And for the ill of the owners are reserved;
And as a mighty load the bearer smothers,
So some to their own hurt rule over others,
Not looking to the account they needs must make,
Nor how their smiling fortune may turn back:
Whose honour like the sea doth ebb and flow,
Whose beauty hath the time to fade and grow:
Whose riches like the eagle hath their wings,
Now lighting down on earth to heaven then springs,
The body's summer *rose* is quickly gone,
By winter's stormy rage all over blowne,
To shew earth's constant changes; and that all
Which here on earth doth spring, must likewise fall:
Thrice happy he, that state who quickly findes,
Which is not shaken by earth's contrare windes:
Hence *solitary* and *poor* content I live,
Since better hap, blind fortune doth not give;
And like *Diogenes*, contemplate all
Within my *cabine*, that doth here befall;
Which gives me subject both to sing and mourn,
The times o'er past which never shall return:
I praise the worthy deeds of martial men,
And I do wish, the whole world may them ken,
I praise their virtues; no, their virtuous deeds
Do praise themselves,—and as most worthy seeds,
Beget like children; so commemoration
Begets them native sons, by imitation.
Native! more native than by blood descended,
Who, with their fame, their fortunes have dispended;
For what avails to paint a noble race,
In long descent of branches, if in face,

Like virtue doth not shine, and equal worth,
Ignoble deeds bely a noble birth;
Maugre all common thoughts, this true shall trie,
Virtue alone is true nobility:
If one most vicious in my line should be,
Five hundred years ago, what is't to me
Who virtuous am? What? Can it derogate
To my good name, or violate my state?
Or if ancestors brave shall me precede,
And I do prove the knave, what shall proceed
By their heroick virtues unto me,
Whose vicious life denies my progeny?
For lineage and forbears *Naso* said,
Are not call'd ours, nor what our selves not made.
To prove this paradox I dare be bold,
With judgement of the learned, but I hold
My pen, for all do know of old what's said,
And I Achilles like most noble rather,
Than I *Thercites*, he to be my father:
True generosity doth so esteem,
Though ignorance the contrare would maintain:
But *Momus* must needs carp, and *Misanthropos*
Be *Areopagita*-like *Scythropos*.
Scarce were these lines as yet come to the birth,
When some false flattering sycophant gave forth
Most foul expressions making rumour spread,
That citing of some ancient stories bred;
No small disgrace unto the present times,
Princes and persons of most ancient stems;
And that I write of purpose to attaint them,
I wish of this the wrong it might repent them.
For as the contrare's true, so I protest
I never had a purpose to infest
The meanest, far less those of better sort,
Where birth and grace do make a sweet consort.
Yea, more, I do protest, against my will,
These lines were reft from under my rude quill.
I never did intend so great a height,
That they should touch the press or come to light:
But now, sith more there is than my design,
I forced am my just defence to bring
'Gainst my traducers who maliciously
With baneful Envy's tooth have snatch'd at me.

The poet accordingly appeals to all readers of candid judgement, and competent to discern, exclaiming:

> If I your approbation do find,
> I care not these *Ardelio*'s catching wind.
> No other patrons do I seek but you,
> To take of this small piece a little view,
> And give just censure join'd with your protection.
> More worth than *Zoilus*' hate *Gnatho*'s affection;
> Your favours shall me shelter, and defend
> Against all envy's rage, to live to end;
> Trusting in God to keep my conscience pure,
> Whose favour most of all shall me secure.

The first part of the threnodie is thus completed and the reader is introduced to the second part of the same work, which is of a broader and more interesting character than the first part precented, and was constantly by much the more attractive of the two.

Henry Adamson is actually the speaker, though he assumes the character of Mr Ruthven. The poem is divided into nine cantos after the number of the muses. Each of these is dedicated to regret for the untimely death of Gall, and that their laments might be diversified, the poet calls on his remaining friends and his "gabions" to lament for the associate whom they have lost. The plan is to celebrate in each of these songs some happy expedition in the neighbourhood of Perth where the three friends, Adamson, Ruthven and Gall have met in the morning at Mr Ruthven's; and each of them accoutring himself with a gabion from the collection which was as chance and choice might determine, a bow and arrow, a bugle horn or one of those carved sticks of which the cabinet contained such a variety. Provided thus for courage and amusement, they had only to direct the excursion of the day to some part of the vicinity of Perth which is perhaps the most romantic in Scotland. There they contended together in blowing the bugle or drawing the bow, went a-fishing for the pearl which is found in some of the rivers, and amused themselves by remarks on the scenery or the antiquarian remains. Even brings them back to Perth, and so at their setting out in the morning, and their return on parting in the evening, to lament the loss of their accomplished companion Gall. The poetry is far from contemptible considered as such, and the antiquarian information refers to such interesting matter as makes us almost acquiesce in Hawthornden's praise of Perth's good fortune in having such over other towns of Scotland whose traditions have been embodied with less care. If there had been many such descriptive poems we might have opposed a national poem to Drayton's *Poly Olbion*.

It is worthy of remark that in the sixth department of the poem or muse, the matter of the Gowrie Conspiracy which was what slander reported as having offence in it, is more plainly alluded to than even in the apologetic passage already quoted. Mention is made of the king's visit to Perth and forgiveness being dispensed to the town for their share in that transaction. It is particularly said that Dr Ruthven was presented to James on that occasion and pardoned for his name having been called Ruthven, for that seems to have been the accession to the conspiracy of which he was guilty or accused. Gall or Adamson smiled at the story altogether, which was a prevailing opinion among the natives of Perth. Ruthven, called by his comrades Monseur, is serious in his own vindication. He was an old man as well as a prudent one, and the king's narrative had with him the same faith which James demanded for it. Indeed his credit stood much higher. James as a sure mode of obliterating the recollection of Gowrie's death while he was provost of the town of Perth, was to take the office of provost on himself. This was on the 15th April 1601 when King James himself visited the city and was openly declared provost at the cross. Our friend George Ruthven was declared a person in favour, healths were drank and glasses broken, and James himself, it seems, was inspired with a prophetic spirit:

> He gave his *Burges* oath, and did enroll
> With his own hand within the *Burges* Roll
> And *Guildrie Book* his dear and worthy name,

> Which extant with his own hand you may see:
> And, as inspired, he thus did prophecie,
> What will you say, if this shall come to hand,
> *Perth*'s Provost *London*'s Mayor shall command.

Sundry interpretations were assigned to this divine afflatus but none, says Ruthven, hit upon the true interpretation; and, to say the truth, if a Daniel had come to judgement it would have required no great penetration to discover the probability that he would [command London's Mayor], moreover and succeed to

Queen Elizabeth. Ruthven proceeds:

> Happy *King James the Sixth*, so I may say,
> For I a man most jovial was that day,
> I had good reason, when I kissed that hand,
> Which afterward all *Britain* did command.
> *Monseur*, said *Gall*, I swear you had good reason,
> So glad to be that day: for you of treason
> Assoilzied was, with your unhappy chief:
> Pray thee, good *Gall*, quod I, wake not my grief.
> Said *Gall*, *Monseur*, that point I will not touch,
> They'll tine their coals that burn you for a witch.
> A witch, good *Gall*, quod I, I will be sworn,
> Witchcraft's a thing that I could never learn;
> Yea, Mr *Gall*, I swear that I had rather
> Ten thousand chiefs been kill'd, or had my father,
> A King is *pater patriæ*, a chief
> Is often borne for all his kinnes mischief.
> And more, I know was neither heart, nor hand
> Did prosper, which that King did ere withstand.
> Therefore, good *Gall*, I prithee let that pass,
> That happy King knew well what man I was.
> While thus we talk, our boat draws near the shore,
> Our fellows all for joy begin to roar
> When they us see, and thus begin to bawl,
> Welcome, good *Monseur*, welcome Master *Gall*;
> Come, come a-land, and let us merry be,
> For as your boat most happily we did see,
> Incontinent we bargained to and fro,
> Some said, It was your barge, and some said, No:
> But we have gained the prize, and pleadges all,
> Therefore come, *Monseur*, come good Master *Gall*;
> And let us merry be, while these may last;
> Till all be spent we think to take no rest.
> And so it was, no sleep came on our head,
> Till fair *Aurora* left *Tithonus*' bed.
> Above all things so was good Gall's desire,
> Who of good company could never tire,
> Which, when I call to mind, it makes me cry,
> *Gall*, dearest *Gall*, what ailed thee to die?

END OF THE SIXTH MUSE OF *THE MUSES THRENODIE*

The reader has now almost a complete analysis of the *Mirthful Mourning* of Mr or Monseur Ruthven whose tomb is thus inscribed in a copy of verses prefaced to the Edition 1638:

Here lies his dust by whose most learned skill,
He and his *Perth* do live, and shall live still.
Of Mr *George Ruthven* the tears and mournings,
Amidst the giddy course of fortune's turnings,
Upon his dear friend's death Mr *John Gall*,
Where his rare ornaments bear a part, and wretched *Gabions* all.

Before leaving a subject on which we did not intend to dwell further than to explain what is meant by "gabions" in the technical language of our late friend Mr Oldbuck and other local antiquaries, we may express our surprize that an age which might be described as peculiarly bibliomaniacal has not been presented with an accurate edition of Mr Adamson's *Muses Threnodie*, with a text corrected from the best authorities and notes corrected and enlarged by the patient labours of some local antiquary of Perthshire. It would be, we will venture to say, one very rich and acceptable addition to the secret crypt in the book-case destined for the reception of the private publication or the rare edition of which only one hundred formed the original impression. This is the more extraordinary as the late well known gentleman (we mean he of Monkbarns), whom we now have to deplore with as many affecting interrogations as are in the *Mirthful Mourning* put to Mr Gall himself to the Hibernian tune "Arrah, why did you die." And we should have hoped that while drawing up sketches such as his own gabions might supply, he should have previously given a genuine and correct impression of Adamson's poems *The Muses Threnodie* which set the example to him of a similar publication. Trusting that the gap in Scottish literature will be supplied by some member of the Bannatyne Club, or some other gifted sage for whom, in the phrase of Cid Hamet Benengali, the adventure may be reward, we hold it our duty to inform the reader by tracing the very miscellaneous plan of these sheets, here presented to him by Mr Oldbuck's trustees, and published by his special directions, partly on the model of the threnodie with which the reader is already acquainted.

Antiquaries, at least if countrymen of Mr Oldbuck, unless men of remarkable steadiness in their persons, are apt to degenerate strangely into a very excursive mode of thinking and of writing, trivial in the sense and still more so in the mode of expression. One of those most important members was said to have announced the discoveries on which he founded his fame by proclaiming them with the voice of a herald through the whole domestic region, from the foot of the stairs to the entrance of the family bed-room at the top, and ejaculating the important fact "My Lady! My Lady! I have found a preen" (*anglice* a pin). Such are the discoveries we make when they happen to be actually real discoveries; for great is our sorrow to be obliged to announce not merely that all is not gold that glitters but neither is every thing a pin which seems to be such at first sight.

It usually happens that your antiquary, especially if he be a preses or censor or secretary, or one of the council of a learned body associated for their common pursuits, is a man of some consideration and, as they say, well to pass in the world. This is not indeed the necessary consequence of being a member of these societies which are seldom opulent enough, and, still more, seldom disposed, to relieve the circumstances of their members should they be so pleased; but it is, on the contrary, that they may have the satisfaction of saying as the talk of their members that the president is a man of certain quality, the secretary possessed of an easy estate, and all of them entitled to please themselves with respect to their pursuits. In this case the learned bodies act according to the principle ascribed by the novelist Fielding to servants in general who, although not very solicitous to vindicate the character of their masters or mistresses in respect to virtue or morality, are nevertheless extremely anxious to make good their claim to riches or quality, because such pretensions communicate a certain degree of respectability even to their servants who, on the contrary, do not rise in respectability although it proceeds that they are dependants upon persons of the purest virtue and the most strict morality. Now, the consequence is that the little preferment which such associations have to bestow, being conferred upon men who are well to live in the world, such are found certainly with some honourable exceptions, are seldom capable of that close and minute attention by which an antiquary must assert for himself the name and fame of a discoverer in his art. The experience of every reader must suggest to himself many a gentleman-like, grave pursuer of this science who cannot be justly termed a great wit or an ingenious discoverer.

Our friend Mr Oldbuck was no exception to this rule. The society to which he belonged was one which adopted no general plan to which any member might contribute his share and, by slow degrees, the whole stock of the society might form one general result to which the aid of all the members might in their turn contribute. In the case supposed, the number of hands employed would, in process of time, produce an effect upon the fruits of their joint labour; and many discoveries which might be beyond the sage enquiries of individuals might be successfully and clearly investigated by the researches of the whole body judiciously persevered in. Like ordinary mechanical processes, that of building for example. A number of common tradesmen who have no knowledge of architecture sufficing for the slightest scientific purpose will yet, if they will condescend to use stone and mortar, build an excellent and serviceable wall to a height at which the labour of a single individual or of the whole gang of masons acting individually and each on his own separate plan, would have produced no visible effect.

It is not ours however to direct the studies or researches of gentlemen, who as Dr Johnson said to the celebrated Jonas Hanway, put perhaps horses to their chariot and were elevated by a wealthy corporation to the dignity of one of its managers. It is sufficient for us while publishing what may be called the sweepings of the study of Mr Jonathan Oldbuck to indicate the cause why his writings are of so miscellaneous a nature.

It seems to be turned up in a principle natural to humanity, to wit that we are delighted not with the acquisition of knowledge as we are pleased with the chase while the game is afoot, but interested in it no longer when the pursuit is prolonged and becomes tedious. Hence Mr Oldbuck, although an acute, sharp man, was unwilling to bestow that attention which is required from every man who is expected to bring the subject of his investigation to a useful and systematic conclusion. Neither fame nor emolument exercised that species of constraint once he gained the leisure which his fortune put at his own uncontrolled command, and his private family fortune was to him what his plunder was to the Roman soldier when he made the memorable answer *Iret ubique perdidit Romam*. If you want a laborious essay on the subject in question go to one who must be bribed to labour by want of the means of life. I profess to enjoy learning but not to slave in the caverns of its mines.

Often too, the love of exercise or the principle of whim induced

our antiquary to immerse himself with experiments on that species of agricultural improvement which is generally practised by
country gentlemen. He was a friend of some distinguished stock-
breeders and must be occasionally distinguished among those
"whose talk was of oxen," although the preacher has asked with a
shrewd inuendo whether the thought of such could be of wisdom; but especially he was like some others of his acquaintance
attached to raising plantations of various sorts and seems to have
meditated an essay partly in defence of an article in the *Quarterly
Review*, which a gentleman had thought himself called upon to
reply to. Some opinions are also offered in this miscellany upon
dressing of ground or landscape gardening as that art is now
termed. These, like other dogmata are rather flitting insinuations
which have crossed the author's mind, than an attempt to follow
up an elaborate dissertation; but the larger part by far of this work
consists in the author's account of his own gabions or those of a
scientific and antiquarian friend.

Mr Oldbuck had often been attacked by his visitors in this
manner; "You say my dear sir, that the merit of all this collection
is chiefly that great part of this catalogue of battle-axes, broad-
swords, steel hats and matchlocks which seem to be bidding
adieu to time, consists in the individual weapons having been
possessed and used in the field of war by men of name who have
left fame behind them in those bloody paths where they gathered
their renown."

Friend. And how do you think, friend Oldbuck, if we had the
misfortune to lose you, we will be able to pronounce, let alone to
spell, these unbaptized names of Saxon and Celt to which you
appropriate the weapons in question? They will be, I am afraid,
forgotten before the time of your successors, so they will have but
anomalous hob-nails out of the commodity.

Mr Oldbuck replied with a long pinch, which is a great assistant to persons of his habits if they chance to be sharply pressed in
a dispute. Having gained such time for recollection as could be
decently expended in the act of taking snuff, he replied, "To
prevent the risk of that catastrophe which is infinitely to be de-
precated, no doubt I have written a note of the particulars which
render these memorials interesting and laid them up with the
general articles to which they have reference."

Friend. Ah! Jonathan, these old women's tales may do well

enough while you and I live who have seen Rob Roy and Sergeant More Cameron; but when you and I are gone and one or two old grey heads more besides, these memorials, as you call them, will be at the mercy of the cook-wench and unquestionably will singe many a good fat hen.

Mr Oldbuck's brown complection turned more dark upon this insinuation which it was easy to see went to the quick. "I will take care of that catastrophe," said he, "for I will make it the business of my trustees to bestow a part of the rents of Monkbarns upon printing and publishing with suitable decorations my catalogue of the curiosities of Monkbarns, and I shall take good care, Mr Patrick, to commit the charge to persons who shall be disposed in this as well as in other respects to carry my intentions fully into effect."

"No doubt, Mr Oldbuck," continued his friend, "the persons who were chosen for this purpose are very highly favoured and I will frankly own that I was greatly gratified by those hints by which you led me to suppose that I myself, if God please to prolong my life, might find myself one of the chosen number, but frankness is a jewel, my old friend, and I would far rather forgo the honour of crowning a long life of friendship with acts of regard which should continue after death than I would, for the paltry consideration of a legacy, bind myself to lend my aid to diminish your fair fame by lending my hand to a publication which, to say the least, would multiply your follies and blaze them through the world instead of lapping them in the friendly mantle of oblivion. What could we learn from your *Reliquiæ Trotcosienses*, as you are pleased to call them, except that you have been led into foolish bargains by interested individuals who, every way inferior to yourself, continued to impose upon you by a little flattery and an appeal to your ruling foible of giving hard names and detailed histories to bits of trumpery; which they continued to make you purchase at an exorbitant rate. If you expect me to perform the part of a manager in this farce I must tell you plainly, friend Oldbuck, that you are mistaken; I have too much respect for you to suffer myself to be mingled up with an affair from which, believe me, your memory is like to come off halting."

"Very well sir," said the senior. "I am glad we understand each other and I shall take care that the necessary alterations are made in the deed in order to secure myself against the possibility of wounding the feelings of a friend by leaving him a task which he was unwilling to discharge, or disappointing the regulations which I myself have made for disposing of a valuable property which has cost me considerable sums of money in a way which I think of consequence to historical information and the encouragement of good letters."

"This is speaking in plain terms indeed," said the other interlocutor (whom we shall call Crites), "and so the issue of it is that you break with an old friend because he is unwilling to join in proclaiming you after your death to have been an old fool during your whole lifetime."

"It is at least somewhat short of the rules of civility," said Mr Oldbuck, "to proclaim me such in my own life time to my own face and in my own parlour."

"I do you a kindness in such plain dealing," replied Crites. "Remember the fate of Woodward who brought every wit in London upon his head by his antiquarian essays."

"And do you not call him a learned man, Mr Crites?" said the antiquary.

"Perhaps so," replied the critic, "but his learning was as absurdly employed as the wisdom, good breeding, gentlemanlike feeling and other amiable qualities which Don Quixote employed in the course of his adventures, and which did not the less render him an ingenious but most ludicrous madman."

"O very well," retorted Mr Oldbuck. "We understand each other perfectly and as you have no inclination to be mixed up, as you call it, in my affairs *post mortem* so I can have no motive for choosing a trustee who would think himself degraded by undertaking the duty which my settlement imposes on him. Let us therefore speak no farther about the matter and leave me to order my will as I think proper."

The testator and his trustee parted upon these terms and we, who were to have had the assistance of Crites in the discharge of our duty, are now compelled either to see abandoned the execution of our friend's will in a matter particularly interesting to his feelings and which, in fact, occupied a great part of his own thoughts while alive, or by contradicting the opinion of Crites and producing in print that catalogue which was the subject of debate between them, fix perhaps a storm of ridicule upon the character of our old friend.

We have thought, however, that it was very possible to take a medium view of the subject, and although we are far from adhering to, and battling for, all the opinions of our deceased friend, of which we are far from maintaining the justice any more than maintaining the truth and sanctity of those relics to which Mr Oldbuck has stood commentator at considerable length, yet we conceive that the public may obtain amusement certainly, and at times information also, from studying the freaks and gambades into which an active and ingenious mind will, to use Sterne's celebrated metaphor, sometimes force his hobby-horse. Nor are we to suppose that such amusements of the mind are always to be considered as serious exertions of the understanding, or taken as proofs of the real intention or serious belief of the author. The thousand opinions which shoot through the gloom like exhalations glitter, dazzle and disappear, are no more frequently the spoil of the imagination than the grave conclusions of the understanding. And in receiving them the author is often found to have been amusing himself when he seems most serious. In such a case the promulgating such lucubrations can, in the thought of sensible readers, form no subject of accusation against the author. On the contrary, the essays will be prized in proportion to the entertainment which the readers may derive from that source. Mr Oldbuck's peculiar foibles will not be more widely blazoned than what they were before by his very title of the antiquary, and whether his character be rendered more or less estimable, we shall but do him more justice in giving way to the manner in which he himself chose to be represented to the public.

The taste of the reverse to what is usually termed pure and classical, and more probably entitled to the name of bizarre or whimsical, may, in many points, be nevertheless referred to principles which have a claim to be really founded upon taste, even when in fact they may be charged with extravagance. Now the ideas of men whose taste has been thought exact, even when compared to each other, has varied so much even in our own days from the extremity of ornate beauty to the pastoral extreme of absolute simplicity; from the correctness of classical models to the richness of the gothic and splendid vanity of the manorial style, that truly we hold it stuff of the conscience to suppress any opinion on account of its supposed incompatibility with the taste of the day. We live at a time when Sir Uvedale Price, a man of most unblemished taste, has been one to bring back the fashion of going up and down stairs in the open air, a fashion which Horace Walpole, also one of those judges whose decrees passed without challenge, had almost entirely tarnished. Such indeed and so great have been the vibrations of humble opinion in architecture, landscape and gardening as tempts us to believe that as nature in her own abundance seems disposed to distinguish itself by the most singular variety so she gives to those whom she may intrust with the power of imitating her works an unbounded variety of invention, and a collection of materials perpetually varied and equally inexhaustible. We think, therefore, there is room for hesitation before we take upon ourselves to draw the line with a strong and decided hand and to shut out anything which may be in itself beautiful, or denounce as incapable of entering into a composition anything which shall lay just claim to the character of taste. On the contrary, we are tempted to hold that every manner which is powerful enough to attract a class of followers is permissible, except one which shall be so unfortunate as to meet with no admirers, and in this manner we must certainly be of opinion that the ideas of Jonathan Oldbuck, though we are far from laying them down as incontrovertible, are still as worthy of explanation as those of more gifted men or persons who are more widely admitted in the capacity of authorities.

PREFACE BY
THE LATE JONATHAN OLDBUCK ESQ.
OF MONKBARNS L.L.D. AND A.S.S.

As I HAVE left charges to my friends who are to take the trouble of executing my *post mortem* arrangements, that these following sheets be printed and given to the public independently of their own opinion of their merit, I must of course be obliged in honour to assure the reader that what he may find of tediousness, of whimsy, or of obstinacy in the perusal is entirely owing to me, the said Jonathan Oldbuck, by whose positive bequest the trouble of perusal has been inflicted upon them; and these circumstances of my last will shall serve to shew that I, the aforesaid Jonathan Oldbuck, called an antiquary (that is the owner of a small trade in literature ridiculed by those who occupy shops in the same trade upon a grand and liberal scale) having thus freed my trustees from all blame which might be annexed to the task imposed upon them, I hope I shall not be esteemed exorbitant in exacting for myself any little merit if such should be due to the author of the *Reliquiæ*. Suum cuique is our Roman justice,* and so the last point of debtor and creditor which I have to settle with the world is finally, and I hope fairly arranged.

The following very loose remarks divide themselves naturally into four subjects each comprehending a principal department of that which has amused me during what I venture to term my course of antiquarian existence.

The first of these is my house or the place which I have chosen for the depository of my gabions, or if not copied from the mansion house of Trotcossey the reason is, that venerable house, founded for monastic mortification, is not so well adapted for the convenience of a scholar and student as I would wish to have the credit of living in. I have therefore borrowed from a friend, who chooses to have his name concealed, the description of a house in the south of Scotland built as much on the system of free will as heart could desire; for in the words of Coleridge the place is both in its elevation and interior, "a thing to dream of not to tell," and it

* Shakespeare.

24

is the opinion of many of the most respectable inhabitants of the neighbourhood that the halls themselves are haunted and the tenant bewitched. The elevation and interior therefore of ——————— ——————— will serve me in which to arrange my gabions and give a rude idea of my thoughts on domestic architecture so far as adapted to the pursuits of such a student as I am. I think it was Lucian—but I suffer far too much under the rheumatism to reach the book from the shelf—but I think it *is* Lucian who recommends to an orator to divide his speech into copartments according to the well-known chambers of the house which he inhabits. The division hath this advantage; that it is not easily forgotten when the speaker, like the man in the play, is involved in the distress of literally wanting words. With the walls and distribution of the house we will commence our description.

Secondly, I will invite my supposed guest to look at the interior of the library and notice a few books of rare occurrence or peculiar curiosity. The number, however, which require to be mentioned is not great, although I will not withhold the light of my magic lantern wherever I think it can convey illumination.

Thirdly, the gabions (of the meaning of which word I trust the reader has formed a perfect idea from the account given in the first part of this proem) will furnish ample materials for a third part of the *Reliquiæ* and in this part it is our purpose to include such snatches of real or feigned narrative as appear to illustrate various of the said gabions, which have their only merit from the names of the persons to whom they have belonged, or the account of the deeds in which they have been employed.

Fourthly and lastly, as we must suppose the reader well-nigh choked with the accumulated dust of centuries while he passes through the books and gabions, it is but fair that we take a look from the balconies of the castle or a walk in the gardens, or generally in the grounds in the neighbourhood, where the ingenious proprietor takes pride to himself for having planted on a small estate about four hundred Scottish acres of excellent wood, some of which is above twenty or twenty-one years of age.

Thus like a skilful traiteur I have shewn my bill of fair, taking care according to the custom in like cases, not to omit any topic of recommendation which my subject and its boundaries admit of. Your more favourable opinion or satirical expression are probably now of equal indifference to those whose fate he must share before these pages shall have been given to the public. Meantime the purpose and tendency of the following sheets are it is hoped so far explained as not to involve any reader farther than the persusal promises to confer upon him a corresponding share of instruction and amusement.

RELIQUIÆ TROTCOSIENSES
PART I
THE ANTIQUARIENSES

Chapter One

MY ANCIENT FRIEND and my regretted labourer in the vineyard of Scottish antiquities Jonathan Oldbuck Esquire has fixed
upon my unworthy premises to play the part of such a Conundrum Castle as I, or any other more whimsical man can recall,
dedicated as it is to hobbihorsical persons as a proper place of
deperdition for the gabions or curiosities by a collector aspiring to
fill the rank of *Ruthvenus Secundus*. Having myself been ambitious
of filling this character I may notice one or two peculiarities in
setting about my plan.

Firstly, it is the custom of others who are not moved by the
antiquary's peculiarities, to procure from an architect of emin-
ence first an *elevation* as it is called erected to the situation, and an
interior plan corresponding to the elevation. And thus the builder
may form an idea at once how his mansion will look from the
outside, and, on the other hand, how it will answer his internal
accommodation and display the gabions of its proprietor to the
best advantage. This is the more becoming if the proprietor
has occasion to testify his gratitude to the public in the way of
acknowledgement, for as he can hardly be expected to entertain
in the inside of his mansion all those gentle readers to whom he is
indebted for things, it at least shews a becoming sense of obligation to make the outside of his house so far different from the
ordinary style as to call for a second and more attentive gaze as he
passes by the mansion of an old friend. Not able, therefore, to
make the interior of his house a *shew-house*, such decorations may
be bestowed on the exterior as may attract the traveller's attention, and which may one day be celebrated in such Doric verses as
those below, that is if Scotland be a name some score of years
hence.

Dialogue between a Traveller and a Countryman

1.

What's that House? is it new or auld
An Abbot's tower or Baron's hauld?
There's mop-moss in and out a hundred fold.
    It has a fuer on
As if 'twere whirled fanning on the mold
    Of some mad mason.

2.

Country man: Aye Sir, 'twas a grand place anes,
But fancies change and all is . . .

The plan of the whimsical building is so miscellaneous that it requires some explanation to shew how, consulting the best artists, the builder found it possible to obtain a building so anonymous, yet the reader will not probably be surprized at hearing that he possessed the advantage of Mr Atkinson's experience (Saint John's Wood, London) for the whole interior arrangement of the little mansion, so that the inhabitant was as completely provided for in point of domestic commodation as the perfect skill of one of the best architects who ever drew a plan could devise for him. Thus he not only escaped the grosser errors of these amateur artists who have built their houses without stairs, and their rooms without windows, but also steered clear of some errors of a less gross nature, but which have the tendency to constitute a perpetual if not frittering blister: falling plaster (which for the most ordinary regular artist would not have fallen), or the vexation of a cross-light or an awkward communion, or the position of a door which opens unhappily, is sufficient to teaze a man a very little perhaps, but a little every day where he houses. The laying out of the apartments of the house was therefore regularly and most exactly provided, which will account for the good proportion of their rooms and their convenient communication with each other. When these great points were gained, Mr Blore, whose extensive acquaintance with gothic architecture exceeds perhaps that of any other artist living, had the kindness to assist the writer to erect towers, throw forward windows, and borrow external decorations proper to the manorial system of architecture; and these being added to the outside plan, afforded a variety of outline and depth of light and shade, or in professional phrase, gave a picturesque effect to the whole. It is true that the mixing of plans by different artists mingled with ideas of his own did not escape the error proper to such a mixture of plans by different gentlemen of taste and skill, and was not entirely doing fair play by any of the architects, and may be truly charged with bizarrerie. But my idea of such a villa as I have built is that it might be formed on such a plan as some of the novels which formed its principal foundation, where every style of composition is admitted save that which was decidedly tiresome. In other words I have a supreme contempt for the argument which is so often put in the words of Mr Dibdin's song:

> Lord! what will all the people say,
> Mr Mayor, Mr Mayor,

though it is repeatedly placed before me by well-meaning advisors. Men are apt not to be moved from their own opinions once formed and adopted. The reader will therefore scarce be surprized if he at first finds some opinions perhaps both offensive as well as singular from their novelty, since their author is far from recommending them to example, and will in general state his reasons why he preferred adopting them in his particular case. With this explanation the author will enter upon the account of his mansion, although by persons of a very correct judgement he may be censured as glorying in the anomalies which are in fact his shame.

The entrance opens into the hall through a stone porch flanked by two towers, and to compare small things with great, the plan of which has been taken from the entrance of Linlithgow palace by the ascent from the town of Linlithgow. The hall is of a good size, and so far as colouring, it is fitted up in a pleasing and uniform tone.

Its dimensions are as follows. The walls from the floor to the height of eight or ten feet are panelled with black oak, which was once the panelling of the pews belonging to the church of Dunfermline, celebrated as containing the sepulchre of the Scottish hero-monarch Robert Bruce. In this panelling are inserted many separate pieces of carved oak of the same kind. The south side of the hall is furnished with two or three bay windows which are filled with painted glass representing the arms of different families of the name of Scott. On these we can only observe that, from the Duke of Buccleuch to the smallest esquire of that numerous clan, the only circumstance proper to all of the name is that field *Or* upon a Band of that tincture. They almost all bear two stars or mullets and a crescent *Or*. But as this Band belongs to the Murdeston family in particular, the Scotts of Harden and the branches descended from that flourishing family carry the mullets and crescent *Azure* on the field *Or*.

The ceiling of the hall, about fourteen feet high, is vaulted and ribbed and decorated with a line of scutcheons going round both sides of the hall with the following inscription:

> These be the Coat Armouris, of ye Clannis, and Men of name, quha keepit the Scottish Marches, in ye days of auld. They were worthie in thair tyme and in thair defens God thaim defended.

The name of each clan is above its proper scutcheon. The number according to tradition is eighteen, which accordingly is the same as those depainted in this rank, but whether the number is quite correct or not is difficult to discern.

There is also a large range of shields running east and west along the top of the hall, understood to be the various escutcheons belonging to the proprietor, and it is worthy of notice that three of the eighteen ancestors are omitted, the escutcheons being filled with clouds with the inscription *premit nox alta*, by which it is intimated that the family estate of Rutherford of Hunthill having passed out of the family, no clue is left by which their alliances can be ascertained, and the party concerned has boldly avowed the fact. As there is no likelihood of any of his children standing for a canon of Strasburgh the damage is the less irreparable. Having said so much on the propriety of the introduction of this blazonry, upon principle we may add that in point of taste the splendid tinctures of heraldry mix in very pleasing correspondence with the dark brown colour of the carved oaken panelling, which time has brought to dark complexion, and on the side on which the windows admit the light through the storied house, bear a pleasing uniformity with the tint predominating in the whole.

We may also notice the ingenuity of a collector in the use which has been made of particular parts of the carved wood above mentioned. On the right side of the hall above mentioned, the close observer is aware of two species of presses formed of the same carved wood with the rest of the panelling. The visitor is rather astonished, and if a very strict Presbyterian, perhaps somewhat shocked to be informed that these presses aforesaid are, or rather were, the pulpit and precentor's or reader's desk of Mr Ebenezer Erskine, upon whom descended the new light which fructified so well that he became the venerable father of the Scottish Associated Synod of Non Jurors, otherwise termed the *Burgher Seceders*.

The author in question, or to speak more plainly, I myself, may safely disclaim all irreverence towards Master Ebenezer Erskine and his followers, many of whom I have myself known as personally very excellent men. The idea of pulpits and precentors' seats being *inter res sacros* is in no sense Presbyterian, although such an idea may prevail in the High Church of England, and is one of the doctrines with which *Jack* sometimes upbraids brother *Martin* as being directly derived from the heresies of Father Peter. But with Jack himself the maxim is held unchallengeable, that a church when there is no service in it is but a heap of stones and mortar; a pulpit, a collection of planks of a peculiar shape and thickness *de ceteris*. It is shrewdly suspected by many members of the Antiquarian Society that John Knox himself would not have approved of the heathenish veneration with which his own pulpit is preserved in certain buildings upon the mound in Edinburgh.

For my own part I cannot see any harm in applying Ebenezer Erskine's pulpit and precentor's box to the purpose of keeping a few bottles of wine cool in such boiling weather as the present, when we sometimes, for the sake of taking our meal *al fresco*, make use of the hall instead of our eating room. It is true the ancient panelling may upon such an occasion hear a Bacchanalian chorus, or a Jacobite rant with which it was not wont to be assaulted in the good days of Master Ebenezer, but we are not afraid of disturbing his good-natured spirit by such orgies. In fact, instead of repenting for the misapplication of these relics of Dunfermline, I cannot but suspect that I have hit upon the very purpose to which the Kirk Synod of Dunfermline would have desired their relics should be turned; and if the well known seat of repentance had come with the other holy remains, I will appeal to all who have once been infatuated with the mortar tub whether it is not, of all other parts of the church, that for which the builder is most sure to find occasion.

From the line formed by where the armories of the ancient border clans are depicted, to that where the carved panelling is terminated by a sort of festoon, extends a space about four feet high, not panelled with the Dunfermline wood, but with strong fir deals painted the colour of oak; it being thus easily penetrated with nails or hooks of iron the space is reserved for the occupation of such gabions the size and character of which have recommended them to that situation. They are generally arms both gothic and modern, offensive and defensive, together with the spoils of wild animals, mineralogical specimens, and other articles which will claim the dignity of more particular mention in the part of these idle pages which is dedicated to such gabions as appeared to be deserving of so much attention.

The massive chimney-piece of the hall with other works of the chisel which could be pointed out, does very great honour to the execution of Mr John Smith of Darnick, builder, who modelled the said chimney-piece in free stone from what is called the Abbot's Seat in the cloister of Melrose. The chimney or grate inserted under this ancient arch was the property of the celebrated and unfortunate James Sharp, created Primate of Scotland on the revival of prelacy after the Restoration, one of those unfortunate men whose character neither depends for moral good or bad upon what he himself said, thought or did or how he behaved, he being always judged of according to the principles espoused by the persons who pretended to be his judges, and his apparent weight being made to depend upon the justices of the scales in which for the time his character was balanced. A prelatist of the old Scottish church and a Presbyterian of the original tenor would give a very different interpretation of the emblems which can be traced upon his chimney-grate.

The motto is *Fides dona superat*, illustrating the figure of a muffled man, that is a ruffian having his cloak so closely wrapped about him as to disguise his features, who offers to bribe with meat a mastiff dog which sturdily rejects the temptation. On the hearth before the grate is placed a bronze pot of the largest size, which was found about twenty years since in the domain of Riddell in Roxburghshire. It happened that the housemaid, with an unnecessary prodigality of domestic labour, had bestowed several coatings of black-lead when burnishing the utensils of the kitchen with that substance. It chanced at a sale of household goods by auction, that the present proprietor and a gentleman of rank in the neighbourhood were contending with emulation for possession of what they well knew was, especially from its size, a gabion of great merit, to the no small surprise of the uninitiated of whom there were a considerable number present, when an old woman, after a long look at the countenance first of the one bidder and then at the other, at length ejaculated with a sigh at the extremity of the contention, "Heigh Sirs! the foundery wark* must be sair up in Edinburgh to see the great folk bidding that gate about a kail pot. A weel," she added with a tone of submission, "it is needless for me to wait for the frying pan if the kail pot is gaun to gae off for three guineas." With which declaration, the good lady left the auction.

The eastern end of this room is fashioned into two niches modelled in Paris plaister from those splendid sculptured niches which formerly held the saints and apostles of the Abbey of Melrose. Both these niches are each of them occupied by what is very rarely seen in Scotland, namely a complete suit of feudal steel armour. The one was designed for a French knight or one of the *gens de arm* of the middle ages. He must have been a man considerably under the middle size, and the suit of armour exhibits one peculiarity which will be interesting to those who are students of the learned Dr Meyrick. The shield, which is very rarely companion of the suit of armour, is not only present in this case, but secured in an unusual manner by nails with large screw-heads instead of being hung round the neck as was commonly the case during a career, the hands being left free, the right to manage the lance, and the left to guide his horse's bridle. To complete this suit of armour a lance is placed in the one hand exactly after the measure of one in Dr Meyrick's collection, and a drawn sword in the other which last is carved over with writing and contrived so as to keep a record of the days of the Catholic saints. In a word, it is a calendar to direct the good knight's devotions. The other suit of armour, which is also complete in all its parts, was said when it came into my possession to have belonged to a knight who took arms upon Richmond's side at the Field of Bosworth and died I think of his wounds there. If one was disposed to give him a name, in all certainty the size of his armour might claim that he was John Cheney, the biggest

* cast iron ware.

man of both armies on that memorable day. I venture to think—
for I feel myself gliding into the true musing style of an antiquarian disposed in sailors' phrase "to spin a tough yarn"—I incline, I
say, to think that the calendar placed in the hand of the little
French knight in the right-hand niche, originally belonged to the
gigantic warrior of Bosworth Field. I think it was withdrawn for
the purpose of supplying its place with a noble specimen of the
sword of the mountaineer of nearly six foot length and wielded
with both hands. This we must consider as the *gladius militis levis
armaturæ*, or the sword of the light-armed soldier. It was with such
weapons that men in old times fought at barriers, in passes, in the
natural straits of a mountainous country, or upon the breach of a
defended castle. They are often mentioned in the wars of Swit-
zerland and in the feuds of the Scottish clans. The Scottish poet
Barbour gives a most interesting account of the successful defence made by his hero against the Gaelic vassals of John of Lorn,
three of which armed with these dreadful weapons attacked the
monarch at once after the rout of Dalry and were all slain by him.
There are several other swords of the kind in my small collection
as I may afterwards call upon the reader to observe; but none of
them are like that placed in the grasp of the warrior of Bosworth
which, to speak truth, may match even with the tremendous blade
of the *Castle of Otranto*.

I am, however, infringing on my order, such as it is, in anticip-
ating what I have to say upon my gabions before going through the
account of the apartment. Before I quit the hall I ought to say that
the end which terminates it upon the west or left side of the
entrance is garnished with spoils from the immortal field of
Waterloo, when I collected them in person very shortly after that
immortal action. There are two or three cuirasses both of brass
and steel. The cuirass of the former metal has become very rare,
because they were at once knocked to pieces by the peasantry who
could sell the copper of which they were made at a certain rate for
so much a pound. The belts, swords and axes of the train are also
come to anchor on this whimsical place. There are caps of the Polish lancers, whose love of liberty never seems to have prevented
them from being the foremost to rivet their own chains and those
of any other country *cum multis aliis quæ nunc me scribere longum est.*

On the same end of the hall with the relics of Waterloo are
stationed in niches casts of two of the few saints whose images

Melrose continues to exhibit. These are the figures of St Peter and St Paul which still look down from the vennel walls of the chancel. The one apostle wears his keys, his usual emblem, as the other displays "that two handed engine" as Milton calls it, with which he is supposed to maintain the discipline of the Church and is said to have suffered his own martyrdom.

In the centre of this end of the hall occur two specimens in most beautiful preservation, which would be valuable to naturalists. The one which is uppermost is a noble pair of stag's horns found in a morass called Doorpool belonging to the estate of Abbots-rule. My friend the late Robert Shortreed, Esquire, to whom I was obliged for this curiosity, assured me that this creature was found at no great distance from the surface; a skeleton which must have stood nearly seven feet high and not a bone of which was a-wanting; and the remains of the elk preserved in the museum at Edinburgh were the only thing with which he could compare it. I have learned from one whose private regard I could fully estimate, however imperfectly I was able to comprehend the extent of his scientific knowledge, I have learned, I say, from Mr Humphrey Davy that it is sufficiently evident these remains have belonged to a creature now extinct, since its immense antlers are partly palmated like those of the elk and fallow deer, and partly branched like red deer.

Beneath the antlers of this species of stag are nailed those of the wild cattle of this country described by our old historians and of which we find the relics very often with the antlers of the stags of former days. It was said to have an unconquerable aversion to the human race, refusing to accept of food from them, pining to death if reduced to captivity and abhorring to feed even upon grass or branches which men had handled or trode upon. About a century since this very shy breed of animals was said to be pre-served as an object of chase at three places in Scotland; Drum-lanrig, Cumbernauld and Hamilton Palace. I have myself seen them long since at Drumlanrig and also at Chillingham, the seat of the Earl of Tankerville near the village of Wooler. The present relic is, I think, of many which I have seen and some which I possess, by far the largest one, excepting that in possession of his Grace the Duke of Buccleuch and Queensberry.

The size of the hall is thirty-three feet in length, thirteen in breadth and fourteen in height.

Chapter Two

Proceeding to notice the various apartments in the Babylon which we have built, the most important in point of size and in point of utility is certainly the library, and two apartments of different sizes are dedicated to this purpose, both in the eastern end of the house and communicating with each other, as each also has a separate entrance from the hall.

The largest of these two apartments is a proper library; that is a room dedicated to the preservation of books, whether of value or of curiosity only. It is accordingly a sizeable apartment which, oftener than I could wish, is dedicated to the purposes of ordinary society; but a house such as I was able to build in respect to extent had not space enough to afford a drawing-room exclusively fitted for the purpose of social reception. The library, therefore, is rather more than sixty feet long and eighteen feet broad. It is in general appearance a well-proportioned room but unless varied by some angles it would have the objection of wanting relief or, in the phrase of woman-kind, having the inestimable fault of wanting a flirting corner.

To remedy this defect an octagon is thrown out upon the northern side of the room, forming a recess of twelve and a half feet in length and eleven feet in depth which, corresponding to the purpose of the whole apartment, contains two bookpresses with doors of latticed wire which are for the purpose of containing books of small size and rarity which would otherwise be in danger of being lost or mislaid.

On the general system of locking up bookpresses my ideas coincide with those of the great Burke who, pointing to a collection so secured, declared it reminded him of Locke on the human understanding. The master of the house who uses this practice in general will hardly escape the churlish suspicion of a jealousy of his guests like that which should be indicated by adopting the St Giles's custom of chaining his knives and forks to the table, yet the wickedness or meanness of the times is so great that a man who bestows much expense upon a collection of what are termed the gems of a bibliomaniacal collection, without taking some pains to secure himself against depredation, especially where the public are admitted as visitors, will have some cause to repent his confidence. I have found it the best way to reserve five or six cases which can be locked at pleasure for security of such books as are peculiarly valuable, as well as those which are for any reason unfit to be exposed to the general class of readers.

The only precaution which I know besides the security afforded by lock and key is that which is afforded by a good double catalogue, one exhibiting the contents of every press in the library, and another affording an alphabetical catalogue according to the authors' names for reference upon occasion. I need not add that the proprietor must make himself intimately acquainted with the individual appearance of every book in his collection and with the shelf which it occupies. This is a species of knowledge which is very frequently acquired and to a surprising extent by individuals who are otherwise not properly speaking men of literary habits, and could not in common phrase be said to read books for the purpose of acquiring a knowledge of their contents.

Thus a gentleman very eminent in the trade, as it is called, that is in the professional art of bookselling, came to such a pitch of accuracy that he would suffer his eyes to be blinded while his guests or friends put into his hands at pleasure such books as they selected from a private press in his drawing room, and he could disseminate them one from an other, and affix the proper title to each, merely by examining them with his fingers, by the form and size of the volume. So much was this the case that some of the guests, having put into Mr C.'s hand some books which had not been in the cabinet alluded to, he said, not suspecting the trick which had been played him, "Well I must own that my memory is not so good as I thought—if those books which I now hold were any part of the contents of the cabinet referred to, I must own that I do not remember them." This corollary of his proposition was the more singular because the books were selected as being of the same size and external form with those which lived recorded in the memory of the gentleman I allude to. I own such an exertion, of the truth of which I am perfectly satisfied, seems to me even more extraordinary than that of a shepherd who, lying upon the hills among his flock for many weeks, makes himself master of the personal appearance of every sheep which it contains and knows them individually from each other as an officer becomes acquainted with the faces of his regiment.

To return to the description of the library, the roof which is on a level with that of the hall is fourteen feet high and the presses rise to the height of eleven feet leaving a space of three feet accordingly intervening between the top of the shelves and the ceiling. This was a subject of great anxiety to me as I wished to save room, which circumstances rendered precious; in one point of view the difference of three foot in height all around a room of sixty feet long and eighteen broad would have added greatly to my accommodation; but on the other hand, a bulky and somewhat ancient person climbing up to a height to pull a book down from a shelf thirteen feet high at least, augurs an operation somewhat too like the situation of the "seaboy upon the dizzy shroud" to be entirely inviting to my imagination. Indeed, being one of those who are inclined to hold that good people are valuable as well as scarce, I have remarked with anxiety that the lives of such worthies as myself are very often embittered at least, if not closed, by the consequence of a fall from the steps of their own library staircase. I recollect with a degree of horror, for I cannot suppose a more excellent and valuable man in a more precarious situation, a late eminent literary character progressing around the shelves of his own library not on "the unsteady footing of a spar" but by the still more precarious assistance of the shelves themselves, alongst which he transported himself by the assistance of his feet and hands, sidling along, now at a great height from the ground, now making astounding exertions to possess himself of the volume he wanted and consulting it with the assistance of a single hand in the lofty situation which he had obtained: and where, as a fall would most likely have been death, he was weighing his valuable life against five minutes gained in ascertaining the precise date of some obscure event in history which perhaps in fact never happened at all.

In these days I myself have no books at least worthy of being mentioned as a collection, and I remember wasting my invention in endeavouring to devise a mode of placing my volumes in an order easily attainable for the purpose of consultation. But I never could hit upon an idea more likely to answer, than supposing a librarian who, like Talus in Spenser, should be in point of constitution, "an yron man made of yron molde;" a creature without hopes, views, wishes, or studies of his own, yet completely devoted to assist mine; an unequalled clerk with fingers never weary, possessing that invaluable local knowledge by which I might, availing myself of his properties, command my volumes like the dishes at King Oberon's banquet, to draw near and to retire with a wish. I have never been able to find for myself a mechanical aid of such a passive description, and the alternative to which I am reduced, is a working room or study in addition to my library where I keep around me dictionaries and other books of reference or those which my immediate studies may require me to consult.

This private apartment is fourteen feet high like the others, twenty feet long, by about fourteen broad, and a space of about seven feet in height to the ceiling of the apartment affords room for a small gallery filled up with oaken shelves, running around three sides of the study, composed of oaken plank, and resting upon small projecting beams also of oak. The gallery and its contents are accessible by a small stair about three feet in breadth, which gains room to ascend in the south-west angle of the room and runs in front of the books, leaving such a narrow passage as is sometimes found in the front of the balustrades of old convents and more certainly designed for the use of the lay brethren alone. After going round to the south-east angle of the room, a small door incloses at pleasure a staircase which leads about seven paces higher and by another private entrance reaches the bed-room story of the house, and lands in the proprietor's dressing room. The inhabitant of the study, therefore, if desirous of arranging his dress, or unwilling to be surprised by visitants, may make his retreat unobserved by means of this gallery and the private stair-case which combine the proprietor's study with his bed-room, a facility which he sometimes found extremely convenient. The library properly so called contains only one picture, that of a young Hussar officer nearly related to the proprietor and which is worthy of attention in as far as it is painted by the eminent historical artist William Allan.

Chapter Three

The apartments of the house designed for the reception of friends are, like the fortunes of the possessor, formed upon a limited scale. There is, in the first place, a small drawing room twenty-four feet by eighteen and in height the same as the others. When this apartment is inadequate to the accommodation of our fine friends, especially if a dancing or musical party be in contemplation, we have only to open the door of communication between the drawing room and the library in order to obtain all the space necessary for the purpose at least in a poor man's house.

The furniture of the drawing room is from Baldock's, consists of curious antique ebony chairs, and an antique cabinet bought at Linlithgow, and said to have been a part of the furniture which found its way out of the palace when burnt the night after the Battle of Falkirk, and verifying by its appearance its alleged antiquity. There are also in the drawing room some paintings, chiefly relations of the family, which we may perhaps afterwards notice. The contents of the Linlithgow cabinet may likewise be afterwards inserted in their proper place among my gabions.

The drawing room, besides one door into the entrance hall and another into the library, has a third serving for a communication with a small room which for want of a better name has acquired that of the armoury. It is not a sitting apartment, and chiefly is useful in insulating the drawing room and interposing a proper space between that apartment and the eating room to which we are now approaching. This armoury consists of two parts; the one of which looking southward is about ten feet in length and filled with water-coloured portraits of members of the family, and the other portion of the armoury being twenty-five feet in length is entirely hung round with gabions, some of which may be hereafter more particularly commemorated. The two portions of the armoury communicate by an archway shut occasionally by an oaken wicket of gothic carving, and when this is shut, a private passage is open from the southern part of the armoury for the purpose of communication between the drawing room and the household apartments below stairs.

The said southern armoury also affords entrance to a species of conservatory where the plants it must be owned, do not thrive particularly well. Proceeding outwards by means of a passage between the lower end of the dining room and the back of the conservatory aforesaid, and communicating with a stair-case which leads upwards to the bedroom story and downwards in the words of the old Scottish song "to the regions below which men are forbidden to see," we come to the eating room, a quiet apartment, not very large indeed, yet ample enough for all the common wants or purposes of a private family, and capable of accommodating a larger company of guests than the proprietor would often desire to see together. The dimensions of this room are thirty feet in length including a considerable bow, and seventeen feet in breadth. The ceiling is not above twelve feet in height, and is apparently supported by ribs of carved oak which nevertheless are only stucco, but so ingeniously moulded and painted, and tied with ornaments and escutcheons at the places where they cross each other, that they can hardly be distinguished from the more permanent material, so that what we have said respecting the roof of the library may be held as repeated in this place. The eating room contains a beautiful dining table of Scottish oak capable of dining thirty people and clouded in the most beautiful style. It is indeed an especial proof of the power attained in the present day of working the produce of our native forests into furniture as elegant as is to be seen anywhere in England, though manufactured out of West Indian or South American timber. I believe that my deceased friend Mr Bullock, who had his manufactory in Hanover Square opening into Oxford Road, was the first person who employed our native wood in this useful and elegant manner, and I am indebted to his memory for the extreme pains which he bestowed in toiling his own fine genius to meet my wild wishes respecting my furniture at this place, and furnishing me with various ideas which I must myself have been altogether unable to have suggested. I must say on this subject that the taste which before Mr Bullock's appearance influenced the manufactory of our domestic furniture had in it an extremity of poverty and *meschinnerie*. It seemed to be the object of the artist not to unite beauty of contour with apparent strength and solidity, but on the contrary to employ on the article the least possible degree of material of which it is possible the article should consist. Thus the legs of tables, of chairs, and the supporters of furniture in general, assumed a pyramidical form tapering downwards to the resting point which was invariably the narrowest point of the supporting limb. The outline thus wanted both grace and solidity, and it required an accomplished person like Mr Bullock (who was bred an artist) to discard a false taste which had become general and introduce into modern upholstery the fine forms of ancient art as well as the rich and varied tints which might be derived from the patriotic use of our own native wood.

In this last subject, and *apropos* of the set of dining tables which are valuable in the eyes for more reasons than one; they were made of particular parts of the growth of certain very old oaks which had grown for ages and at length became stag-headed and half dead in the place where they originally grew in the old and noble park of Drumlanrig Castle. These trees were put up for sale by the late Duke of Queensberry, along with the more thriving plantations growing upon the domain around the castle, but no one being aware of the curious and valuable purposes to which they might be applied, they fetched low prices, and some of those who became purchasers did not even think it worth their while to cut them down, since the payment must have been a necessary consequence of concluding their bargain.

So stood the matter when the Duke of Queensberry concluded an unusually long life and the bargain, so far as it respected these old trees, became in every respect forfeited. Mr Bullock, who chanced to be in attendance at Drumlanrig about the time, had no hesitation in giving it as his opinion that the progress of time had exactly brought these ancient oaks to the point of perfection when their wood would make most beautiful furniture. The set of tables designed for the mansion we are talking of was accordingly taken in hand, and turned out most beautifully, so that it was one of the singular chances, that accident in this world will often bring a commodity to that purpose for which it is best adapted. A case made also by Bullock out of the root of elm and yew trees which had been grown in the woods of Rokeby completed the set of tables, forming a convenient and useful receptacle for the separate leaves of the original when they were not wanted for use.

Of the rest of the furniture of this eating room there is nothing remarkable to say until we are called upon to state the peculiarities of the gabions which it contains, a name which may be also conferred upon such paintings as hang upon the walls, since the proprietor has no judgement at all to enable him to prize them as paintings, and merely possesses them as having some hobbi-horsical point of recommendation which has little or nothing to do with the opinion of a man who is so much of a connoisseur as really entitles him to form a judgement on paintings.

A breakfasting parlour, or a *boudoir* if the word be more fashionable, serves the woman-kind of the family for making their tea or sewing their samplers, and it contains a rich harvest of art by modern masters of the brush which fell into my hands in the following manner, and therefore, upon the maxim laid down may be chiefly considered as *paintings*, that is to say as works of merit rather than *gabions* of which I have possessed myself merely from the attraction of some whim of my own. Several artists some years ago united to club their talents for the sake of sending forth a work of copperplates which should be called the *Provincial Antiquities of Scotland*. Whether the plan was too vague and extensive, or whether it had no combining quality to give the whole unity and precision, it is not for me to say, but the talents and names engaged ought to have found for it a warmer reception from the public. The artists furnished, agreeable to a certain engagement, a number of valuable drawings which were engraved, and being applied to for the purpose of writing suitable descriptions, I did what I thought was my best in that capacity and have the pleasure to think that, if I failed, it was not for want of sufficient labour bestowed on my subject. Although the gentlemen concerned were desirous to make a suitable pecuniary recompense to the humble prose-man who had furnished the descriptions, I did not think it proper for me to accept of such remunerations and the gentlemen concerned put an end to our amiable debate by making a gift in my favour of the original paintings and drawings, coloured and plain, to which I had contributed descriptions; a recompense far too valuable for my deserts, and which few circumstances could have inspired me with the self denial necessary for refusing.

These valuable relics by Turner, by Calcote, Williams, Blore and other artists of the first name, form the furniture of the *boudoir* in which they are hung, and bear witness of the deserved fame of the artists engaged in the enterprize. Since the work has been announced as finished, the demands of the public have considerably increased and will one day I hope be carried as high as its deserts seem to warrant.

Having thus exhibited the bounds prescribed by society to those who shew their houses, or to those whom they are shewn, I flatter myself that there is no occasion for going into further details. The sunk story of the house contains cellarage, servants-hall, kitchen accommodations, laundry and bedrooms for servants on a scale suitable, as the advertisements say, for the use of a genteel family.

The bedroom story contains a number of apartments for the accommodation of members of the family or guests. The attic story also contains a number of sleeping places for upper servants and others, for occasional anglers or muirfowl shooters, or in case of need, for amateur tourists warranted not to walk in their sleep, as the place being rather high, the ascents and descents require a stranger to have all his senses about him. All this is easily understood and imagined, nor will I proceed any further with my description in compassion for the curiosity of those who are edified even by that part of a strange house which can be supplied by peeping through a key-hole, whom I would hereby refer to the animadversions of the fair authoress of *Destiny*.

PART II

𝔄rticle 𝔒ne

THE LIBRARY, as it is properly the most useful and instructive part of the collection which the pains of the antiquary has heaped together, may justly claim a distinction immediately after the apartments of the house which take precedence of it for the same reason that we crack the shell of a nut before approaching the kernel. Upon the system of utility there are many books the real use of which in an antiquarian collection is so small as to reduce them to the class of mere gabions, volumes that is which are not prized for the knowledge they contain but for some peculiarity which renders the individual copy unique, like that of the celebrated Boccaccio. When we are informed that a facsimile of the celebrated Boccaccio which sold for several hundred pounds at the Roxburghe sale can be obtained for about five pounds and is inappreciably different from the original or true copy only in the position of a single letter, we are tempted to suppose that the curiosity is scarce worthy of the difference, and that in no respect is more valuable than a broken earthen jar, or an old broad-sword or javelin corroded with rust and disowned by the modern fashion of the fight but valued because supposed to have belonged to the Roman Agricola or the Caledonian Galgacus. Both are curious gabions upon George Ruthven's system and neither are anything more. I do not intend to make a proper classification of such printed gabions as I may happen to be possessed of, nor do I think that Jonathan Oldbuck of Monkbarns, although classed as an antiquary, is at all fit to unveil the treasures that would charm a bibliomaniac, or discover to the uninitiated the peculiar charms on which the value of the books contained in such a collection are likely to be reposed. I have indeed some books worthy of being marked with a twice or even thrice repeated "R.," but —tell it not in Gath—I have often forgot the peculiarity which adds a choice flavour to the particular article and like the man in the Arabian tale who forgot the charm of "open sesame," my treasures are useless to me because the spell is lost which is the mainspring that gives access to them. I shall not therefore dip deep into this species of lore nor attempt to shew my knowledge where it is possible I might only display my ignorance.

In branches of information I would only say that my collection of historical works relating to England and Scotland, in particular, is extensive and valuable. For example, few English chronicles are sought for in vain in the foresaid catalogue, as indeed is the reprint by the London booksellers, although, owing to the giddiness of the public, it has somewhat failed in a commercial point of view, rendering it inexcusable for any person terming himself a collector to want any of these valuable and inexpensive reprints.

Nothing indeed is more apt to exhale a sigh than to recollect the catalogues we have seen and the prices of former days. When I, for example, recollect that a catalogue of black-letter books, chiefly beautiful copies of romances of chivalry and chronicles, was offered to me as curator of a library of considerable extent and renown, I am ready to gnaw my nails to the quick when I remember what a lot might have been purchased for less than thirty pounds which would now be esteemed a price not more than sufficient for one of their number.

One of our curators however was a man of sense, taste and interest, and from all these considerations his opinion had great weight when he objected to fitting up our shelves upon the principle of Don Quixote's collection which perished in the celebrated *auto de fé* held in his native village. My proposition however was not entirely rejected, but being admitted only to the extent of five or six pounds, it served to purchase a valuable sample of the works which were rejected. They were in fact the sweepings or remainder of the curious works of the collection of books formerly belonging to the celebrated Messirs Foulis, printers of Glasgow.

In like manner Mr Lamb, vicar of Norham, in his reprint of the curious and contemporary poem of "Flodden Field" (afterwards reprinted by Henry Weber) has a lamentation over the fate of the poor student who is unable to pay five or six pounds for the *Chronicles* of Holinshed and others which, to the affliction of the vicar, were currently purchased at the above prices by the late John Kemble Esquire, of Covent Garden Theatre.

There is however a way of viewing the subject which we are convinced would have pleased the philanthropic clergyman. Mr Kemble, when the changeful taste of the public and the unjust persecution of a party of the town had injured a fortune honourably acquired in his own art, was, in his latter days, respectably provided for by the sale of the collection which he had formed by the assistance of considerable wealth added to great scholarship, liberality and knowledge of the subject which made, if I may so call it, the theme of his collection. This curious library, being the most complete collection respecting the history of the British drama, was purchased by the Duke of Devonshire at a price so liberal as to insure to the original proprietor the comforts to which no one who knew him would have endured to think of his wanting while they secured to the halls of Chatsworth the possession of a literary treasure worthy of the House of Cavendish. To this great collection I had the honour of contributing a copy which my friend Mr Kemble had never even seen of Settle's *Emperor of Morocco* which was the first play illustrated with prints; a circumstance so offensive even to the great John Dryden, that as his biographer Johnson observed, his invidious criticism is thereby greatly envenomed. It was given to me by the Rev. Henry White of Litchfield, and I question if there is another fair copy in the world except that in the collection which was founded by John Kemble now the property of the Duke of Devonshire. I mention this because a collector founds his fame not only upon the treasures which he possesses but upon those curiosities which have passed from him; and I need scarce add that I am happy that anything which has been mine should have changed its destination so much to the better.

To begin with my remarks on those books which still remain with me, I must take notice that the foot or lower line of the library is occupied by a handsome cabinet also wrought out of Rokeby yew, and serving to sustain an exact cast of *the Poet*, Shakespeare, taken by Mr Bullock from his monument at Stratford-upon-Avon, which having been erected by the players who were his companions in life, and being an image executed under their eyes was like to be the most exact resemblance. The interior of this cabinet contains some manuscripts of various value and a small unadorned snuff-box made of the wood of the celebrated mulberry tree, and inclosing the following inscription commemorative of the kind friend who bestowed it on the present proprietor:

> *This Box, made out of the wood of Shakespeare's Mulberry Tree, originally the property of David Garrick & by him given to Rob. Bensley Esqr is presented to ———— by Mr Thornhill who acquired it by Inheritance.*

This remnant of the Jubilee bears the arms of Shakespeare cut upon the lid and must be considered no doubt as a gabion of great curiosity.

Two presses on the left hand of Shakespeare's cabinet contain a miscellaneous collection of dramatic pieces being modern reprints, as well as a great number also in the small quarto form which was the original mode of publishing plays or dramatic works at the Restoration, and for several years afterwards. There is a complete collection of Congreve's original pieces, and those of Dryden might, without much trouble, be also rendered perfect. One circumstance is to be remarked: that the original offences quoted by Collier against the profanity and indecency of the stage are completely verified by these copies of the *editiones principes*, although even the second edition in its alterations from the first shews sometimes bungling attempts at repentance and atonement indicating shame at least, if not repentance. It is believed that a small sum of money and some time bestowed in rummaging the London catalogues and some trouble bestowed in collation and comparison of editions would make this branch of the collection an interesting and curious one.

Article Two

L'Antiquité Expliquée, Et Représentée En Figures Par Dom Bernard de Montfaucon. This superb copy of a most copious and valuable work upon antiquities, the merit of which is acknowledged in all parts of the world, is here bound in fifteen volumes scarlet morocco, in which capacity it reached the author as a present from his most excellent majesty, King George the Fourth of happy memory. Anyone who had the honour of having access to the person of that most excellent prince will pardon the vanity which records his kindness in this, and other instances of his goodness, which the object may record with grateful feelings:

'Twas meant for merit though it fell on me.

Article Three

Libri Classici cum Notis Variorum. This edition, comprehending all the approved classics with many other Latin authors with notes of the best commentators, extended to one hundred and thirty-nine volumes and splendidly bound, was the gift of Archibald Constable and Company by way of handseling the new library of the author. Between author and bookseller, such as they went in our day, this exchange of courtesy might be compared to that of Lintot thrusting upon Pope a well-printed edition of Horace, and requesting the bard amuse himself by turning an ode during the time of a temporary stop upon the ride to Oxford. It must be owned that the splendid gift was bestowed in the present instance on an author not very worthy of it:

> For long, enamoured of a barbarous age
> A faithless truant to the Classic page;
> Long have I loved to list the barbarous chime
> Of minstrel harps, and spell the Gothic rhime.

I am however as sensible of the value of the treasure thus kindly put within my reach as I was when my old friend Dr Adams used to say, "I might be a good scholar if I would give competent application." At any rate, the superb present of Messirs Constable and Company set me up in the line of classical antiquities, and I may add to it a few volumes of old favourites, companions of my early studies which I did not care to part with, although their place was amply supplied by this complete edition.

Article Four

Ballads and Popular Poems. My reader will probably expect that I should mention some curiosities in a line which may be thought peculiarly my own. Accordingly, on opening a locked press, in the first book which occurs I find, among an immense quantity of such gear, as many as six volumes of stall copies of popular ballads and tales. The memorandum on the first leaf of these which here follows appears to have been written as far back as eighteen hundred and ten, which throws back the date of the collection for at least thirty years more:

> This little collection of stall tracts and ballads was formed by me when a boy from the baskets of the travelling pedlars. Untill put into its present decent binding it had such charms for the servants that it was repeatedly and with difficulty rescued from their clutches. It contains most of the pieces that were popular about 30 years since and I dare say many that could not now be purchased for any price.
>
> 1810   W.S.

To this the author has great reason to adhere, especially when he considers how very soon tracts become extinct after having been degraded into stall editions. In fact the very circumstance which seems to insure their antiquity is a sign of its being actually a modern edition. This may be gathered when we consider that the lower sort of printers became stocked in the beginning of last century with all those black-letter types which were originally used by the artists of a superior degree, which is the reason that the most ordinary tracts, dying speeches, ballads and the like were now performed with the black-letter, which had served the highest purposes of the trade from Miller and Chapman down perhaps as low as Watson. However, this desultory and juvenile collection comprehends many articles, and some not to be elsewhere found, indispensable to a history of Scottish printing.

Article Five

This is *Wit and Mirth: Or PILLS to Purge Melancholy; Being A Collection of the best Merry Ballads and Songs, Old and New. Fitted to all Humours, having each their proper Tune for either Voice, or Instrument: Most of the Songs being new Set.* It is announced as being in five volumes, the fourth edition. It is however a made-up copy from more editions than one, though very tall and uniform, and, affording accordingly at a time when I became proprietor of it, a remarkable instance of the insane degree in which the passion of a bibliomaniac sometimes exerts itself. This appears from these documents which are bound up with the volume:

> The foregoing documents relate to the attempt to *condiddle* as it has been fondly and technically termed this copy of D'Urfey's Pills out of McLauchlan's Saleroom by whom it was disposed of with other stock

of Mr Blackwood winter & spring 1819. The thief or condiddler took a check of conscience or rather was seized with an apprehension of disclosure which occasioned his returning the volume of which I became the purchaser.

The auctioneer's advertisement is long and too tedious to insert. The letter of the unfortunate *condiddler* is peculiar and worthy of insertion.

Copy of the letter received with D'Urfey's *Pills*:

What demon possessed the mind of him who is now supplicating for forgiveness for the offence committed in carrying off these volumes he cannot pretend to say, unless it was the mean & pithy desire of the perusal; but he humbly prays that he may be forgiven for this almost atrocious act of delibrate robbery.—In hopes that Mr McLachlan will take no more notice of the subject and thanking him for so kind and private an intercession he ventures to Sign himself A (once mean but now he hopes reclaimed) Villain.—

It is impossible to pass this document without remarking how often men in a moral point of view are willing to exchange popular opinion and self-applause for an equivalent as inadequate as a mess of pottage compared with the birthright of Esau; but trusting that the reformation announced by the ill-fated young man has continued lasting, we have only to observe that the editor of D'Urfey's *Pills*, as his collection is elegantly styled, enjoyed a certain sort of half-reputation and was half celebrated, half ridiculed, by Addison, Dryden, and other Augustan writers in the end of the seventeenth century. He was a musician as well as a poet, and his collection goes to prove two curious facts. First, that a variety of songs falsely called Scotch, for example, "'Twas within a mile of Edinburgh Town," and others besides, were in fact songs composed for the players and they are sung. Secondly, that it is a mistake to suppose that the English had no style of national music although they have suffered it to drop almost out of memory. A great number of tunes which are of genuine English origin are to be found along with the words in the *Pills to Purge Melancholy*. The tunes of the *Beggar's Opera*—so many of them at least as are of English origin—go to establish the same proposition, and shew in what a short time a nation may be bullied into the abandonment of its own music.

Article Six

John Bell's *Ballads and Tales*. These ditties, of which there are some repetitions, are another copy of reprints of the ancient stall editions of popular vaudevilles. The north of England had at all times afforded a rich collection of such minstrel poetry, and Mr John Bell, who if not now deceased has at least relinquished his trade as a printer and bookseller, had a good deal of the spirit dear to a person who is desirious of keeping the old minstrelsy afloat in the popular recollection. He called his own little shop upon the Quay, Newcastle, his Patmos and his anchorite's cell. The author of "Chevy Chase" was his *Magnus Apollo* and even his children were an evident token of his love of minstrelsy being christened by such chivalrous names as Spearman Bell, Percy Bell, &c. while nothing could more gratify the father than the opportunity of preserving and reprinting some of the lines which had of yore cheered the heart or inflamed the passions of Canny Newcastle. When Mr Bell retired from business I became purchaser of his stock of trade, which of course added no less than forty or fifty volumes, valuable as reprints, to the contents of the locked press already mentioned.

Article Seven

I find in the same crypt a collection contained in three volumes of *Old Ballads, Corrected from the best and most Ancient copies extant, with* INTRODUCTIONS Historical and Critical. This collection is the more curious as, excepting perhaps the commentary of Addison upon "Chevy Chase," it contains the very first attempt to treat the productions of the popular or suburban muse or, in other words, ballad poetry, as the proper subject of criticism. The public even in the time of *The Spectator* was so far from esteeming "Chevy Chase" as worthy of the pains which Addison bestowed upon it, that he was ridiculed out of the intention of pointing out in the same manner the simple beauties of "The Babes of the Wood" to which modern poets have so often and so justly paid a tribute of panegyric. The editor of the octavo collection therefore, is the first who boldly avowed the taste for ballad poetry already sanctioned by Addison, and since his time correctly and elegantly illustrated by Bishop Percy, who has been equally careful in editing the fragments of it which remained, and curious in applying the same to the illustration of Shakespeare and other legitimate subjects requiring annotation. It cannot be said that the editor of these three volumes has in any degree either the taste, learning, or powers of composition of Bishop Percy, but he has exerted himself, and man can do no more.

Article Eight

The Tea-Table Miscellany or a Collection of Choice Songs Scots and English, in four volumes, by Allan Ramsay. This copy of a memorable work has for me the recommendation contained in the following inscription and which the reader will hardly fail to appreciate:

> This copy of Allan Ramsays Tea table miscellany belonged to my Grandfather Robert Scott & I was taught Hardyknute out of it by heart before I could read the ballad myself. Automathes which I have also & Josephus's Wars of the Jews added to this collection made my library. Hardyknute was the first poem I ever learned—the last I shall ever forget.

Having spoken of the *Tea-Table Miscellany* in some remarks upon Scottish ballad poetry not long since published, I shall here only observe that it is difficult to say whether the poetry of Scotland is most obliged to Allan's memory for making verses with his ingenious young friends to known tunes, or should complain of him for rendering those originally intended for them no longer applicable, and consequently contributing his share to render them obsolete. The question is perhaps somewhat difficult of decision.

Article Nine

The three thin volumes which next occur are necessarily extremely rare, being a collection of Scottish minstrelsy collected by the Reverend Gustavus Von Bergmann, Pastor of Ruien in Livonia,

printed at his own private press and never published. The account
of it is contained in the following note:

> The Collector of these very curious popular songs was a Livonian
> Clergyman who had no more types than would set up one sheet of
> his work at a time which he afterwards wrought off with his own
> hands. They are therefore singularly rare as the impression could
> not but be extremely small & as besides they were never designed
> for sale. I owe this copy to the friendship of Mr Robert Jamieson.

These curious volumes were lately for some weeks in possession of Dr Bowering, who has made some translations
shewing the tone and simplicity of the Lithuanian relics. Mr
Jamieson, to whom I was obliged for this work above mentioned, is the collector and editor of a collection of *Popular
Ballads and Songs, from Tradition, Manuscripts, and Scarce Editions;
with translations of similar pieces from the Ancient Danish Language,
and a few originals by the editor.*

One remarkable discovery was originally made by Mr Jamieson
and has not perhaps been sufficiently attended to by the *Docti
utriusque linguæ.* It is the near resemblance betwixt the ballads of
the Scottish and those of the Danish people, a resemblance so
very accurate as almost to realise the conclusion that the bards of
one nation have merely been the copiers of the other. To this
subject we shall have occasion to recur when on the subject of
Danish minstrelsy. Before quitting the press with which we are
now engaged, we may observe that it contains almost the whole of
Joseph Ritson's publications, a most industrious and zealous antiquary, although unfortunately he suffered himself to be led far
astray in some of the idle debates in which antiquaries are apt to
involve themselves farther than discretion warrants. Some of
poor Mr Ritson's publications which have been lost by fire are
here preserved, which makes the collection interesting.

PART III

Article One

TURNING NORTH-WEST-WARD from the depository of old ballad poetry, the visitor turns into the projecting space which is described as an octagon, having space for two book-presses, both of which are furnished with doors and locks on the plan of those last mentioned. We must here notice that though it would be a vain attempt to arrange a library of ordinary size according to its subjects, yet this can be attained in a small degree when the subjects treated of are handled in volumes of the same size, and resembling each other in height and taking their place on the same shelf. Thus the press whose contents were last treated of chiefly was occupied by popular poetry, and that to which we now turn being that on the right of the octagon, is occupied by two sets of books of both of which I have been a collector.

The first of these presses may be distinguished by the general term of "demonology," a subject upon which as strange and wild nonsense has been published as that of any other which is known to me, but I do not mean to abuse the patience of the reader by going very deep into this subject.

Article Two

The present is a very curious edition of a very curious book being *Satans Invisible World Discovered; or*, A choice Collection of Modern Relations, proving evidently against the *Saducees* and *Atheists* of this present Age, that there are *Devils, Spirits, Witches*, and *Apparitions*, from Authentick Records, authentic Attestations of Famous Witnesses, and undoubted Veracity. To all which is added, That Marvellous History of *Major Weir*, and his Sister: With two Relations of Apparitions at *Edinburgh*. By Mr *George Sinclair*, late Professor of Philosophy, in the Colledge of *Glasgow*.

Mr George Sinclair is in respect of demonology the same sort of author that the Reverend Mr Glanville is in England. Both were persons of some sense, and learned education, which gives them a degree of credit; their powers of understanding—as the vulgar supposed that circumstance perfectly extrinsic—were nevertheless essential to the credit of a witness. Thus in *Much Ado About Nothing*, Benedict says while overhearing Leonato and Don Pedro, "I should think this a gull, but that the white bearded fellow speaks it. Knavery cannot sure hide itself in such reverence." In the same manner the vulgar are naturally of opinion that they have rendered their tale undubitable when they have said that their authority was an Oxford scholar. Glanville, I remember, was the first author who, by his mode of applying logic, gave me some idea of the practical use of that art of reasoning. Mr George Sinclair, the author of *Satan's Invisible World Discovered*, was a person of considerable knowledge in relation to the manner in which he employed it, and whose character upheld, and among the ignorant at least in some degree upholds, the popularity of his metaphysical doctrines among the common people, for whose use numerous editions have been at different times, and some very lately, reprinted. I had never seen, though I had long looked for it, a copy of this edition printed by Reid in 1695 which is undoubtedly the original, until Mr David Laing most kindly and handsomely made me a present of this copy.

The following articles in the first edition are omitted in the latter ones:

First. The dedication to George Seaton, Earl of Winton and Tranent.
Second. The copy of a Latin encomium upon the work and the author by Patricius Sinclarus.
Third. A note of the author himself on the Cartesian Philosophy.
Fourth. A preface to the reader, consisting of fifteen pages, concluded by what Mr Sinclair calls *Carmen Steliteuticon*.

Of these variations one point is rather curious. In the dedication the natural philosopher gets completely the better of the metaphysician; for the professor of philosophy expands upon his admiration not only of Lord Winton's family, descent, prudence and heroic valour, but also of his extensive coal mines. An extract from which passage may amuse the reader, it being indeed an exquisite morsel of singular pedantry:

This treatise is called *Satan's Invisible World Discovered*, but I have ascertained, that by Your transcendant Skill, you have discovered an Invisible World, far beyond what any of your Ancestors could do; I mean your subterraneous World, a work for a Prince, and a Subject to Write of, by that great Philosopher Kircher. What Meanders and Boutgates are in it, are rather to be admired than believed. There Dædalus for all his skill would mistake his way? What running of Mines, and Levels? What parting of Gaes? What cutting of impregnable Rocks, with more difficultie, than Hannibal cutted the Alpes.

Qui montes rupit aceto.

What Deep-Pits, and Air-holes are digged! What diligence to prevent Damps, which kill Men and beasts in a moment! What contriving of Pillars, for supporting houses and Churches, which are undermined! What floods of Waters run through the Labyrinths, for several miles, by a free Level, as if they were conducted by a Guide! How doth Art and Nature strive together, which shall advance Your Lordships Interest most! What curious Mechanical Engines has Your Lordship, like another Archimedes, contrived for your Coalworks, and for drawing Coal-sinks! What a moliminous Rampier, hath Your Lordship begun, and nearly perfected, for a Harbour of deep Water, even at Neip Tides!

Portus ab accessu ventorum immotus & ingens.

How bountifull has Nature been in forming a choice Coal under ground, within a stone-cast of your New-haven?

Your Experimental Skill in improving your Coal, for making of Salt, is praise worthie. Your defending of the Salt-pans against the imperious Waves of the raging Sea, from the N.E, is singular. Your renting of Rocks, for clearing of Passages into Your Harbours, which none of your Predecessors were able to do, is stupendous.

As the Result of the wise Government of your Affairs, redounds to your self, so does it to the public Advantage of the Country, and others, so that men may say,

Te toti genitum credere genti.

How many hundreds of Young and Old have their Being and Livelihood, by their dependence on your Lordships virtuous Actions about the Coal and Salt, and things belonging thereunto, who art your self the greatest Coal and Salt-Master in Scotland, who is a Nobleman, and the greatest Nobleman in Scotland, who is a Coal and Salt-Master; Nay, absolutelie the best for skill in both, of all Men in the Nation. What fruitfull Corn-fields, where Ceres hath her chief habitation lie within the Prospect of your dwelling house at Seton? Which perswades me to maintain this Paradox, There is no Subject in Britan has so much Casual and Land-Revenue within a mile of his house, as your Lordship has.

In a word, your Affability in Converse, your Sobriety in Dyet and

Apparel, your Friendship and Kindness to Your Friends, your Candor and Ingenuity, with the prudent management of your Affairs, have endeared all Men to You; So that I may say, If your Predecessors were famous of Old for their Feates of War, in the time of War, so is your Lordship famous for your Arts of Peace, in the time of Peace. But, my Lord, I fear I am wearisome, and therefore I shall close as I began, imploring your Patrocination to this small Enchiridion. And as I have been long since Devoted to You in all Dutie and Love, so shall I ferventlie pray for Your Preservation and Happiness here and hereafter, while I live, and shall think my self happy to be under the Character of Your Lordships,

Most Dutifull and Obedient Servant,
GEORGE SINCLAIR.

Mr Sinclair has, besides the above *morceau*, given another instance in which he strangely mixed his dissertations upon the certain sciences with his visionary studies. It is in a treatise upon hydrostatics, containing a short history of coal, and winded up with a cock-and-a-bull story of a demon or fiend which haunted the house of one Gilbert Campbell, a weaver of Glenluce in Galloway. The book is dated 1672, and the spirit was supposed to be raised by a bold and sturdy beggar, one Alexander Agnew afterwards hanged at Dumfries for blasphemy. He was a sort of atheist who declared that he knew no God but salt, meal and water.

With regard to Mr Sinclair's collection of ghost stories, it contains what has at all times been desirable in such matters; a curious and detailed account of a good number of tales concerning gothic superstition not to be found elsewhere, and some that are famous to this day in Scottish history and tradition. I am informed that one which came to the hammer sold as high as four pounds, and in evidence of its rarity Mr Constable long regretted a copy which he possessed and which disappeared through the intervention, it was supposed, of such a demon as we have formerly mentioned, who in the present day more frequently haunts the shops of booksellers than the huts of weavers. With this observation we dismiss the subject of this father of fables who appears, however, to have been a man of honesty and good faith in his speculations.

The press containing this masterpiece of the terrible comprehends a great many other volumes of the like character, of whom it may be said in general that the authors are themselves no conjurors. I would not willingly prolong the subject by mentioning them individually.

Some of these may be just noticed; for example, Bekker's *Monde Enchanté*, with the whole seven volumes, one of which is rare. Edition, Amsterdam, 1699.

De La Lycanthropie, Transformation, Et Extase Des Sorciers. Le tout composé par J. De Nynauld, Docteur en Medecine. Paris, 1615.

The Discovery of Witches, in Answer to Severall Queries Lately Delivered to the Judges of Assize for the County of Norfolk. And now published by Mathew Hopkins Witchfinder, for the Benefit of the whole Kingdome. London, 1647. This tract I conceive to be scarce, as well as the print prefixed, where may be seen Mathew Hopkins by whose evidence a number of old women were consigned to the stake, two of whom are presented in the portrait along with him, besides portraitures of their imps, of which we are informed the names are Ilem Quazer, Pye Wackett, Peckt in the Crown, Grizzel Greedygut, Sack-a-Sugar, Vinegar-Tom, &c., all of whom are depicted in such hideous shapes as shews the coarse imagination of those who devised their names.

For Hopkins's character and fate see Dr Grey's notes upon *Hudibras*.

Pomponatius, his work upon enchantments being full of abstruse philosophy. Basileæ, (no date).

The Certainty of the Worlds of Spirits, Fully evinced by the unquestionable Histories of Apparitions, Operations, Witchcraft, Voices &c. Proving The Immortality of Souls, The Malice and Misery of Devils and the Damned, And the Blessedness of the Justified. Written for the Conviction of Saduccees & Infidels, by Richard Baxter. London, 1691. This collection, which in point of authenticity may be classed with that of Glanville and Sinclair, builds its evidence upon the character of the worthy dissenting minister Richard Baxter (whose doctrine was distinguished among the dissenters) that no sect of religion might be free from the disgrace attending follies of this nature. The book has had its day of popularity, but the reverend author is now rather pitied than credited for the prodigies which he has amassed together. Those who collect books of such a nature will, however, hardly choose to be without one upon which a pen has been employed

which in its day has been so celebrated.

Witches Apprehended, Examined and Executed, for notable villainies by them committed both by Land and Water. With a Strange and most true triall how to know whether a woman be a Witch or not. A coarse plate shews that the new method of trying a witch is something near akin to the old; for two clowns are engaged in dragging the wretched female through the sluice of a mill and their progress is observed with great gravity by several respectable looking persons who hold their hands with great composure in the pockets of their immense Dutch slops.

Another of these wonderful histories belongs perhaps to the celebrated persecution of the witches of New England. It is termed *An Exact Narrative Of many Surprizing Matters of Fact Uncontestably wrought by an Evil Spirit or Spirits, in the House of Master Jan Smagge, Farmer, in Canvy-Island, near Leigh in Essex, upon the 10th, 13th, 14th, 15th and 16th of September last, in the Day-time; In the Presence of The Reverend Mr Lord, Curate to the said Island, Jan Smagge, Master of the House, and of several Neighbours, Servants and Strangers, who came at different times, as Mr Lord's particular Care to discharge his Duty, and their Curiosity led them to this Place of Wonders. Together with &c., &c.* London, 1709.

We have also another of these rare tracts inscribed to the Right Honourable Sir Edward Coke Knight, Lord Chief Justice of England. The full title is *The Triall Of Witch-craft, Shewing The True And Right Methode of the discovery: With A Confutation of erroneous wayes.* By John Cotta, Doctor in Physicke. London, 1616.

The next treatise is the well-known Boy of Bilson which has furnished so many quotations to the commentators on Shakespeare. The full title runs thus; *The Boy Of Bilson: Or, A True Discovery Of The Late Notorious Impostures Of Certaine Romish Priests in their pretended Exorcisme, or expulsion of the Divell out of a young Boy, called William Perry, Sonne of Thomas Perry of Bilson, in the County of Stafford, Yeoman. Upon which occasion, hereunto is premitted A briefe Theologicall Discourse, by way of Caution, for the more easie discerning of such Romish spirits; and judging of their false pretences, both in this and the like Practices.* At London, 1622.

A class intimately relating to the imaginary studies with which we have of late been conversant are tracts regarding astrology which, of all mystical sciences, is perhaps that which lays the

From the title-page of *Witches Apprehended, Examined and Executed.*

strongest hold upon the imagination and even yet asserts by its beauty if not by its credibility, a hold upon the imagination of the most stubborn infidels. This collection contains the lives of Ashmole and Lilly, the one a celebrated dupe to the astrologers of his day, the other an equally remarkable impostor, or more probably one who having commenced by deceiving himself, ended by becoming one of the most remarkable impostors of his period. It is remarkable how his reliance upon his art—founded on having bought a bargain of astrological books at half price—leads him on in full faith until the predictions of astrology come to rank as one and the same thing with whichever course is recommended by his own interest. We have only time, however, to add that Lilly was a shrewd and cunning philomath, as the term then went, and that, besides his memoirs written by himself and addressed to Ashmole, this library contains a good many of his contemporary tracts and astrological disquisitions.

We have not now time to enter upon a subject which would probably be tedious and prefer making mention of a book written by Lord Henry Howard afterwards created Earl of Northampton: *A defensative against the poyson of supposed Prophesies: Not hitherto confuted by the penne of any man, which being grounded, eyther uppon the warrant and authority of olde paynted bookes, expositions of Dreames, Oracles, Revelations, Invocations of damned Spirites, Judicialles of Astrologie, or any other kinde of pretended knowledge whatsoever, De futuris contingentibus: have been causes of great disorder in the common wealth, and cheefely among the simple and unlearned people: very needefull to be published at this time, considering the late offence which grew by most palpable and grosse errours in Astrolog., &c., &c.* London, 1583.

Lord Henry Howard was a great politician and faithful adherent of James the Sixth's claim to the succession to the crown of England, and the person whom Cecil, Earl of Salisbury, chiefly employed in the private treaty which he secretly carried on with the Scottish monarch at the risk of his total ruin had it been discovered by Queen Elizabeth. His Lordship was a Catholic, but not a bigoted one, and certainly a person who would sacrifice no point of his interest to the most important article of his religious belief. The *Defensative* is a warning against those supposed prophesies with which Froissart says that the English in his time were always well furnished, and which were then invented especially among the Catholics to keep up the cause of Queen Mary, when contrasted with that of her son, which was doing James at the time the greatest possible service. The style of this nobleman was admirably suited to the taste of James the First, bristling with quotations and rendered mystic by inversions of speech. The original edition now in my hands is known by a typographical distinction, to wit, that the pages are not numbered, for which, no doubt, the learned lord had a reason if he had pleased to make the same known to us.

It is enough however to observe that the *Defensative* was considered as having done eminent service to King James and that the noble author was in process of time rewarded both with wealth and promotion.

Without stopping to dwell upon less remarkable articles, we may say, that besides several tracts of the Reverend Mr Cotton Mather allied to the subject of demonology, and other articles of the same class, this part of the library contains a great number of tracts of different kinds, being that which is termed by those skilled in such subjects "eccentric biography" being the lives of remarkable criminals and the history of their crimes, as also of humorists who have attracted public attention by their peculiarities, of impostors, and in short, of those originals who fill up the twelfth class of Granger's engraved British portraits, which he describes to contain "Persons of both sexes, chiefly of the lowest order of the people, remarkable for only one circumstance in their lives; namely, such as lived to a great age, deformed persons, convicts, &c."

It is obvious that though the classification is very ample, yet a private collector can seldom have advanced far in fitting it up. The following books are perfect, although they may be termed rare.

A General and Rare History of the Lives and Actions of the most Famous Highwaymen, Murderers, Street Robbers, &c. To which is added, A Genuine Account of the Voyages and Plunders of the most Noted Pirates. Interspersed with several Remarkable Trials Of the most Notorious Malefactors at the Sessions House in the Old Baily, London. Adorned with the Effigies, and other material Transactions of the most remarkable Offenders, engraved in Copperplates. By Capt. Charles Johnson. Birmingham, 1742. A considerable part of this work is filled up with imaginary occurrences, from which we are induced to conclude that it has been in its original concoction the device of some hack bookseller, and the same may be said of the following book on the same subject in a more commodious shape.

A Compleat History Of The Lives and Robberies Of the most Notorious Highway-Men, Foot-Pads, Shop-Lifts, and Cheats, of both Sexes, in and about London and Westminster, and all Parts of Great Britain, for above an Hundred years past, continu'd to the present Time. Wherein the most Secret and Barbarous Murders, Unparalell'd Robberies, Notorious Thefts, and Unheard of Cheats, are set in a true Light, and expos'd to publick View, for the common Benefit of Mankind. To which is prefix'd, The Thieves New Canting-Dictionary, Explaining the most mysterious Words, New Terms, Significant Phrases and Proper Idioms, used at this present Time by our Modern Thieves. By Capt. Alexander Smith. The Fifth Edition, (adorn'd with Cuts) with the Addition of near Two Hundred Robberies lately committed. London, 1719. On this book which may be supposed to have been then just published, Sir Richard Steele, then engaged with the paper called the *Englishman*, makes the following observation: "There is a satisfaction to curiosity in knowing the adventures of the meanest of mankind and all that I can say in general of these great men in the way recorded by Capt. Smith, is that I have more respect for them than for greater criminals who are described with praise by more eminent writers." *Englishman*, No. 48.

It is singular enough that the *Englishman* in which this censure is justly passed, though of rare occurrence and written by a classical author, sells for half a crown, while Captain Smith's memoirs run to two or three guineas. The first edition in two volumes was printed for Markhew.

Ausführliche Relation von der Famosen Zigeuner Diebs Mord und Räuber Bande &c. That is, A detailed account of the bands of Gypsy thieves who committed robbery and murder and suffered death at the Town of Grieson by cord, sword and wheel with a prefixed historie of the aforesaid Gypsies. These judicial proceedings are very curious especially to such as consider the history of the gypsy tribes with their origin as matter of curiosity. The collection we have cited affords the quotations used in the *Quarterly Review* in the article upon Mr Hoyland's gypsies where some account is given of this alsatian band which committed diverse cruelties.

With these volumes, especially the former part of them, we may connect the part entitled *A Recantation Of an ill ledde Life: Or, A Discoverie of the High-way Law. With Vehement Disswasions to all (in that kinde) Offenders. As also, Many cautelous Admonitions and full Instructions, how to know, shunne, and apprehend a Theefe. Most necessarie for all honest Travellers to peruse, observe and Practise.* Written by John Clavell, Gent. London, 1628. This tract is a proof among many that the trade of saying "stand to a true man" was by no means so discreditable in former times as in ours. Anthony Wood mentions with great commiseration more than one brave fellow who had fought gallantly for the king—"but weary fa the waefu wuddy." Neither need we wonder that high-way robbery is represented as the readiest resource of a ruined gentleman, and scarcely disgraceful to those who have practised a more honourable mode of cutting out a living with their swords. Clavell appears to have been a man of good parts, and of a family on which no stain could be thrown. His honoured friend, his ever dear and well-approved good uncle, and his mother and sisters seem also to have been according to the time persons of worship.

The following verses on the transitory nature of their booty are rather a favourable specimen of the penitent highway-man's poetry:

> But makes no matter, whether more or lesse,
> 'Tis soon consumed againe in wickednesse,
> Ill gotten goods can never prosper well,
> Nor can they thrive that have no place to dwell,
> The rolling stone can hardly gather moss:
> Those that live on, do always live on loss.
> You have no trade, no calling, no vocation
> Whereby to live, and save; you have relation
> To nothing that is good, wastfull expense
> So of your lawlesse gains the recompense.
> Thus to be furnish'd then, is just as though
> A man should thatch his dwelling house with Snow,
> Which melts, drops, soulters, and consumes away
> E'en in the time of one sun-shining day.
> For when to Innes and Taverns you do run
> That note your ways, then are you twice undone.
> For well they know their bills you dare not chide,
> If you presume your actions they must hide;
> And so to make them rich, you forfeit all
> That men may wise, or good, or honest call.

And as you sinned in gaining, so are fain
To bee in spending cozened, not complain
Although you know't, so thriftless is their way
That do on ruins of their Country prey.

With this species of tracts is associated, though perhaps without much propriety, the numerous miscellaneous works of the celebrated Daniel Defoe. These were collected according to the list of the celebrated antiquary George Chalmers; at the same time he may have fallen into error both in ascribing some of the miscellaneous tracts to Mr Defoe, and also in excluding some from the list which were certainly the production of that author. The collection in the library extends to thirty-five volumes in number, which is uniformly bound, and I suspect that several ought to be added to the lists of singular works besides those we have mentioned.

We may also notice Topsell's *History of Four footed Beasts and Serpents, collected out of the writings of Conrade Gesner*. Folio. London, 1658. This is an extremely curious and elaborate work on natural history.

Burton's *Anatomy of Melancholy, What it is. With all the Kinds, Causes, Symptoms, Prognostics and severall cures for it. In three Partitions with their several Sections and Members and Subsections, with a Satyrical Preface &c. by Democritus Junior*. London. 8th edition. Folio. 1676.

The Voyages And Adventures, Of Ferdinand Mendez Pinto, a Portugal: During his Travels. This book is remarkable for affording Mr William Godwin a happy motto for his Romance of St Leon: "Ferdinandez Mendez Pinto was but a type of me thou liar beyond all bounds of credibility."

I might proceed with the catalogue and mention *The Divine Weekes and Works* of Du Bartas, translated by Sylvester.

The *Sylva Sylvarum* of Lord Bacon, Folio, London, 1651.

Thomas Heywood's *Nine Books of Women*. London, 1624.

The Hierarchie of the blessed Angels by the same. London, 1635.

Reginald Scott's *Discovery of Witchcraft*. London, 1665. A rare book in excellent order which may also be said of great part of its companions.

THE *Will Dunbar 1767*

HISTORY

OF

SERPENTS.

OR,

The second Book of living Creatures:

WHEREIN IS CONTAINED

Their Divine, Natural, and Moral descriptions, with their
lively Figures, Names, Conditions, Kindes, and Natures of all venomous
BEASTS: with their several Poysons and Antidotes; their deep hatred to
Mankinde, and the wonderful work of God in their Creation, and Destruction.

Necessary and profitable to all sorts of Men: Collected out of divine Scriptures,
Fathers, Philosophers, Physitians, and Poets: amplified with sundry accidental
Histories, Hierogliphycks, Epigrams, Emblems, and Ænigmatical Observations.

By EDVVARD TOPSELL.

The Boas

London, Printed by E. Cotes, 1658.

Article Three

The opposite side of the octagon is occupied by a very few of those Dalilahs of the collector's imagination which are acquired at too great a price to admit of their being anything beyond a mere example.

So many pages have been thrown away upon the style and character of the old romances of chivalry as may excuse the compiler of this catalogue for only mentioning two or three of the most curious of the contents of this library in the department alluded to. The first example which I shall produce is a fine copy in black-letter, 3 Tom, in Folios, of the *History of Lancelot du Lac* nouvellement imprime a Paris, MDXXXIII, On les vend a Paris en la rue saint Jacques par Philippe le noir libraire et lung des deux relieurs jurez de juniversite de Paris a l'enseigne de la Roze blanche couronnee.

[A folio of manuscript is missing at this point.]

Marked by de Bure in his catalogue both as one of the oldest and one of the most valuable of the numerous class which belong to the Round-table.

The next which we shall mention is a romance in six folio volumes, bound in three, being *La Tres elegante Delicieuse Melliflue et tresplaisante hystoire du tres noble Victorieux et excellentissime Roy Perceforest Roy de la grant Bretaigne fundateur du franc palais et du Temple du souverain dieu. &c.*

This romance is also held in good esteem and we will only mention a third of the said class which the admirers of black-letter also hold sacred: *Le Premier Livre de la Cronique du tres vaillant et Redoute Dom Flores De Grece, Sur Nomme Le Chevalier De Cignes, Second Filz D'Esplandian, Empereur de Constantinople. Histoire non encore ouye mais belle entre les plus recomandées. Mise en Francois par le Seigneur des Essars Nicolas de Herberay, commissaire ordinaire en l'Artillerie.* A Paris, Pour Jan Longis, libraire tenant sa boutique au Palais, en la galerie par ou l'on va en la Chancellerie. 1552.

These last mentioned *novelles* are remarkable for being a

species perfectly distinct from the poetical, or, as they are properly called, romances of chivalry, which generally pretend to be in some degree at least founded upon real history, although such traites as they may really exhibit amongst the great wars of fable are like the shipwrecked sailors of Virgil thinly scattered amidst the immense gulph. It was only the vulgar, however, who demanded with Audrey in such cases whether the recital made to them concerned *a true thing or no*; and it may be doubted whether supposing the answer to be in the negative, it would not be more satisfactory on that account to the unsuspicious audiences. At any rate, when a successful author had written the life of a distinguished hero, it almost always gave rise to continuations of the same story without end. Thus Flores of Greece is himself descended from Bellianis of Greece, famous for being quoted with approbation during the criticism held by the curate and barber upon the books of chivalry in Don Quixote's library. Flores of Greece is also called into review and, although the author, or at least translated by Nicolas de Herberay who has in France the credit of being the author, he undergoes an unsparing condemnation at the hands of the unpitying censors.

The next book which we are brought to notice is a French romance called the *Story of the Swan or Cheuelere Assigne* printed for the Roxburghe Club by the learned Mr Utterson; a fable which exists in various languages and in different countries of Europe.

Although the collection which we speak of is by no means extremely rich in this kind of works which were in very high degree *recherché*, yet we have already said enough to shew that it contains several articles of value and rarity, among them the following, remarked high among the canons: *Les prouesses et faictz merveilleux du noble huon de bourdeaux per de france duc de guyenne*. This rare folio is thus named as the folio novellement imprime a Paris pars Jehan Petit. It is remarkable as having been the foundation of the very gay and pleasant tale of knight-errantry and faery to which Wieland has given a new existence, which is translated by Mr Sotheby with a spirit equal to the excellent original. It is singular that two trains of composition can be discerned in the original, one in the usual cast of knight-errant fiction, the other of another mood, being neatly embroidered, as it were, with fairy fiction which happily and beautifully blends with the original fiction. The hero visits the earthly paradise and has a *rencontre* with the fratricide Cain, which has a cast of Rabbinical fiction leaning to the oriental vein. This is perhaps one of the most curious books in the collection. It belonged to the celebrated Roxburghe collection.

The same copartment of books holds the works of Rabelais, both the original edition by Du Chat, celebrated for the annotations, and also the Scottish edition of Sir Thomas Urquhart in broad Scottish. To compare them is very curious, although the extreme coarseness of the language renders the task at times disgusting. It goes far, however, to establish the similarity between the English and the broad Scotch which approach each other much more nearly than the mere English antiquary can form a conjecture.

The editor is here again stopped by a volume of some rarity, being an example of what he before mentioned of the manner in which a popular romance was followed by continuations. It seems that after his tragical death, Yseult, the unfortunate mistress of Tristrem's affection, became sensible that she bore a child between her sides, destined to be a posthumous pledge of their criminal but faithful love.

NOTE ON THE TEXT

The manuscript of *Reliquiae Trotcosienses* is owned by the Faculty of Advocates and is held in Scott's library at Abbotsford. It is half bound in morocco, and consists of 126 quarto leaves numbered 1–126, with a final, un-numbered leaf containing only a few lines. Folio 122 is missing. It is partly in Scott's hand, and partly in that of his amanuensis William Laidlaw. A portion of *Reliquiae Trotcosienses* has been published previously. The description of Abbotsford which begins with the hall and ends with an allusion to the 'attic story' was edited by Mary Monica Maxwell Scott and appeared in *Harper's New Monthly Magazine.*[1] She later also edited a section describing some of the books beginning with Scott's account of the library and ending with the reference to Richard Baxter's *The Certainty of the World of Spirits*. This appeared in *The Nineteenth Century And After.*[2] While these extracts follow the manuscript with some care there are notable errors and omissions and, not surprisingly, there is no attempt to include the large section at the opening of the text and a smaller portion at the end which is in Scott's difficult hand. The current editors have therefore based this edition on the manuscript throughout, and have edited it to produce a printed book such as Scott might have expected.

That part of the manuscript in Scott's own hand shows clear signs of failure in motor skills resulting from Scott's strokes of 1830, that 'stammer' in his handwriting which he describes so poignantly in his *Journal* for the period.[3] The result is a marked deterioration in the formation of individual letters when compared to Scott's writing in, for example, all but the final Waverley Novels. There is also evidence that Scott frequently loses the thread of a sentence in the course of writing it, leading one sentence to collapse in on another. The result is a text which displays all the brightness and wit of Scott's intellect, and a continuing grasp of underlying structures; but it is also one where what Scott intended to write is not always fully articulated on the page. These considerations have all played their part in the editing process.

The deterioration of Scott's motor skills and verbal fluency, and their implications for editing *Reliquiae* can, for example, be seen in the sentences at 27.17–28 of the present edition. In the manuscript, Scott writes:

> And thus the builder may form an idea at once how his mansion will look from the outside and on the other hand how it will answer his internal accomodation and display the Gabions of its proprietor to

> the best advantage this is the more becoming if the proprietor his
> occasion to testify his gratitude to the public in the way of acknow-
> legement for as he can hardly be expected to entertain in the inside
> of his mansion all those gentle readers readers to whom he is
> indebted for thinks it ⟨et⟩ at least shews a becoming sense of obliga-
> tion to make the outside of his house so far different from the
> ordinary stile as to call for a second & more attentive gaze as ⟨he⟩ he
> passes by the mansion of an old friend

This passage shows, too sadly, Scott's failing powers. Some features are
to be found in all Scott's work in manuscript: the repetition of the word
'readers' for example, or the idiosyncratic spellings of 'acknowlegement' and 'accomodation'. Other features, however, are seldom found
in Scott's earlier work. While Scott's manuscripts are generally very
lightly punctuated he usually give some indication of where he wishes a
new sentence to begin. Here, however, sentences flow into each other—
such as at the junctures 'advantage this' and 'acknowlegement for'. The
error of replacing a word with a homophone such as in the cases 'thinks'
for 'things' and 'his' for 'has' is also far more common in Scott at this late
stage. In instances such as these the current editors have attempted to
interpret as best they can what Scott appears to have intended. The case
under discussion has been rendered as follows:

> And thus the builder may form an idea at once how his mansion will
> look from the outside, and, on the other hand, how it will answer
> his internal accommodation and display the gabions of its pro-
> prietor to the best advantage. This is the more becoming if the
> proprietor has occasion to testify his gratitude to the public in the
> way of acknowledgement, for as he can hardly be expected to
> entertain in the inside of his mansion all those gentle readers to
> whom he is indebted for things, it at least shews a becoming sense
> of obligation to make the outside of his house so far different from
> the ordinary style as to call for a second and more attentive gaze as
> he passes by the mansion of an old friend.

This edition of *Reliquiae Trotcosienses* is, consequently, based closely
on the manuscript but has been edited with the aim of providing a
readable printed text. As the editors of the Edinburgh Edition of the
Waverley Novels have pointed out, Scott's manuscripts underwent a
process of 'socialisation' before they appeared before the public, a process by which 'intermediaries' (the collective term used by the EEWN
for compositors, proof-readers, and master printer) prepared the text
for publication following a series of 'standing orders'.[4] While *Reliquiae*
was never itself published in Scott's lifetime it was his intention that it
should be, and the current editors have therefore corrected the text in
ways consistent with the mandate given to Scott's contemporaries.[5] As
David Hewitt outlines in the General Introduction to the EEWN, the
role of the intermediaries was fairly extensive. They not only normalised

spelling and supplied a printed-book style of punctuation, but also corrected minor errors and removed words repeated in close proximity to
each other. The editors of *Reliquiae* have therefore applied these 'standing orders' to the current text.

Those changes typical of the work carried out by the intermediaries
have been made silently by the editors of *Reliquiae*. They include
the minimal punctuating of the manuscript according to early nine-
teenth-century conventions. Sentences, as can be seen in the example
quoted above, have been given capital letters at their beginnings
and a full stop at the end. First letters of words have been rendered
as lower case except where capitals are clearly required. Except where
they are also found in printed versions of texts quoted by Scott,
ampersands have been spelled out, as have abbreviations such as
'wh.' for 'which', or 'Dr' for 'Doctor'. An example of this can be
found at 18.12–13 where Scott writes in manuscript 'to use stone
& mortar build an excellent & serviceable wall to a height at wh.
the labour of a single individual'. Both of Scott's ampersands have
been translated into 'and' and the contraction 'wh.' expanded to
read 'which'. The final *d* with which Scott concluded past participles
has been expanded to *ed* in words such as 'called'. The manuscript,
for example, reads 'followd' at 5.11 and 'formd' at 16.19 but these
words appear as 'followed' and 'formed' in this edition. Obvious
misspellings and malformations have been corrected, although where
a degree of editorial interpretation has been required, the emendation
is noted. Inadvertent repetitions of words (e.g. 'readers' at 27.24
in the passage quoted) have been deleted. The double *ll* used by
Scott and Laidlaw in words such as 'powerfull' and 'beautifull' has
been silently altered (the manuscript reads 'usefull' at 18.31 for example), as has the *ck* form in words such as the manuscript's 'fantas-
tick' at 5.30. Where Scott has indicated that a new paragraph should
begin, or a word be italicised, his instructions have been followed
in print except where noted. A standardised presentation for all headings has been adopted: this involves *inter alia* the consistent use
of either 'chapter' or 'article', and the use of words instead of numerals
for numbering the chapters and articles. Consistent typographical
conventions have been imposed—titles of books have been printed
in italics, for example, while chapter and section headings have been
centred and printed in bold.

These types of change can be seen by comparing the manuscript and
printed versions of the passage at 10.13–22 of the current edition. The
manuscript of *Reliquiae* reads:

> The account of the Gabions of which it may be now not easy to
> trace the humour which the contemporaries of the poet discernse
> therein is concluded by a species of Apology as to an address by the

Mourning poet to the Lovers of learing & having given in an
account of the first of "the Muses Threnodie" we ought to hold it
our duty Scandal it seems had spread a rumour that instead of a
harmless and playful satire the Author was about to take up the
melancholy history of the Gowrie Conspiracy To this he replies in
the Apology aforeside which connects both parts of his threnody
and states his actual purpose in writing them

The printed version reads as follows:

> The account of the gabions of which it may be now not easy to
> trace the humour, which the contemporaries of the poet discern
> therein, is concluded by a species of apology as to an address by the
> mourning poet to the lovers of learning; and having given an
> account of the first of *The Muses Threnodie*, we ought to hold it our
> duty to continue. Scandal, it seems, had spread a rumour that
> instead of a harmless and playful satire, the author was about to
> take up the melancholy history of the Gowrie Conspiracy. To this
> he replies in the apology aforesaid which connects both parts of his
> threnody, and states his actual purpose in writing them:

Punctuation has been added to render the sense more intelligible (the
commas after 'humour' and 'therein' for example); the capitals which
seem to denote new sentences have been matched by full stops at the
end of the sentence which precedes them; the words 'discernse', 'learing' and 'aforeside' have been interpreted as 'discern', 'learning' and
'aforesaid'; capitalisation has been removed in words such as 'mourning', 'lovers'; and 'author'; and the inverted commas around 'the Muses
Threnodie' have been removed and the title italicised. This passage is
typical in the kinds of change made by the current editors in order to
follow what would have been the practices of the intermediaries in
'socialising' the manuscript of *Reliquiae Trotcosienses* for its appearance
in print. This class of emendation has not been noted in the Emendation
List.

However, *Reliquiae Trotcosienses* was written at a late stage in Scott's
life and the manuscript is not always fully coherent. At times, therefore,
more overt editorial intervention has been required to convey what
appear to have been Scott's intentions. Several examples illuminate the
typical editorial repair to the text. The manuscript, for example, at
6.1–3 reads:

> The remarkable numbres of this kinds of friends were Dr Ruthven
> himself who was distinguished by his professional knowledge and
> particularly by his good humour and actitity

Correcting the obviously hurried composition here which includes, in
context, elements of tautology and incompletely articulated logic, the
text has been emended to:

> These friends, were, firstly, Dr Ruthven himself who was distin-

guished by his professional knowledge and particularly by his good humour and activity.

Another example where straightforward semantic 'tweaking' of the text yields up its underlying meaning is found where the manuscript reads:

> The taste of the reverse of what is usually termed pure and classical, and more probably entitled to the name of bizarre or whimsical, may, in many points if it may never the less be referred to principles which have a claim to be really founded upon taste, even when in fact they may be charged with extravagance.

At 22.28–32 this is emended to read:

> The taste of the reverse to what is usually termed pure and classical, and more probably entitled to the name of bizarre or whimsical, may, in many points, be nevertheless referred to principles which have a claim to be really founded upon taste, even when in fact they may be charged with extravagance.

Clear omissions of sense have also been rectified: the manuscript's 'These trees were by the late Duke of Queensberry' becomes, for example, at 42.7–8 'These trees were put up for sale by the late Duke of Queensberry'.

Word order and word form have sometimes been changed to reach a more clearly balanced sentence, both semantically and stylistically (reflecting the normal treatment of Scott's manuscripts when being converted into type). The manuscript's 'The artists engaged ⟨from⟩ furnished agreeably to a certain engagement, a number of valuable drawings which were engraved' for example, thus becomes 'The artists furnished, agreeable to a certain engagement, a number of valuable drawings which were engraved' (43.14–15).

Numerous examples of tautology and careless penmanship have also been eliminated; for instance: 'In this pannelling are inserted many separate pieces of carved oak of the same king with the same pannelling' becomes 'In this pannelling are inserted many separate pieces of carved oak of the same kind' (29.36–37). Occasionally, hurriedness in the manuscript would seem to have led to mistaken deletion, which the editors have restored; for instance, 'very old oaks [. . .] grew at ⟨the⟩ in old & noble park of Drumlanrig Castle' which is, consequently, emended to 'very old oaks [. . .] grew in the old and noble park of Drumlanrig Castle' (42.4–7).

While considerable intervention has been required to turn Scott's manuscript into a coherent and readable text the intention of the editors has been to intervene as little as possible in what Scott has actually written. They have, consequently, left unchanged several sentences which are semantically opaque, but which cohere grammatically and where the context provides very little guidance to potential alteration. Cumulatively, the editors have made changes to the text where these are strongly urged by the internal sense of the manuscript, but they have not sought to force upon the text an absolute logic for its own sake. The manuscript is over ninety per cent intelligible, but problems of exact meaning in one or two instances remain. All changes made to the manuscript text which require a degree of editorial interpretation are recorded in the emendation list.

Following the practice of the intermediaries, factual errors, where appropriate, have also been corrected. For example, at 15.40 Scott writes 'End of the 8th Muse of the Muses Theronadie'. This has been corrected, on the basis of the evidence of the printed text, to read 'END OF THE SIXTH MUSE'. Such corrections are also noted on the Emendation List.

All emendations in the list are editorial apart from those in the special category of being derived from a printed source. Where Scott is citing or quoting from a printed text he seldom offers any punctuation, but would certainly have expected it to be supplied; the punctuation of printed sources has therefore been used to punctuate Scott's quotations without note in the Emendation List as has the capitalisation of printed texts and book titles. However, where Scott's spelling is appropriate it has been retained; where it is faulty the printed text has been followed as the basis for emendation.

However, in some instances Scott appears to be quoting from memory, and thus semantic variants in Scott's manuscript have been retained, if what Scott has written makes sense.[6] For example, at 50.35 the note in Scott's book at Abbotsford reads 'an attempt to *condiddle*'. However, the manuscript reads 'the attempt' as if reflecting the familiar tone with which Scott is recalling the event; the 'the' has therefore been retained. However, in cases where no sense can be made of Scott's holograph, an emendation has been made on the basis of the published book or the holograph notes contained within Scott's personal copies. This is indicated in the emendation list by 'PB'. This policy on emendations from printed sources is based on the assumption that it may be of more interest to the modern reader to know how Scott remembered his sources than that they are always presented in a strictly accurate form.

One particularly interesting set of emendations involves those from Henry Adamson's *The Muses Threnodie*. The note at 6.40 of the current text seems to make it clear that Scott is following James Cant's 1774 edition of the poem.[7] Internal textual evidence also suggests that this is the edition which Scott is quoting from. For example, in both the manuscript of *Reliquiae* and Cant's edition the word 'Buffoons' is added for clarification at 7.13 although the word is not present in the first, 1638, version of the poem.[8] So too, at line 11.3 both Cant's edition and *Reliquiae* read, somewhat oddly, 'paradise' while the 1638 version has the word 'paradoxe'. Similarly, while both Cant and Scott read 'Since better' at 11.29, the 1638 text reads 'Sith bitter'. Most tellingly of all, Cant's 1774 version has several lines which transpose the line order of the first edition; for instance, at 9.33–36 in the 1638 version the couplet 'Here lies a book . . . *Kennett*', comes before 'Here lies a turkass . . . grammar', but both Cant and Scott transpose them.

There is, on the face of it, no evidence that Scott had ever seen the 1638 version of the poem; there is no copy of this edition at Abbotsford. However, internal evidence in Scott's *Reliquiae* version may suggest that he had read it at some time. Several of the spellings in the Adamson portion of *Reliquiae* seem to be of particularly archaic construction, far more archaic than those we would normally find in Scott, and, interestingly, more archaic than those found in Cant's version of the *Muses*. For example, at 9.13 the 1638 version has the word 'Pantheraes'. While Cant has 'pantheras', Scott has written 'panithaeras'—a word which is in itself incorrect but which seems in some way to reflect the more antiquated spelling of 1638. A similar situation arises at 11.26 and 27 where Scott uses the more archaic form 'windes' and, as if in an attempt to bring it into line, fineds'. While Cant has the more modern 'winds' and 'finds', Scott's spellings echo the 'windes' and 'findes' of 1638.

Such features of the manuscript suggest that while Scott's source is definitely Cant he may have some memory of the older version of the text. This is feasible, because there is much in Scott's manuscript to suggest that he is not copying directly from Cant, but is indeed, at times at least, quoting from memory. For example, in many cases, in spite of the occasional attempt at archaism, Scott has modernised the spelling of Adamson's text. At 9.33 Cant uses the form 'lys' while Scott uses the more modern 'lies'. Similarly, at 11.11 while Cant uses the form 'dignitie' Scott has 'dignity'. More compelling evidence for Scott quoting from memory is offered by the fact that there are at times significant semantic variants between Scott's version and Cant's. Scott frequently exchanges a word of similar sense; for example, he exchanges 'six' for Cant's 'ten' at 8.37, 'evil' for 'ill' at 8.16, and 'bad' for 'good' at 10.36. He is particularly likely to change a word in this way if it falls at the end of a line and the word he has chanced upon happens to rhyme; Cant's 'hing' at 9.27 becomes 'swing' in Scott's version, while the 'Burges scrole' in Cant at line 14.29 becomes 'Roll' in Scott and his 'quill' at 16.2 becomes 'skill'. Perhaps the most convincing evidence of all of the fact that Scott is relying on his memory lies in the fact that certain lines of the text have been missed out in *Reliquiae* ; of these the most interesting is the line 'I rather that *Thercites* were my daid' omitted between 12.17 and 18, possibly because its sense is largely repeated at 12.19.[9]

Such evidence seems to suggest that Scott is often quoting from a memory of Adamson's poem rather than copying directly from a printed version of it. And while the evidence suggests that this memory is predominantly of Cant's 1774 version, certain aspects of the manuscript might imply that he may have a more distant memory of the earlier 1638 version which at times is colouring what he writes. With this in mind the following policy has been applied to the sections of the text where Scott is quoting from Adamson. Scott's punctuation in these sections is, as is usual in his manuscripts, minimal; as editorial policy has been determined by the aim of producing a readable book, punctuation has been supplied, but here by reference to Cant's edition. Cant's capitalisation and italicisation have also been followed. (On the very rare occasions where the punctuation or capitalisation supplied by Cant has seemed clearly incorrect the manuscript has been followed or an editorial emendation made with a note outlining the basis for the decision.) On the other hand, Scott's, rather than Cant's, spelling has been followed wherever it makes sense, including those archaic spellings which might reflect his memory of the 1638 text of *The Muses Threnodie*. Where Scott's spellings are clearly incorrect Cant's text has been used as the basis of emendation. In the case of semantic variants a similar policy to that on spelling is followed: if what Scott has written makes sense in context his word has been retained; where what Scott has written does not make sense Cant is used as the basis of emendation. Thus, Scott's 'brother' at 8.36 is emended to 'brethren' on the authority of Cant on the basis that Scott's word does not make grammatical sense, while his choice of 'dearest' at 15.39 is retained rather than emended for Cant's 'sweetest'. All semantic variations which have Cant's text as their authority are identified on the emendation list by '*Muses*, 1774'.

In some cases emendations are derived from artefacts at Abbotsford House or from the building itself. These are marked by 'AH' on the emendation list. To a degree, Scott maintains the conceit that he is not writing about Abbotsford itself, which is never mentioned by name. But it is clearly Abbotsford that is being described and so, in the case of measurements, lacunae in the manuscript have been filled according to actual measurements, and internal inconsistencies rectified. However, measurements supplied in the manuscript by Scott but not factually correct have been left unchanged, except where they are clearly nonsensical. The introductory section to *Reliquiae Trotcosienses*, published here for the first time, makes it clear that Scott was not writing a mere description of the building of Abbotsford and its collections but offering a quasi-fictional account as if given by a friend of Jonathan Oldbuck. The editors felt that above all, anything in the text which adds to the flavour of this conceit should, where possible, be retained.

NOTES

1 'Gabions of Abbotsford: A Hitherto Unpublished Fragment', ed. Mary Monica Maxwell Scott, *Harper's New Monthly Magazine*, vol. 17, no. 467 (April 1889), 778–88.

2 'Sir Walter Scott on his "Gabions"', ed. Mary Monica Maxwell Scott, *The Nineteenth Century And After*, vol. 58, no. 344 (October 1905), 621–33.

3 See Scott's entry for 1 January 1831 in *The Journal of Sir Walter Scott*, ed. W. E. K. Anderson (Oxford, 1972), 621.

4 See David Hewitt's General Introduction to the Edinburgh Edition of the Waverley Novels where a full account is given of the role of the intermediaries in the production of Scott's texts. The editors of the current volume are greatly indebted to the Edinburgh Edition both for the insight it offers into Scott's working methods, and the example of editorial practice which it provides. They are also indebted to the Edinburgh Edition for the skills they have acquired while working on it as researchers, and for the background to Scott's work provided by the notes to the novels.

5 Evidence that Scott intended *Reliquiae* to be published is provided by his *Journal* and by several references to a contract for the work. A note in the fly leaf of Robert Cadell's diary for 1831 outlines its author's publishing plans for the forthcoming year and states 'I have a contract with Sir Walter Scott for a work in 2 Vols to be named Reliquæ Trotcosienses . . .' (NLS MS 21021, f. 1r). The contract itself for 'a little work to be entitled Reliquiæ Trotcosienses' is to be found at NLS MS 745, f. 211 and is dated 6 September 1830. It appears that Scott was paid £750 for *Reliquiae* and that five thousand copies were to be printed. In his *Journal* for October 1831 Scott writes 'Something of a *journal* and the *Reliquiae Trotcosienses* will probably be moving articles and I have in short no fears on pecuniary matters': *The Journal of Sir Walter Scott*, ed. W. E. K. Anderson (Oxford, 1972), 659–60.

6 The fact that Scott may be quoting from memory is supported by the fact that he frequently replaces the published word by one near to it in sense.

7 Henry Adamson, *The Muses Threnodie; Or, Mirthful Mournings on the Death of Mr Gall. Containing variety of pleasant Poetical Descriptions, Moral Instructions, Historical Narrations, and Divine Observations, with the most remarkable Antiquities of Scotland, especially of Perth*, with explanatory notes and observations by James Cant (Perth, 1774). This is the edition of the poem which Scott owned and which is listed in J. G. Cochrane's *Catalogue of the Library at Abbotsford* (Edinburgh, 1838: *CLA*, 17).

8 Henry Adamson, *The Muses Threnodie, Or, Mirthfull Mournings, on the death of Master Gall. Containing varietie of pleasant Poëticall descriptions, morall instructions, historicall narrations, and divine observations, with the most remarkable antiquities of Scotland, especially at Perth* (Edinburgh, 1638).

9 Further information about missing lines is given in the Explanatory Notes.

EMENDATION LIST

In the following list the reading in the present text comes first; the authority for the emendation (if relevant) follows in parentheses; this is followed by a slash; the MS reading which is replaced by the emendation appears to the right of the slash. Where no authority for the emendation is given (and this is the most common situation) the emendation may be presumed to be editorial. As Scott would have expected his quotations to be aligned with their printed source there are places where there is a different authority for an emendation. The principal authorities are: the 1638 and 1774 editions of *The Muses Threnodie*, cited as '*Muses*, 1638', and '*Muses*, 1774' (see page 96 for bibliographical details); other printed authorities are indicated by 'PB' (printed book). Some details of Scott's manuscript text are emended by reference to Abbotsford House and artefacts within it, and this authority is indicated by 'AH'. The reference system gives the page and line number on which an emendation entry begins. Angle brackets indicate material deleted in the manuscript, while an up arrow indicates the beginning of material added in the manuscript and a down arrow the ending of the additional matter.

1.5	MONKBARNS / Monk Barns
3.4	three (PB) / thre
3.5	towmont (PB) / towmonth
5.3	voluminous writer, that / voluminous if a that
5.5	meaning, yet which does not lead / meaning ⟨or⟩ ↑ nor ↓ leads
5.6	injury by / injure of
5.14	than / that
5.14	would have been / would been
5.14	ago in the year 1700 / ago for when in the year 1700
5.15	perhaps by a few / perhaps a few
5.16	Perth, who would / Perth would
5.16	"Gall's gabions." / Gauls' Gabions
5.17	gabions." These words / Gabions words
5.17	"gabions" / Gabions
5.24	hobby-horse / hobby horse
5.24	his own and / his and
5.26	hobby-horse / hobby horse
5.26	he is impelled / and impelld
5.27	*Nos hæc mirum esse nihil* / Nos haec murmus esse nihil
5.27	*nihil*. Such could be said of the / nihil—. The
5.29	seventeenth / 17
5.30	Perth, and / Perth during the seventeenth ⟨and⟩ century and
5.32	"gabions," / Gabions
5.33	those / him
5.34	Ruthven's / Ruithvens
6.1	These friends / The remarkable numbres of this kinds of friends
6.1	were, firstly, Dr / were Dr

6.3   activity / actitity
6.8   than / for
6.8   first. [run on] The / first [new paragraph] The
6.8   next / head
6.9   acuteness / acquntenens
6.13   Caiaphas / Cayphaeas
6.13   and is the subject of the / and the the
6.15   third / fourth
6.15   these / Doctor Ruthvens
6.16   the fame / the poetical fame
6.17   *The Muses Threnodie* / the Muses Threnoden
6.21   collection, the / Collection was the
6.28   miscellaneous curiosities in (*Muses*, 1774) / miscellanious in
6.29   described (*Muses*, 1774) / describled
6.31   *Gall's Gabions* / Galls Gabions
6.32   collections / collection
6.36   William Drummond of / William of
6.38   send / sent
7.2   Hawthornden / Hawthorden
7.7   Sir, [new line] These (*Muses*, 1774) / Sir [run on] These
7.10   Sphinges (*Muses*, 1774) / Sphnges
7.10   Chimæras (*Muses*, 1774) / chimæras
7.10   inwardlie (*Muses*, 1774) / inwardice
7.11   rich jewels (*Muses*, 1774) / rich h
7.13   Your two (*Muses*, 1774) / You her
7.13   zanys (*Muses*, 1774) / zanius
7.13   us (*Muses*, 1774) / as
7.20   nor delighting nor instructing (*Muses*, 1774) / neither nor delighting
        instructing
7.29   Muses (*Muses*, 1774) / Musus
7.34   (1639) (*Muses*, 1774) / 1639
7.35   Adamson), / Adamson
7.38   accurate / auderate
8.1   *Threnodie* / Therodie
8.8   Of (*Muses*, 1774) / O
8.21   horns (*Muses*, 1774) / hons
8.21   *Bident* (*Muses*, 1774) / *Brident*
8.22   buckie (*Muses*, 1774) / buskie
8.25   Wherewith (*Muses*, 1774) / Whom with
8.27   purtrayed (*Muses*, 1774) / pourtraid
8.30   shield (*Muses*, 1774) / sheilf
        The Muses Threnodie, 1774, has a full-stop after 'shield', but this has
        been omitted as it does not make sense, even although the text follows
        that edition.
8.31   never (*Muses*, 1774) / neve
8.34   Hot (*Muses*, 1774) / How
8.36   *Cyclophes* (*Muses*, 1774) / *Cyclopus*
8.36   brethren (*Muses*, 1774) / brother
8.37   they (*Muses*, 1774) / the
8.41   use't (*Muses*, 1774) / use'd
9.2   thought (*Muses*, 1774) / though
9.4   including / included
9.4   centurae / centurue

9.9   crispe (*Muses*, 1774) / crisp
9.13   pantheras (*Muses*, 1774) / panithaeras
9.14   livelike (*Muses*, 1774) / livelircke
9.17   Acteon's (*Muses*, 1638) / Acteons
9.20   buckies (*Muses*, 1774) / Buckives
9.32   And in another (*Muses*, 1774) / And another
9.36   Kennett (*Muses*, 1774) / Brumit
         Brumit is presumably the name of a dog, but has no generic implications,
         unlike *Kennett*.
9.37   Mantua (*Muses*, 1774, and MS derived) / Mantuan
         Scott attempts, and fails, to wash out the terminal 'n'.
9.37   bannet (*Muses*, 1774) / Banner
9.39   strangular (*Muses*, 1774) / trangular
10.1   athorter (*Muses*, 1774) / athatur
10.4   bairnes (*Muses*, 1774) / bairns
10.5   whistle (*Muses*, 1774) / whistles
10.6   mussel (*Muses*, 1774) / muscle
10.16   learning / learing
10.16   given in an / given an
10.18   duty to continue. Scandal / duty Scandal
10.21   aforesaid / aforeside
11.3   paradise (*Muses*, 1774) / Paradise
11.4   prime (*Muses*, 1774) / prim
11.12   it's / its
         There is no apostrophe in *Muses*, 1638, nor 1774, nor in the ms.
11.14   load (*Muses*, 1774) / loady
11.15   hurt rule (*Muses*, 1774) / hart rules
11.18   Whose (*Muses*, 1774) / Where
11.26   findes (*Muses*, 1638) / fineds
11.29   not (*Muses*, 1774) / me
12.15   paradox (*Muses*, 1774) / paradies
12.18   And (*Muses*, 1774) / An
12.23   Be (*Muses*, 1774) / or
12.26   making (*Muses*, 1774) / malking
12.27   citing (*Muses*, 1774) / city
12.27   stories (*Muses*, 1774 derived: storeys) / storees
12.31   might (*Muses*, 1774) / migh
12.32   contrare's (*Muses*, 1774) / contraris
12.33   I never had (*Muses*, 1774) / I had
12.43   have (*Muses*, 1774) / him
13.1   accordingly / according
13.2   discern / decencer
13.4   Ardelio's (*Muses*, 1774) / Ardeleo's
13.6   view (*Muses*, 1774) / viw
13.7   your (*Muses*, 1774) / que
13.8   Zoilus' / Zoilus
         Both the 1638 and 1774 editions of *Muses* also lack the apostrophe.
13.19   Ruthven. The / Ruthven the
13.23   "gabions" / *Gabions*
13.23   associate whom / associate to whom
13.26   have met / have ⟨formerly⟩ deceased freind met
13.32   the vicinity / the romantic vicinity
13.34   went / go

13.34   a-fishing / a fishing
13.34   the pearl / the river Pearl
13.35   the rivers / thems
13.35   amused / amuse
13.37   and / or
13.37   their / they
14.1   matter / master
14.5   *Poly Olbion* / Poly Albion
14.7   Conspiracy / conspiracy
14.11   particularly / particular
14.21   mode of obliterating / mode obliterating
14.22   take / taken
14.23   15th / 15
14.24   city and was / city was
14.25   cross. Our / Cross our
14.28   Burges (*Muses*, 1774) / Burgesss
14.29   Burges (*Muses*, 1774) / Burgess
14.40   would [command London's Mayor], moreover / would moreover
15.17   borne (*Muses*, 1774) / born
15.18   more (*Muses*, 1774) / mine
15.26   a-land (*Muses*, 1774) / a lauest
15.27   your boat most (*Muses*, 1774) / your most
15.32   these may (*Muses*, 1774) / thus nicey
15.33   rest (*Muses*, 1774) / est
15.35   The apostrophe following 'Tithonus' is in the manuscript, but does not
         appear in either *Muses*, 1638, or 1774.
15.40   SIXTH / 8th
15.41   a complete / a compleat an complete
15.42   Ruthven / Ruthvens
16.1   1638 / 1614
         There is no 1614 edition of this poem. The verses quoted appear in the
         1638 edition.
16.2   whose (*Muses*, 1774) / whom
16.9   "gabions" / *Gabions*
16.11   an age / in a age
16.13   accurate edition of / accurate of
16.19   which / whom
16.24   hoped / hope
16.25   supply / suppling
16.26   given / have supplied
16.26   *The Muses* / who Muses
16.29   Club / club
16.32   tracing / traced
16.34   directions, partly / directions on partly
16.34   threnodie / Thremodie
16.35   already acquainted. [new paragraph] Antiquaries / alrea [new para-
         graph] Antiquaries
         Scott's holograph breaks off at this point. The manuscript continues in
         the hand of his amanuensis William Laidlaw.
16.37   of / if
16.37   to degenerate / to such degenerate
16.39   sense and still more so in the mode of expression. / sense & mode of
         expression & still more so in the mode of expression.

17.4	bed-room / bed room
17.5	preen" (*anglice* a pin). / preen." (anglice a pin)
17.5	pin). Such / pin) such
17.6	they / the
17.10	It / I
17.15	these societies / the society
17.28	it proceeds / it is proseed
17.33	exceptions, are seldom / exceptions seldom
17.35	art. The / art⟨s⟩ the
17.36	gentleman-like / gentleman like
18.4	contribute. [run on] In / contribute [new paragraph] In
18.5	fruits / produce
18.6	be / by
18.23	miscellaneous / messalaneous
18.32	once he gained the leisure / once the leisure
18.35	*Iret ubique perdidit Romam* / Ibit que perditit Lonam
19.1	with / whith
19.6	whether / whither
19.8	various sorts and / various &
19.20	battle-axes / battle axes
19.20	broad-swords / broad swords
19.24	fame / ↑ fame ↓ renown
	Scott forgot to delete 'renown' when he added the word 'fame'.
19.26	*Friend.* / Friend
19.26	how / who
19.32	is a great / is great
19.34	could / good
19.36	which is infinitely / which infinitely
19.40	*Friend.* / Friend
20.4	cook-wench / Cook ⟨maid⟩ ↑ wench ↓
20.25	multiply / multify
20.36	an / a
21.7	interlocutor / interloquitor
21.27	*post mortem* / post mortem
21.32	trustee / Trutees
21.34	abandoned / abandon
22.9	Sterne's / sterns
22.10	hobby-horse. Nor / hobby horse nor
22.11	amusements / amusement
22.15	disappear, are no / disappear no
22.20	author. On / author⟨s⟩ on
22.24	title / little
22.27	public. [new paragraph] The / public. [run on] The
22.28	to / of
22.30	points, be nevertheless referred / points if it may never the less be referred
23.3	passed / past
23.14	denounce / denounced
23.15	composition anything which / composition which
23.16	taste. On / taste on
23.17	which / whose
24.2	Esq. / Esqr.
24.5	*post mortem* / post mortem

24.13   antiquary (that is / antiquary, that as
24.15   scale) having / scale, & having
24.19   *Reliquiae.* [run on] Suum cuique / reliquae. [new paragraph] Suum
        Cusque
24.19   is our Roman / is a Roman
24.26   The first of these is my / The first of these is in the first place my
24.29   founded / founder
24.35   interior [run on] "a thing to dream of not to tell," [run on] and / interior
        [new line] "A thing to dream of not to tell" [new line] and
25.7   Lucian—but / Lucian but
25.10   well-known / well Known
25.12   play, is involved / play involved
25.13   words. With / words with
25.17   curiosity. The / curiosity the
25.20   gabions (of / Gabions, of
25.28   lastly, as / lastly. As
25.28   well-nigh / well nigh
25.35   twenty-one / twenty one
27.3   Antiquarienses / Antquarenses
27.4   Chapter One / [   ]
        No chapter given in manuscript. This has been added editorially for the
        sake of consistency.
27.6   has / having
27.8   can / whom
27.8   recall, dedicated as it is / recal like me and detetided
27.9   hobbihorsical / hobbihorsebatar
27.10   deperdition / Deperitation
27.10   curiosities / curiosity
27.11   *Ruthvenus Secundus* / Ruthvenus Secundus
27.14   Firstly / And first
27.16   *elevation* / Elevation
27.21   advantage. This / advantage this
27.22   has / his
27.25   things / thinks
27.32   those below, that / those that
27.33   hence / since
28.2   1. / [   ]
        No number given in manuscript. This has been added editorially for the
        sake of consistency.
28.3   What's that House? / Whats ⟨the⟩ House?
28.7   if 'twere / it twere
28.7   whirled / wirld
28.7   fanning / faning
28.10   *Country man*: Aye Sir, 'twas / Aye Sir ⟨I mind the bigging o't⟩ ↑ country
        man ↓ twas
28.10   'twas a grand place anes / twas ance a grand place⟨thought⟩ ↑ anes ↓
28.11   all is / alles
28.14   yet / and
28.16   experience (Saint John's Wood, London) for / Experience [Saint Johns
        Wood London for
28.20   architects / domestic
28.20   ever / evry
28.24   constitute / constitutute

28.25   perpetual if not / perpetual not
28.25   blister: falling plaster (which for the most ordinary regular artist would
         not have fallen), or / frittering blister having plaster of which which the
         most ordinary ⟨nature⟩ regular artist would not fallen for
28.26   or / for
28.27   cross-light / cross light
28.29   houses / horses
28.33   were / was
29.3   mingled / mixd
29.4   taste / tast
29.5   skill, and was / skill was
29.6   bizarrerie / Bezarerie
29.15   though it is repeatedly / Nor it it though repeatedly
29.15   before me by / before by
29.15   well-meaning / well meaning
29.16   advisors. Men are apt not to be moved from / advisors men are apt from
29.16   their / my
29.18   he at first finds some / he first some
29.21   adopting them in / adopting in
29.26   opens / enters
29.29   Linlithgow / Lithgow
29.30   it is fitted up / is fitted up it is fitted up
29.32   follows. [run on] The / follows [new paragraph] The
29.36   hero-monarch / heroe monarch
29.37   same kind. / same king with the same panelling.
30.2   that, from / that the only point in which from
30.2   Buccleuch / Buckcleuch
30.4   *Or* / or
30.8   *Azure* / azure
30.8   *Or* / or
30.9   fourteen (AH) / [   ]
30.12   These (AH) / This
30.12   be (AH) / are
30.12   Armouris, (AH) / Armour
30.12   ye (AH) / the
30.12   Clannis, (AH) / Clannes
30.12   quha (AH) / quho
30.13   Marches (AH) / Maches
30.13   ye (AH) / the
30.13   days (AH) / dayes
30.14   thair tyme and in thair defens (AH) / thair defens
30.14   thaim (AH) / them
30.14   defended (AH) / defendit
         This motto has been emended to reflect the way in which it appears at
         Abbotsford House.
30.15   above (AH) / below
30.17   as / of
30.25   passed / had
30.29   said / had
30.33   on the / once the
30.38   parts / maps
31.1   panelling. The / pannelling the
31.5   Erskine / Ereskin

31.7	Associated / associated
31.7	Synod / synod
31.7	of / or
31.7	Non Jurors / non jurors
31.10	Master / Mas.
31.10	Erskine / Ereskin
31.13	*sacros* / *sacris*
31.13	Presbyterian / presbyterian
31.14	High / high
31.15	*Martin* / Martin
31.19	thickness / thick
31.19	*de ceteris* / de ceteris
31.21	Society / society
31.25	Erskine's / Ereskins
31.30	Jacobite / jacobite
31.31	Master / master
31.32	good-natured / good natured
31.35	Synod / synod
32.1	by where the / by the
32.4	high, not / high but not
32.11	mention in / mention. In
32.14	chimney-piece / Chimney piece
32.17	chimney-piece / chimney piece
32.17	free / fee
32.18	Seat / seat
32.21	Restoration / restoration
32.23	thought or did / thought did
32.23	did or how he behaved / did or behaved
32.24	behaved, he / behaved. He
32.28	Presbyterian / presbyterian
32.30	chimney-grate / chimney grate
32.31	*superat* (AH) / *spernit*
32.37	happened / happens
32.39	black-lead / Blacklead
33.11	kail pot / Kail-pot
33.11	gaun / ga'n
33.12	three / thee
33.19	French / Frence
33.20	*gens de arm* / Gens de arm
33.26	screw-heads / screw heads
33.33	Catholic / catholic
33.33	word, it is a / word, a
33.39	he was John / he John
34.1	think—for / think for
34.3	yarn"—I / yarn." I
34.5	right-hand / right hand
34.9	*gladius . . . armaturae* / gladius . . . armatura
34.9	light-armed / light armed
34.23	*Otranto* / Ottranto
34.23	*Otranto* [new paragraph] I / Ottranto [run on] I
34.31	cuirass of / cuirass also of
34.31	former / latter
34.31	metal has / metal which has

34.35	There are caps / The caps
34.38	*cum multis aliis quæ* / cum multis aliis quiæ
34.38	*longum* / longam
34.40	casts of two / two casts of two
35.15	a-wanting / a wanting
35.16	Edinburgh were / Edinburgh was ↑ were ↓
35.27	days. It / days it
35.37	excepting that in / excepted in
35.38	Buccleuch / Buccleugh
35.39	size / breadth
35.39	thirty-three / 33
35.39	length, thirteen / length & 13
35.40	fourteen / 14
36.3	important in / important certainly in
36.13	drawing-room / drawing room
36.14	reception. The / reception; the
36.15	eighteen (AH) / 10
	The library is described as eighteen feet wide below; it is, in fact, seventeen and a half feet wide.
36.16	well-proportioned / well proportioned
36.18	woman-kind / woman kind
36.21	twelve and a half feet (AH) / [　　　]
36.22	eleven feet (AH) / [　　　]
36.28	Burke / Burk
36.29	Locke / Lock
37.6	precaution / precautions
37.14	to a surprising / to surprising
37.21	they / she
37.31	corollary / coralary
38.2	fourteen / 14
38.3	three (AH) / five
38.5	a / the
38.5	wished to save room / wished for the purpose of saving room
38.7	three (AH) / 6
38.10	height to pull / height pull
38.11	too / two
38.13	imagination. Indeed / imagination; indeed
38.17	stair-case / stair case
38.19	situation, a / situation. A
38.20	progressing around / progressing it around
38.24	sidling along / sidling it along
38.37	Spenser / Spencer
38.38	constitution, [run on]"an yron man made of yron molde;" [run on] a (PB) / constitution. [new line] An yron man of made of yron molde [new line] A
38.40	an / &
39.11	of / from
39.12	apartment affords / apartment which affords
39.16	are / is
39.17	south-west / south west
39.17	angle / ingle
39.21	south-east / S E
40.1	twenty-four / Twenty four

40.7 consists / consisting
40.8 chairs, and an / chairs an
40.9 Linlithgow / Linlithgo
40.11 Battle / battle
40.14 Linlithgow / Linlithgo
40.22 approaching. [run on] This / approaching [new paragraph] This
40.24 water-coloured / water coloured
40.25 twenty-five / twenty five
40.33 to a species / to species
40.37 stair-case / stair case
40.40 see," we come to the eating / see". The ⟨dining⟩ ↑ Eating ↓
40.40 room, a / room is a
41.6 breadth. The / breadth the
41.8 tied / tyed
41.18 West Indian / west indian
41.18 South / south
41.20 Square / square
41.20 Road / road
42.2 *apropos* / apropo
42.3 one; they / one. They
42.6 grew in the old and noble / grew at ⟨the⟩ ↑ in ↓ old & noble
      Scott appears to have deleted the wrong word.
42.7 were put up for sale by / were by
42.25 commodity to / commodity through mere accident to
42.27 trees / tree
42.36 as having / as being having
42.40 *boudoir* / boudoir
43.1 woman-kind / woman kind
43.10 *Scotland.* Whether / Scotland" whether
43.14 The artists furnished, agreeable to a certain engagement / The artists
      engaged ⟨from⟩ furnished agreeably to a certain engagement
43.18 failed / fail
43.26 too / to
43.31 *boudoir* / Boudoir
43.32 artists / authors
43.33 have / has
43.39 servants-hall / servants Hall
44.13 key-hole / key hole
45.8 kernel. Upon / kernel upon
45.16 is inappreciably different from the original / is different from the un-
      appreciable original
45.20 broad-sword / broad sword
46.8 indeed is the / indeed the
46.11 rendering / renders
46.15 days. When / days when
46.16 black-letter / black letter
46.17 chronicles, was / chronicles of black letter was
46.20 remember / recollect
46.27 *auto de fe* / auto de fe
46.31 the collection / the curious collection
46.35 Field / field
46.39 vicar, were / vicar of Norham were
46.40 Garden Theatre / garden theatre

47.6   formed by the assistance of / formed in his more ⟨wealthy⟩ days by the
        assistance of
47.8   made / formed
47.15   House / house
47.23   which was founded / which founded
47.23   Kemble now / Kemble is now
47.34   Stratford-upon-Avon / Stratford upon Avon
47.36   and being an / and an
47.37   their / whose
47.39   snuff-box / snuff box
48.3   Mulberry Tree (AH) / mulberry tree
48.3   originally the (AH) / originally contained the
48.4   Esqr (AH) / Esquire
48.5   Inheritance (AH) / inheritance
48.12   also / both
48.14   Restoration / restoration
48.14   afterwards. There / afterwards there
48.16   perfect. One / perfect one
48.19   *editiones principes* / editiones principes
48.23   money and some time bestowed / money sometime bestowed
48.37   goodness, which / goodness of which
49.5   thirty-nine / thirty nine
49.6   bound, was / bound were
49.10   well-printed / well printed
49.11   bard amuse / bard to amuse
49.30   press, in the / press the
49.31   occurs I find, / occurs in which I find
50.16   black-letter / black letter
50.18   tracts / tarks
50.19   black-letter / black letter
50.23   Scottish / scottish
50.28   *Set.* [run on] It / set." [new paragraph] It
50.33   This / It
50.35   an (PB) / the
50.36   been fondly and (PB) / been [lacuna] &
51.3   detection (PB) / disclosure
51.4   the preferd purchaser (PB) / the purchaser
51.5   insert. The / insert the
51.11   paltry (PB) / pithy
51.14   on (PB) / of
51.19   self-applause / self applause
51.21   ill-fated / ill fated
51.24   half-reputation / half reputation
51.30   sung. [run on] Secondly, that / sung. [new paragraph] secondly. That
51.34   words / music
52.2   *Tales.* [run on] These / Tales" [new paragraph] These
52.6   John / Robert
52.11   *Magnus Apollo* / magnus Ap⟨p⟩ollo
52.12   minstrelsy being christened / Minstrelsy christened
52.13   Spearman / spearman
52.24   Critical. [run on] This / Critical" [new paragraph] This
52.29   in the time / in time
52.29   *The Spectator* / The Spectator

53.12   Ramsay. [run on] This / Ramsay." [new paragraph] This
53.19   Wars (PB) / War
53.19   Josephus's (PB) / Josephus
53.24   whether / whither
53.25   verses with his ingenious / verses. He & his ingenious
53.26   or should complain / or complain
53.34   Von Bergmann (PB) / Fonberbman
54.3   these (PB) / those
54.3   was a Livonian (PB) / was Livonian
54.4   Clergyman (PB) / clergyman
54.20   Scottish / scottish
55.3   north-west-ward / north west ward
55.7   here / hear
55.17   "demonology" / Demonology
56.1   sense, and learned / sense learning & learned
56.2   credit; their / Credit ↑ which ↓ their
        The 'which' was added at a later point but the original sense has been
        misunderstood.
56.2   understanding—as / understanding as
56.3   circumstance / circumstances
56.3   extrinsic—were / extrinsic were
56.4   *Much Ado About Nothing* / Twelfth Night
56.19   had / have
56.19   had / have
56.25   First. The / First the
56.27   Sinclarus (PB) / Sinclair
56.36   an exquisite morsel of / an exquisite morsel a morsel of
56.38   have (PB) / am
57.15   Archimedes / Archemides
57.30   genitum credere / genitum se credere
57.39   perswades me to (PB) / perswades to
58.11   Lordships, [new paragraph] Most / Lordships [run on] most
58.12   Servant, [new paragraph] George / servant [run on] George
58.14   *morceau* / morceau
58.20   dated 1672 / dated in 1672
58.22   blasphemy. He was a / blasphemy a
58.28   elsewhere / else-where
58.35   haunts / haunt⟨s⟩
59.4   Bekker's / Beckers
59.13   1647.[run on] This / 1647." [new paragraph] This
59.16   along / alongst
59.31   1691. [run on] This / 1691. [new paragraph] This
59.32   Glanville / Glandville
61.1   celebrated. / celebrated a one.
61.4   *not.* [run on] A / not." [new paragraph] A
61.12   celebrated persecution / celebrated ⟨New England⟩ historie & persecu-
        tion
61.22   Right / right
61.26   *wayes.* [run on] By / ways" [new paragraph] By
61.26   Physicke. [run on] London / Physicke [new paragraph] London
61.28   well-known / well known
63.3   contains / contain
63.8   art—founded / art founded

63.9   price—leads / price leads
63.20   Northampton: [run on] *A* / Northampton. [new paragraph] A
63.22   and (PB) / or
63.29   *Astrolog.* [run on] *&c.* / Astrology [new paragraph] &c.
63.31   Sixth's / sixth's
63.40   then / at present
64.4   First / I.
64.18   termed by those / termed those
64.19   "eccentric biography" / eccentric Biography
64.23   twelfth / 12th
64.23   Granger's / Gramgers
64.32   *Lives and Actions* (PB) / lives actions
64.39   1742. [run on] A considerable / 1742. [new paragraph] Considerable
65.14   *Thieves.* [run on] By / Thieves. [new paragraph] By
65.16   committed. [run on] London / committed. [new paragraph] London
65.16   1719. [run on] On / 1719. [new paragraph] On
65.17   Steele / steel
65.30   *Ausführliche* / Ausfureliche
65.36   cited / quoted
66.6   1628. [run on] This / 1628 [new paragraph] This
66.11   wuddy." Neither / wuddy" - neither
66.11   highway / high-way
66.15   Clavell appears / Clavell as he appears
66.16   friend, his / friend is ↑ His ↓
66.17   well-approved / well approved
66.31   lawlesse (PB) / lawfull
67.3   is (PB) / in
67.9   ascribing / asriding
67.12   thirty-five / thirty five
67.15   mentioned. [new paragraph] We / mentioned. [run on] we
67.16   Topsell's (PB) / Topsail's
67.25   *Adventures* (PB) / adventure
67.31   *Weekes* (PB) / meeks
67.31   Sylvester. [new paragraph] The / sylvester". [run on] "The
67.32   1651. [new paragraph] Thomas / 1651" [run on] "Thomas
67.33   1624. [new paragraph] *The* / 1624" [run on] "The
67.34   *Hierarchie* (PB) / Hierchy
67.34   1635. [new paragraph] Reginald / 1635" [run on] "Reginald
69.3   which are acquired at / which at
69.10   to. [run on] The / to [new paragraph] The
69.10   black-letter / Black Letter
69.11   nouvellement (PB) / vouvellemont
69.16   Marked / Ked
            This is the first word on the new folio.
69.22   du (PB) / due
69.26   black-letter / black letter
69.27   sacred: [run on] *Le* / sacred [new paragraph] "Le
69.29   *Esplandian* (PB) / Esplandran
69.29   *Empereur* (PB) / L'empereur
69.30   *les* (PB) / le
69.31   *Essars* (PB) / Essais
69.31   *Nicolas de Herberay* (PB) / Nicolas Herberay
69.32   *Artillerie.* [run on] A / Artillerie." [new paragraph] A

69.35	*novellas* / novelles
70.4	traites as they / traites they
70.5	shipwrecked sailors of / shipwreck of
70.7	Audrey / Audley
70.15	criticism held / criticism of held
70.23	Club / club
70.23	Utterson; a fable / Utterson. A Fable
70.27	kind / king
70.27	high degree *recherché* / high recherche
70.28	that it contains / that contains
70.30	remarked / remarks
70.30	canons: [run on] *Les* / canons [new paragraph] Les
70.30	*faictz* (PB) / faits
70.34	knight-errantry / Knight errantry
70.38	knight-errant / Knight errant
70.40	original fiction. / original and probably the original fiction
71.1	*rencontre* / rencontry
71.4	books / book
71.13	more / ner
71.15	editor is here / Editor here
71.17	continuations. [run on] It / continuations [new paragraph] It
71.18	his tragical death, / the tragical deaths
71.18	death, Yseult / deaths of Yseult
71.19	Tristrem's / tristrems
71.19	affection, became / affection she became

EXPLANATORY NOTES

All the items described in *Reliquiae* pertaining to the 'shew-house' described from page 27 onwards are still to be found at Abbotsford unless otherwise indicated.

In these notes a comprehensive attempt is made to identify Scott's sources, and all quotations, references, historical events and historical personages, and to translate difficult or obscure phrases (single words appear in the Glossary). The notes are brief; they offer information rather than critical comment or exposition. When a quotation or reference has not been recognised this is stated: any new information from readers will be welcomed. Literary references are to standard editions or to the editions Scott himself used. Books in the Abbotsford Library are identified by reference to the appropriate page of the *Catalogue of the Library at Abbotsford*. When quotations reproduce their sources accurately, the reference is given without comment. Verbal differences in the source are indicated by a prefatory 'see', while a general rather than a verbal indebtedness is indicated by 'compare'. Biblical references are to the Authorised Version. Plays by Shakespeare are cited without authorial ascription, and references are to *William Shakespeare: The Complete Works*, edited by Peter Alexander (London and Glasgow, 1951, frequently reprinted).

The following publications are distinguished by abbreviations, or are given without the names of their authors:

CLA [J. G. Cochrane], *Catalogue of the Library at Abbotsford* (Edinburgh, 1838).

EEWN Edinburgh Edition of the Waverley Novels, Editor-in-chief David Hewitt (Edinburgh, 1993–). EEWN volumes of Scott's novels have been cited where these are available unless otherwise stated.

Letters The *Letters of Sir Walter Scott*, ed. H. J. C. Grierson and others, 12 vols (London, 1932–37).

Demonology and Witchcraft Walter Scott, *Letters on Demonology and Witchcraft* (London, 1830).

Lockhart J. G. Lockhart, *Memoirs of the Life of Sir Walter Scott, Bart.*, 7 vols (Edinburgh, 1837–38).

Magnum Walter Scott, *Waverley Novels*, 48 vols (Edinburgh, 1829–33).

Muses (1638) H[enry] Adamson, *The Muses Threnodie, or, Mirthfull Mournings, on the death of Master Gall. Containing varietie of pleasant Poëticall descriptions, morall instructions, historicall narrations, and divine observations, with the most remarkable antiquities of Scotland, especially at Perth. By Mr. H. Adamson* (Edinburgh, 1638).

Muses (1774) Henry Adamson, *The Muses Threnodie; Or, Mirthfull Mournings, on the death of Master Gall*, ed. James Cant, 2 vols (Perth, 1774).

ODEP The *Oxford Dictionary of English Proverbs*, 3rd edn, ed. F. P. Wilson (Oxford, 1970).

OED The *Oxford English Dictionary*, 2nd edn, 12 vols (Oxford, 1989).

Poetical Works Walter Scott, *Poetical Works*, [ed. J. G. Lockhart], 12 volumes (Edinburgh, 1833–34).

'Popular Poetry' Walter Scott, 'Introductory Remarks on Popular Poetry', the 1830 Introduction to *Minstrelsy of the Scottish Border*, reprinted in *Poetical*

Works, [ed. J. G. Lockhart], 12 volumes (Edinburgh, 1833–34).
Prose Works *The Prose Works of Sir Walter Scott, Bart.*, 28 vols (Edinburgh 1834–36).
The Antiquary Walter Scott, *The Antiquary*, ed. David Hewitt, EEWN 3 (Edinburgh and New York, 1995); originally published 1816.
The Statistical Account *The Statistical Account of Scotland 1791–1799*, ed. Sir John Sinclair; re-ed. Donald J. Withrington and Ian R. Grant (Wakefield, 1976), Vol. 11 (see *CLA*, 84).

1.1 Reliquiæ Trotcosienses *Latin* Relics of Trotcosey. In Scott's third novel *The Antiquary* (1816), Trotcosey is the name of the monastery upon the lands of which the house of Monkbarns (see note to 1.4–5) is built. The name is derived from the Scots word for a 'hood', punningly referring to a monk's dress.

1.3 Gabions *The Dictionary of the Older Scottish Tongue* defines *gabion* as a 'wicker basket filled with earth used in fortification', and cites uses in John Knox's *Historie of the Reformatioun of Religioun in Scotland* (London, 1644; completed 1572: *CLA*, 2), and Robert Lindsay of Pitscottie's *History of Scotland* (Edinburgh, 1728; completed 1580: *CLA*, 8, 259). Adamson defines the term as 'the ornaments of his Cabin, which, by a Catachrestick name, he usually calleth *Gabions*' (*Muses* (1638), 6). Scott adopts this catachrestic use (i.e. misuse) of the term to describe curious antiquarian collections.

1.4–5 Jonathan Oldbuck Esq. of Monkbarns the fictitious antiquary of Scott's novel *The Antiquary* (1816). Monkbarns is the name of his estate.

3.2 nicknackets small knick-knacks, ornamental bits and pieces.

3.4 Lothians three the three counties of West, Mid, and East Lothian, around Edinburgh.

3.7 the Flood Noah's flood.

3.8 Burns' Verses to Captain Grose Robert Burns, 'On the Late Captain Grose's Peregrinations thro' Scotland, collecting the Antiquities of that Kingdom' (1789), lines 31–36. Francis Grose (1731–91) wrote *The Antiquities of Scotland*, 2 vols (London, 1789–91: *CLA*, 177), which includes material on ancient armour and weapons.

5.2 an author of the present day Scott himself.

5.16–17 Gall's gabions see notes to 1.3 and 6.8. It was also the familiar title of the first part of *The Muses Threnodie*: see text 6.30–31.

5.20 celebrated book club probably the Bannatyne Club, founded in 1823, of which Scott was the first president. The club was modelled on the Roxburghe Club (see note to 5.21–22) and was founded for the publication of Scottish texts and documents. Scott describes the significance of the club in his article on 'Pitcairn's Criminal Trials' (*Prose Works*, 21.219–23).

5.21–22 Roxburghe itself the Roxburghe Club, established in 1812 upon the occasion of the dispersal of the library of John Ker (1740–1804), 3rd Duke of Roxburghe from 1755. During his lifetime the Duke secured an unrivalled collection of books from Caxton's Press, including Valdarfer's edition of Boccaccio (see note to 45.12–15). To celebrate the sale of this book for £2260 the chief bibliophiles of the day met at St. Alban's Tavern, under the presidency of Lord Spencer and inaugurated the Roxburghe Club, with T. F. Dibdin as its first secretary. The club was dedicated to the reprinting of rare literary works, each of the 24 members being expected to present and pay for a limited edition of some rare work during his career. Scott discusses the significance of the Roxburghe Club at some length in his article on 'Pitcairn's Criminal Trials', where he states that it 'produced upwards of forty reprints of scarce and curious tracts' (*Prose Works*, 21.217). The Author of Waverley was invited to join the

Roxburghe Club after referring to it in *Peveril of the Peak* (1822), and officially became a member in April 1823. Scott agreed to act as *locum tenens* of the 'Great Unknown': see *Peveril of the Peak*, 4 vols (Edinburgh, 1822), i.xv–xvi.

5.23–24 Sterne ... hobby-horse Laurence Sterne (1713–68), author of *The Life and Opinions of Tristram Shandy*, 9 vols (York and London, 1759–67: see *CLA*, 63). The term 'hobby-horse' comes from 'the generous (tho' hobby-horsical) gallantry of my uncle' (*Tristram Shandy*, Vol. 3, Ch. 22) and denotes obsessive whimsical behaviour. It is itself derived from the older sense of *hobby*, meaning 'toy horse'. A note to *The Antiquary* points out that Jonathan Oldbuck is given the credit of using 'hobby' in its modern sense for the first time: see *The Antiquary*, 479. The phrase is a favourite of Scott's: in his essay on 'Pitcairn's Criminal Trials' he writes of 'the particular knot of booksellers who devote themselves to supply these gentlemen's hobby-horses' (*Prose Works*, 21.206).

5.27 Nos haec mirum esse nihil *Latin* there is nothing to surprise us in this. No classical source has been traced.

5.33–34 Dr Ruthven a 'Mr George Ruthven, chirurgeon', is mentioned twice in 'Extracts from the Kirk Session Records of Perth', on 19 March 1593 and 29 December 1595. This is published with *The Chronicle of Perth; A Register of Remarkable Occurrences, Chiefly Connected with that City, from the year 1210 to 1668*, ed. James Maidment for the Maitland Club (Edinburgh, 1831: *CLA*, 281). Cant (*Muses* (1774), 1.vi) describes him as descended from the noble family of Ruthven and says that he was a physician and surgeon in Perth. Ruthven was about 92 years of age when the poems were published.

6.4 Gowrie Conspiracy John, 3rd Earl of Gowrie (*c.* 1577–1600; succeeded 1588) and his brother Alexander, Master of Ruthven, probably conspired to murder King James VI of Scots, but were overpowered and slain at Gowrie House in Perth on 5 August 1600. Gowrie, who was educated in Europe, was an accomplished scholar and also the provost of Perth. Cant provides a lengthy note on the conspiracy in his edition of *The Muses Threnodie*, writing: 'Mr Ruthven was a relation of the two unfortunate brothers, and narrowly escaped being swallowed up in the catastrophe. The circumstances of the time required the utmost caution in the poet, while he touched that delicate string; it was dangerous at that time to speak a language different from the Court' (*Muses* (1774), 1.148).

6.8 John Gall younger Cant states that he 'was a merchant, well educated, of sweet dispositions and pregnant wit, and much esteemed. His premature death of a consumption, occasioned the following elegiac and descriptive poem' (*Muses* (1774), 1.vii). A Mr John Gall is mentioned in 'Extracts from the Kirk Session Records of Perth' as appearing as a witness on 3 October 1604 printed with *The Chronicle of Perth; A Register of Remarkable Occurrences, Chiefly Connected with that City, from the year 1210 to 1668*, ed. James Maidment for the Maitland Club (Edinburgh, 1831: *CLA*, 281).

6.13 Caiaphas high priest of the Jewish Sanhedrin at the time of Jesus's execution: see John 18.14 and 24.

6.13–14 is the subject of the first poem respecting them and their gabions the first of the Muses takes John Gall as its subject and is ostensibly written by George Ruthven as he and his 'gabions' mourn for Gall.

6.15 Henry Adamson Cant states that 'the author of the two poems was educated for the pulpit, and appears to have been a gentleman of considerable abilities, a good classical scholar, he wrote some Latin poems above mediocrity. His relations were of considerable rank among the citizens of Perth, he was the son of James Adamson, who was dean of guild in 1600, when Gowrie was murdered, and was provost in 1610 and 1611. Our poet died unmarried in the year after the poems were published' (*Muses* (1774), 1.vii–viii).

6.17   The Muses Threnodie   for the full title of the poem first published in 1638 see headnote. A *threnody* is a song of lamentation.

6.25–29   see *Muses* (1774), 1.vi.

6.27   own coining   this is not correct: see note to 1.3.

6.36–37   William Drummond of Hawthornden   1585–1649, Scottish poet, whose father owned the estate of Hawthornden, near Roslin, in Midlothian. He was associated with the poets who surrounded James VI, but he did not follow the court to London on the Union of the Crowns in 1603, continuing his education at Edinburgh University, and in Bourges and Paris. After inheriting Hawthornden in 1610, he led a retired life, reading widely in European literature, and writing. His first collection was published in 1614, *A Midnight's Trance* in 1619 (republished in 1623 as *A Cypresse Grove*), and *Flowres of Sion* in 1623. Drummond was very much the great figure of Scottish letters when he recommended the publication of Adamson's poetry.

7.6–30   To my worthy friend Mr Henry Adamson . . . W. D.   see *Muses* (1774), 1.viii–ix.

7.9   Alcibiades Seleni   Alcibiades (*c.* 450–404 BC) was an Athenian general and statesman whose personal life was notorious for its dissolute nature: this is presumably why he was associated with Silenus, the attendant of Bacchus. His 'composite' personality, half statesman, half dissolute, may also explain his link with the other mythical creatures mentioned in the same sentence. The phrase 'the Sileni of Alcibiades' (in the plural) became proverbial in ancient Greece and was used to refer to things which, in appearance, seem worthy of contempt but on further consideration seem of more significance and admirable. *Sileni* or *Seleni* were small images divided in half which could be opened out for display; in the 16th century Erasmus writes: 'when closed they represented some ridiculous, ugly flute-player, but when opened they suddenly revealed the figure of a god, so that the amusing deception would show off the art of the carver' (Margaret Mann Phillips, *Erasmus on His Times* (Cambridge, 1967), 77).

7.10   Sphinges   sphinxes. In Greek mythology the *sphinx* was a fabulous winged monster with a woman's head and bust and a lion's body.

7.10   Chimæras   in Greek mythology the *Chimaera*, the mother of the Sphinx, had a lion's head, a goat's body and a serpent's tale.

7.10   Centaurs   in Greek mythology fabulous creatures with the head, trunk and arms of a man and the body and legs of a horse.

7.12   They deservedly   *Muses* (1774) reads 'They may deservedlie'.

7.12   non intus ut extra   *Latin, literally*, internally, not as externally, referring to something that is not as it seems.

7.15–17   founders . . . monasteries   this is described in the third muse of *The Muses Threnodie* (*Muses* (1774), 1.73–91). Perth is reputed to have been founded by the Roman governor Agricola during his campaigns north of the Forth *c.* AD 79. A bridge of ten arches over the Tay at Perth was carried away by floods in 1621. The term *fowse* denotes a 'fosse' or ditch. Adamson claims that a temple dedicated to Mars was found in a field adjoining the Tay (*Muses* (1774), 1.90), and *The Statistical Account* claims it was built by the son of Regam, second daughter of King Lear (11.473). The monasteries are mostly described in the sixth muse (*Muses* (1774), 1.153–59). Until the Reformation, Perth had four monasteries, Carmelite, Carthusian, Dominican, and Franciscan. See *Memorabilia of the City of Perth* (Perth, 1806), 1–54, and *The Statistical Account*, 11.468–518.

7.21   these   *Muses* (1774) reads 'them'.

7.27   afterwards   *Muses* (1774), and *Muses* (1638), read 'after'.

7.32–35 The above letter ... lamented   *Muses* (1774), 1.ix.

7.34–35 the year after ... much lamented   Cant states that Adamson died the year after the poems were published, i.e. 1739 (*Muses* (1774), 1.viii), but *The Statistical Account* claims that Adamson died in May 1637 and that Drummond's letter arrived after this date (11.471).

8.3–9.2 The Inventory ... stale   see *Muses* (1774), 1.1–2.

8.9 workmanship   *Muses* (1774), and *Muses* (1638), read 'workmanships'.

8.11 Centaurs   see note to 7.10.

8.14 Albion   poetical name for Britain, the allusion being to its white cliffs.

8.16 evil   *Muses* (1774), and *Muses* (1638), read 'ill'.

8.16–17 presage good ... Ye gods   Scott here omits a line of *Muses* which reads 'What sprite Daedalian hath forth brought them'.

8.20 Neptune ... Trident   Neptune was an old Italian deity associated with water. In Roman literature he is frequently associated with the Greek god Poseidon and is often depicted carrying a trident or three-pronged fish spear.

8.21 Pan   Greek god of flocks and shepherds.

8.22 Triton ... Buckie   in Greek mythology Triton was a merman, son of Poseidon the god of the sea. He is frequently depicted blowing on a conch shell. 'Buckie' is the Scots word for a whelk.

8.24 Mars   Roman god of war.

8.26 Cyclopean ... Achilles   in *The Iliad* Achilles is the chief hero of the Greeks during the Trojan war. His armour is described as 'Cyclopean', partly because it is huge, and partly because on the day he kills Hector Achilles is wearing armour made specially for him by Hephaestus (Greek god of fire, and of smiths) whose craftsmen were said to be the Cyclops.

8.27 Venus ... Apelles   Apelles was the greatest painter of antiquity. He was born in the first half of the 4th century BC in Ionia. His most famous picture was of Aphrodite, or, as the Romans called her, Venus, the goddess of love, rising from the sea. Cant has a note which reads: 'Apelles was a celebrated painter in the days of Alexander the Great, who would allow no other painter to draw his portrait; he left an imperfect picture of Venus, no painter would venture to finish it' (*Muses* (1774), 1.17).

8.28–29 Hector's ... war   Hector was the leader of the Trojan forces during the war. His story is told in Homer's *Iliad*.

8.30–31 fatal sword ... yield   Ajax was leader of the Salaminians at the siege of Troy. Homer depicts him as a man obstinate in his bravery to the point of stupidity. His shield, made of seven layers of ox-hide, is described in Homer's *Iliad*, 7.219–20.

8.32–33 Herculean club ... Lerne dub   Heracles, or Hercules, was a Greek hero noted for his strength. He was assigned 12 'labours' the second of which was to destroy the Hydra, a poisonous water-snake who lived in the marshes of the Lerna near Argos. A *dub* is a Scottish word for a pool of stagnant water.

8.34 Vulcan ... crooked heel   Vulcan was an early Roman fire-god later identified with the Greek god Hephaestus, god of fire and of smiths. He is represented in Homer as lame from birth.

8.36–39 Cyclophes ... tempering it   in Greek mythology the *Cyclopes* or *Cyclops* were one-eyed giants who acted as the metal-workers of Hephaestus, and made Zeus's thunderbolts. The brethren Allans have not been identified, but were presumably blacksmiths or sword-smiths in Perth, who made a sword for George Ruthven.

8.37 six   *Muses* (1774), and *Muses* (1638), read 'ten'.

8.38 that   *Muses* (1774), and *Muses* (1638), read 'their'.

8.40 **Esculapius** Aesculapius, the Roman name for the Greek god of medicine and healing.

9.1–2 **ale . . . pure and stale** the idea is that rather than use it offensively George Ruthven instructs the Allans to cool the red-hot sword in stale (i.e. strong) ale and warm it up for drinking.

9.4 **centurae** waist bands or girdles.

9.5 **Mercury** in Roman mythology the messenger of the gods represented with a staff.

9.6–29 **And more . . . Amalthean horn** see *Muses* (1774), 1.3–4.

9.8 **contortized** this seems to be a word coined by the poet. It would appear to be derived from 'contortioned', i.e. twisted.

9.9 **works** *Muses* (1774), and *Muses* (1638), read 'work'.

9.12 **chimæras** see note to 7.10.

9.15 **brought them out** produced them.

9.16–19 **monstrous branched . . . hacksaw** in Greek mythology Acteon was turned into a stag by the gods for boasting that he was a better hunter than Artemis, the virgin huntress A *knapsea* or knapscap is a cap of cloth or leather with bars of steel inside.

9.20 **toes of lapsters** lobsters' claws.

9.21 **ensigns for tapsters** signs for inn-keepers or publicans.

9.22 **Gaudie beads** *probably* bright colourful beads making a showy appearance, but also the larger beads in a rosary separating the decades of aves.

9.27 **swing** *Muses* (1774), and *Muses* (1638), read 'hing'.

9.29 **The wealthy Amalthean horn** Amalthea was the goat who, in Greek mythology, suckled the infant Zeus. The horn of the goat, which Zeus later gave away, had the power of producing whatever its possessor wished.

9.31–10.12 **In one nook . . . hunting horn** see *Muses* (1774), 1.4–5.

9.31 **stand** *Muses* (1774), and *Muses* (1638), read 'stands'.

9.31 **Lochabrian axes** Lochaber is an area in the west of Inverness-shire. A Lochabrian axe is a type of halbert with a strong hook behind for laying hold of the object assaulted.

9.35 **book they call the Dennet** this has not been identified.

9.36 **head of old Broun Kennett** head of [a dog called] Brown Kennett. A *kennet* is a small hunting dog.

9.37 **Mantua bannet** cap or hat made of a type of silk from Mantua in northern Italy.

9.38 **robin and a jannet** a 'robin' is an early variety of pear and a 'jannet', or genet, an early variety of apple.

9.40 **buffet-stool sexangular** low stool or footstool, with sides like a folding table, and with three or four legs. However, 'sexangular' may imply a six-legged or six-angled stool.

9.40–10.1 **sexangular . . . Whatever matter** Scott here omits two lines of *Muses* which read: 'A fool muting in his own hand, / Soft, soft my muse, sound not this sand:'.

10.4 **totum** four-sided disc with a letter on each side, which was spun like a top; when the disc fell, the uppermost letter told the spinner's fortune.

10.4 **bairnes taps** *Scots* children's whipping-tops.

10.5 **guardareilly** possibly a variant of Paris criminal slang 'gaudille' meaning poker or sword.

10.6 **Abercorne mussel** Abercorne is a village in West Lothian on the south shore of the Firth of Forth. The Forth was renowned for its mussel fishing.

10.9–10 **sacred games . . . consecrate** ancient games were held in Greece at least 3500 years ago. The Olympic Games, the most important of these, were held in honour of Zeus.

10.12   Diana gave her hunting horn   Diana was a Roman goddess identified with the Greek Artemis, the virgin huntress.

10.15–16   apology . . . learning   see *Muses* (1774), 1.7: 'An Apology of the Author: Done as by the Mourner to the Lovers of Learning'.

10.20   Gowrie Conspiracy   see note to 6.4.

10.23–12.43   An Apology . . . snatched at me   see *Muses* (1774), 1.7–11.

10.24–25   sing Swanlike   the swan was said to sing before death. Compare Emilia in *Othello*, 5.2.250–51: 'I will play the swan,/ And die in music'.

10.30   Heraclitus   Heraclitus of Ephesus (*c.* 500 BC), a philosopher who maintained that all things are in a state of flux and that matter itself is constantly changing.

10.31   reeling   *Muses* (1774), and *Muses* (1638), read 'reelings'.

10.32   Democritus   Greek philosopher born at Abdera *c.* 460 BC. He is sometimes known as the 'laughing philosopher' in opposition to the melancholy Heraclitus. He believed that while bodies decay, the atoms of which they consist are eternal, and proposed that happiness is to be found in recognising the superiority of the soul over the body.

10.36–11.1   For neither . . . order all   see Ecclesiastes 9.11.

10.35   bad   *Muses* (1774), and *Muses* (1638), read 'good'.

10.40   fame   *Muses* (1774), and *Muses* (1638), read 'favour'.

11.2   second causes   from the 17th century secondary causes are explored by many thinkers as a means of discerning the divine will through its materialist manifestations.

11.3   paradise   although the MS and *Muses* (1774) read *paradise*, *Muses* (1638) reads *paradoxe*.

11.10   Thus   *Muses* (1774), and *Muses* (1638), read 'Hence'.

11.12–13   written riches . . . reserved   i.e. it is writings which are preserved (not material wealth), and they keep the record of the ill deeds of their owners.

11.13   And for the ill of the owners are reserved   compare Ecclesiastes 5.13.

11.14   bearer   *Muses* (1774), and *Muses* (1638), read 'bearers'.

11.15   So some to their own hurt rule over others   compare Ecclesiastes 8.9.

11.23   rage   *Muses* (1774), and *Muses* (1638), read 'age'.

11.26–27   findes . . . windes   *Muses* (1638) has 'findes' and 'windes', while *Muses* (1774) 'finds' and 'winds'. The archaic spellings may indicate a memory of 1638.

11.30   Diogenes   (4th century BC), the chief representative of the Cynic school of philosophy, and famed for his extravagantly simple way of life. He is reputed to have lived in a large earthenware tub.

11.33   o'er past   past by.

11.34   I praise the worthy deeds of martial men   compare Ecclesiasticus (in the Apocrypha) 44.1.

11.35   may   *Muses* (1774), and *Muses* (1638), read 'might'.

11.37   worthy   *Muses* (1774), and *Muses* (1638), read 'lively'.

11.38   Beget like children   beget children like themselves.

11.39   native sons   offspring of the same kind, compatriots, fellow-countrymen.

11.42   For what avails . . . noble race   see Juvenal (*c.* 60–*c.* 130), *Satires*, 8.1–2. The argument of the passage from 11.42–12.23 is based on this satire.

11.43 **long descent of branches** i.e. a long family tree.

12.1 **Like virtue** similar virtue.

12.3 **common** *Muses* (1774), and *Muses* (1638), read 'contrare'.

12.3 **this true shall trie** this truth will be tested and found true.

12.4 **Virtue alone is true nobility** see Juvenal (*c.* 60–*c.* 130), *Satires*, 8.20.

12.11 **heroick** *Muses* (1774) has 'heroic', and *Muses* (1638) 'heroick'. Scott's spelling may indicate a memory of 1638.

12.13–14 **For lineage ... selves not made** Naso is one of the names for Ovid, Publius Ovidius Naso (43 BC – AD 17). For the reference see his *Metamorphoses*, 13.42–44.

12.15 **dare** *Muses* (1774), and *Muses* (1638), read 'durst'.

12.17–18 **what's said ... And I** Scott here omits a line of *Muses* which reads 'I rather that *Thersites* were my daid'.

12.18 **And I Achilles like most noble rather** see Juvenal (*c.* 60–*c.* 130), *Satires*, 8.269–70. For Achilles see note to 8.26. Thercites, a deformed officer in the Greek army during the siege of Troy, was famed for constantly railing against his superiors.

12.22 **Momus must needs carp** in Greek mythology Momus was the personification of fault-finding.

12.22 **Misanthropos** a misanthrope, or hater of mankind.

12.23 **Areopagita-like** Areopagus was the hill in Athens where the highest court of the city had its sittings, and thus a name for the court itself; thus *Areopagita-like* means 'judicious', or 'just'.

12.23 **Scythropos** common Greek descriptive adjective used here to represent a sullen, angry-looking person.

12.26 **Most foul ... spread** Cant adds a note stating 'It was dangerous at that time for any person in Perth to express the smallest doubt of the conspiracy of the two noble brothers, or to imagine that the King and his servants had any iniquous [iniquitous] design against them' (*Muses* (1774), 1.11).

12.26 **expressions** *Muses* (1774), and *Muses* (1638), read 'aspersions'.

12.26 **rumour** *Muses* (1774), and *Muses* (1638), read 'rumours'.

12.29 **Princes** *Muses* (1774), and *Muses* (1638), read 'Places'.

12.31 **the** *Muses* (1774), and *Muses* (1638), read 'their'.

13.3–12 **If I ... me secure** see *Muses* (1774), 1.12.

13.8 **More worth ... Gnatho's affection** Zoilus was a rhetorician and critic of the 4th century BC. He wrote nine books of criticism on Homer and his name has become proverbial for a carping critic. Gnatho is an amusing parasite in Terence's comedy *The Eunuch* (161 BC).

13.19–20 **divided into nine ... the muses** the *muses*, Greek goddesses of the literature and arts, were traditionally nine in number: Calliope (epic poetry), Clio (history), Euterpe (flute-playing), Melpomene (tragedy), Terpsichore (dancing), Erato (the lyre), Polyhymnia (sacred song), Urania (astronomy), and Thalia (comedy).

13.24–25 **some happy expedition in the neighbourhood of Perth** Scott himself went on many expeditions of this sort with his friend William Adam. The Blair Adam Club, consisting of Scott, William Adam, Sir Adam Ferguson and William Clerk, and others, met each year around the summer solstice at William Adam's house for antiquarian excursions. According to William Adam (*Blair Adam from 1733 to 1834: Remarks on the Blair-Adam Estate* (Blair-Adam, privately printed, 1834), ix–liv), Scott attended their meetings regularly from 1817 to 1831 but in fact the club met regularly only between 1821 and 1830: see *The Abbot*, ed. Christopher Johnson, EEWN 10 (Edinburgh, 2000), 378.

13.34–35   went a-fishing for the pearl ... rivers   the mussels of the River Tay, which runs through Perth, are the source of the finest Scottish pearls. Pearl fishing is described in the fourth muse (*Muses* (1774), 1.91).

14.5   Drayton's Poly Olbion   *Poly-Olbion* (1612–22) by Michael Drayton (1563–1631). Drayton's poem is a topographical description and celebration of England's present customs and history (*CLA*, 155).

14.7–27   Gowrie Conspiracy ... prophetic spirit   much of the material in this passage is derived from Cant's footnote in *Muses* (1774), 1.11. For the Gowrie Conspiracy see note to 6.4.

14.10   king's visit to Perth   James VI visited Perth on 15 April 1601.

14.12   Dr Ruthven was presented to James   no record of this has been found.

14. 20–25   James ... the cross   in a note Cant writes: 'This anecdote looks so like a ridiculous falsehood and vain-glorious fable; that it is no wonder if strangers laugh it to scorn who know that the King is the supreme Magistrate and fountain of all honour. But, however improbable it may appear, there is a foundation for what is recorded in the poem. In the Gildrie-register is to be seen A. D. 1601. *Parcere subjectis et debellare superbos*, and under this motto, James R. all written with the King's own hand ... In the miscellaneous manuscript in my custody before mentioned, Mr Dundee who was on the spot writes thus: "*Item*, on the xv Apprill in anno a thousand vi hundred ane yeir the Kingis Majestie came to Perth, and that same day he was made provost with ane great scerlane of the courteoures, and the bancait was meid at the crois, and the Kingis Maiistie was set downe thereat, and six dozin glasses brokine, with mony owdir silver pissis and pewdir vescilles; and thair the King maid ane greit solleime aith to defend the hail libertie of this brouche [burgh]."

'Mr Dundee, a man of reputation in the town narrates this strange transaction as done at the Cross in sight of the whole town; if it had been a falsehood, both he and the poet had subjected themselves to public ridicule' (*Muses* (1774), 1.164–65).

In *Memorabilia of the City of Perth* (Perth, 1806) it is stated (250–51) that details of the king's visit are preserved in the 'Mercer's Manuscript' and that a lavish civic reception was held on this occasion where the king, courtiers, chief magistrates and people of the town were entertained at the expense of Perth. In spite of Cant's note no other record of James having become provost of Perth has been found and an appendix to Cant's edition of the poem lists Sir David Murray of Gospetrie as provost of Perth in 1601 (*Muses* (1774), 2.95). *Parcere subjectis et debellare superbos* (*Latin*, to show mercy to the conquered and to overthrow the proud) is from Virgil (70–19 BC), *The Aeneid*, 6.853.

14.26   glasses broken   it was the custom to break one's glass when drinking to the king in person so that it could not be used again on a lesser occasion.

14.28–35   He gave ... command   see *Muses* (1774), 1.165–66; seven lines were omitted.

14.28–30   Burges oath ... Burges Roll ... Guildrie Book   on becoming a citizen (a burges) or freeman of a burgh a man would take an oath promising loyalty to the town, and his name would be entered on the list of citizens and the lists of the appropriate trade or merchants' guild.

14.29   Roll   *Muses* (1774), and *Muses* (1638), read 'Scrole'.

14.34   shall come to hand   come to pass.

14.36   divine afflatus   the miraculous communication of supernatural knowledge. Jonathan Oldbuck uses the original Latin expression in *The Anti-*

quary, 108: see Cicero, *De Natura Deorum* (45 BC), 2.167.

14.38 Daniel had come to judgement see *The Merchant of Venice*, 4.1.218. Daniel is the wise interpreter of prophecy in the Old Testament (see Ezekiel 28.3, and the Book of Daniel), but in Shakespeare the reference is ironic.

14.40–15.1 succeed to Queen Elizabeth i.e. succeed Elizabeth I of England who reigned 1558–1603. James succeeded to the English throne in 1603.

15.2–39 Happy King James ... ailed thee to die? see *Muses* (1774), 1.166–68.

15.11 They'll tine their coals ... witch those who would burn you as a witch will waste their coal. Cant adds a note: 'The King and the Earl's enemies were at a great loss when they debased themselves to bring an accusation of sorcery against him after he was dead, and Lord Cromarty is not ashamed gravely to tell that story, which all the world laughs at. Adamson sneers at the accusation, and poor Monsieur is in earnest to clear himself ... The King was credulous, and had as much learning as made him a Pedant. He was as keen in hunting down witches as stags, and had plenty of dogs for both purposes. He has convinced the world that he was in earnest by his elaborate treatise against witches' (*Muses* (1774), 1.167).

15.16 pater patriæ *Latin* father of his country. This honorific title was bestowed on the emperor Augustus in 2 BC: 'senatus et equester ordo populusque Romanus universus appellavit me patrem patriae'—the senate, the equestrian order and the whole people of Rome gave me the title 'Father of my country' (*Res Gestae Divi Augusti*, 35). James VI and I was fond of proclaiming this role. In *A Collection of Scarce and Valuable Tracts (Somers' Tracts)*, 2nd edn, ed. Walter Scott, 13 vols (London, 1809–15), 3.260, Scott quotes James justifying his paternal role in *Basilicon Doron*, the guide to kingship which James wrote in 1599 for his elder son Prince Henry: 'Kings are also compared to fathers of families: for a king is truely *parens patriae*, the politique father of his people'. The paternal language and the specific phrase *pater patriæ* also occur in James's *The True Lawe of Free Monarchies* (1598): *The Minor Prose Works of James VI and I*, ed. James Craigie (Edinburgh and London, 1982), 53–54.

15.24 and thus begin to bawl *Muses* (1774), and *Muses* (1638), read 'and lowdly thus gan call'.

15.35 fair Aurora left Tithonus' bed in Greek mythology Aurora was the goddess of dawn. She had a child with Tithonus, brother of Priam king of Troy.

15.39 dearest *Muses* (1774), and *Muses* (1638), read 'sweetest'.

16.1 Edition 1638 the first edition of Henry Adamson's *The Muses Threnodie* was published in 1638. It contains this verse (21).

16.2 skill *Muses* (1774) reads 'quill'. The lines are not in the only edition of *Muses* (1638) to have been examined.

16.11–12 an age which might be described as peculiarly bibliomaniacal Scott begins his essay on 'Pitcairn's Criminal Trials' with the words, 'This has been called "the age of clubs;" and certainly the institution of societies which, under no more serious title than that of a festive symposium, devote themselves to the printing of literary works not otherwise likely to find access to the press, will hereafter be numbered among not the least honourable signs of the times' (*Prose Works*, 21.199). John Ferriar (1764–1815) published a verse epistle called *The Bibliomania, An Epistle, to Richard Heber, Esq.* (London, 1809), *CLA*, 186, and Thomas Frognall Dibdin published *Bibliomania; or Book Madness: A Bibliographical Romance* also in 1809 (*CLA*, 247, 197). See also *The Antiquary*, 23–24.

16.23–24 Hibernian tune "Arrah, why did you die." the word 'arrah' is of Anglo-Irish coinage and denotes the exclamation 'Ah!' or 'Indeed!' The phrase is frequently used to denote Irish people in chapbooks, for example, *Joe Miller's Jests* (1739): see *CLA*, 129.

16.29 Bannatyne Club see note to 5.20.

16.30 Cid Hamet Benengeli Cid Hamet Ben Engeli, an imaginary Arabian author to whom Miguel de Cervantes Saavedra (1547–1616) attributes the story of *The Adventures of Don Quixote* (Part 1, 1605; Part 2, 1615): see *CLA*, 101. The book's anonymous narrator is supposed to find Cid Hamet's manuscript in the market place in Toledo: see Part 1, Ch. 9.

17.5 My Lady ... preen Scott himself was the owner of several 'preens' the most significant of which is perhaps a brooch belonging to Helen MacGregor, Rob Roy's wife, now at Abbotsford.

17.8 all is not gold that glitters proverbial: *ODEP*, 317. Compare *The Merchant of Venice*, 2.7.65.

17.13 well to pass in the world well-to-do, comfortably off.

17.16 relieve the circumstances of their members i.e. the antiquarian societies did not act like merchant guilds and did not have funds for the support of the widows and orphans of members.

17.22–30 principle ascribed ... most strict morality see Henry Fielding (1707–1754), *The History of Tom Jones* (1749), Book 12, Chapter 7 (*CLA*, 63).

17.39–40 The society to which he belonged the novel does not make Oldbuck a member of an antiquarian society, but as he develops as a character outside the novel he can easily be imagined as one, and specifically of the Society of Antiquaries of Scotland (founded in 1780); this seems to be implied by the initials after his name in his narrative (see text 24.3 and note, and text 31.20–21).

18.18–19 Dr Johnson ... chariot Samuel Johnson (1709–84) reviewed a book by Jonas Hanway (1712–86), *A Journal of Eight Days' Journey ... to which is added An Essay on Tea* in three pieces which appeared in the *Literary Magazine* of 1756 and 1757. In the second of these pieces, (no. 13, 15 April–15 May 1757) a comment led to the governors of the Foundling Hospital (of which Hanway was a benefactor) to apply for a prosecution of the anonymous writer. Hanway responded to the criticisms in the *Daily Gazetteer* although unfortunately this article does not seem to have survived. Johnson again replied in the *Literary Magazine* (no. 14, 15 May–15 June 1757). In this last piece he comments: 'I have irritated an important member of an important corporation; a man, who, as he tells us in his letters, put horses to his chariot' (518) and later states 'the writer I found not of more than mortal might, and I did not immediately recollect that the man put horses to his chariot' (519): see *Samuel Johnson: The Major Works*, ed. Donald Greene (Oxford, 1984; revised 2000), 518–19 and notes.

18.24 to be turned up in to manifest itself as, to be discovered to be.

18.21–22 sweepings of the study of Mr Jonathan Oldbuck the contract for *Reliquiae Trotcosienses* includes as part of the work's original title 'Being Sweepings of the Study of the Late Jonathan Oldbuck': see National Library of Scotland, MS 745, f. 211.

18.24–25 to wit that is to say, in other words.

18.35–36 Iret ubique perdidit Romam *Latin* he would go wherever he destroyed Rome. No classical source has been identified. It seems odd that such a phrase is in the mouth of a Roman soldier; it would seem to be more appropriate to someone like Hannibal.

19.1–4 that species ... stock-breeders Scott took an active interest in the farming of the Abbotsford estates which included both arable and stock farms. His main interest, however, was in the planting of trees: see Lockhart, 2.360. Scott might number among his stock-breeding friends the author James Hogg (1770–1835) whose youth had been spent as a shepherd.

19.4–7 distinguished among those ... wisdom see Ecclesiasticus 38.25 in The Apocrypha. However, the 'preacher' is the supposed author of Ecclesiastes, not 'Jesus, son of Sirach', author of Ecclesiasticus.

19.9–12 meditated an essay ... landscape gardening Scott himself wrote an essay on landscape gardening which appeared in the *Quarterly Review*, 37 (March 1828), reprinted in *Prose Works* 21.77–151, and which reviews Sir Henry Steuart, *The Planter's Guide; or, a Practical Essay on the best Method of giving immediate effect to Wood, by the removal of large Trees and Underwood*. Scott also wrote an article 'On Planting Waste Lands' (*Quarterly Review*, October 1827, reprinted in *Prose Works*, 21.1–76) which reviews Robert Monteath's *The Forester's Guide and Profitable Planter*.

19.31 anomalous hob-nails out of the commodity see Ben Jonson, *Every Man in his Humour* (1598), 1.5.96–98: 'all old iron, and rusty proverbs: a good commodity for some smith to make hob-nails of'.

20.1 Rob Roy Rob Roy MacGregor (1671–1734), legendary Scottish freebooter. He was the subject of Scott's fifth novel, *Rob Roy* (1818).

20.1–2 Sergeant More Cameron Sergeant Alan Mhor Cameron served in the French army and then with the Jacobites in 1745–46. After a period of cattle-thieving and banditry he was executed in 1753.

20.4–5 at the mercy of the cook-wench ... good fat hen Scott tells a similar anecdote in the Introductory Epistle to *The Fortunes of Nigel* (1822). There, the author recounts how he was approached by the spirit of one who announces herself as 'that unhappy Elizabeth or Betty Barnes, long cook-maid to Mr Warburton the painful collector, but ah! the too careless custodier of the largest collection of ancient plays ever known ... Yes, stranger, it was these ill-fated hands that consigned to grease and conflagration the scores of small quartos, which, did they now exist, would drive the whole Roxburghe Club out of their sense—it was these unhappy pickers and stealers that singed fat fowls and wiped dirty trenchers with the lost works of Beaumont and Fletcher, Massinger, Jonson, Webster—What shall I say?—even of Shakespeare himself.' (*The Fortunes of Nigel*, ed. Frank Jordan, EEWN 13 (Edinburgh, 2004), 11–12). John Warburton (1682–1759) collected manuscript plays, of which all but three and a half or some fifty or sixty by Shakespeare, Massinger, Marlowe, Ford, Dekker, and other early dramatists were supposedly destroyed by his servant, who set hot pies on them or otherwise burned them. (Scott calls her Betty Barnes; she is Elizabeth Baker in the *Dictionary of National Biography*'s account of Warburton.) After sifting the evidence, W. W. Greg concluded that 'we have undoubtedly to lament the loss of a few pieces, perhaps of considerable interest, but not by any means the dramatic holocaust' that Warburton claimed: 'The Bakings of Betsy', *The Library*, 3rd series, 2:7 (July 1911), 259.

20.11–12 Mr Patrick no character has been identified to account for the sudden appearance of this name in Scott's manuscript. However, 'Mr Patrick' might be a rebirth of Peter Pattieson (Patie or Patrick's son) nominal author of *Tales of My Landlord*, series 1, 2 and 3, who is now refusing to collect and edit any more stories. The nominal speaker in the Proem could be considered a kind of Jedidiah Cleishbotham who edited Peter's manuscripts for the press.

20.19–20 frankness is a jewel proverbial: see *ODEP*, 629. An extended version of the proverb, 'plain dealing is a jewel, but they that use it die beggars', could be implied in this context.

20.37   come off halting   retire limping, as from a field of combat.

21.2–4   regulations ... sums of money   Scott here refers tangentially to the circumstances under which he left his own museum and museum objects: see Hugh Cheape, Trevor Cowie and Colin Wallace, 'Sir Walter Scott, the Abbotsford Collection and the National Museums of Scotland', in *Abbotsford and Sir Walter Scott: the Image and the Influence*, ed. Iain Gordon Brown (Edinburgh, 2003), 57–77.

21.8   Crites   *Greek* judge. This is the word for any kind of judge but in Athens the word was also used of the judges in poetic contests.

21.16   fate of Woodward   John Woodward (1665–1728), geologist and physician, owner of an iron shield with a sculptured centre. The shield was the subject of an engraving of 1705, and was described by Henry Dodwell in a tract of 1711 which brought Woodward to the attention of antiquaries and caused much ridicule among contemporary wits. He published *An Essay toward a Natural History of the Earth* (1695), recognising the strata of the earth's crust and identifying fossils as previously living animals, but his conclusions were misplaced as he believed that this matter had all been originally mixed up at the Flood. He also published 'An Account of some Roman Urns ... with reflections upon the Antient and Present state of London', two letters, the first addressed to Sir Christopher Wren (23 June 1707), and the second to Thomas Hearne (30 November 1711). These were reprinted in 1723, and the 1723 version was included in *A Collection of Scarce and Valuable Tracts (Somers' Tracts)*, 2nd edn, ed. Walter Scott, 13 vols (London, 1809–15), 13.855–69 (*CLA*, 29).

21.22–23   which Don Quixote ... course of his adventures   see Miguel de Cervantes Saavedra (1547–1616), *The Adventures of Don Quixote* (Part 1, 1605; Part 2, 1615): see *CLA*, 101.

21.27   post mortem   *Latin* after death.

21.32   testator and his trustee   a testator is one who makes a will, a trustee one to whom property is entrusted to be administered for the benefit of another.

22.8   freaks and gambades   pranks and capers.

22.9–10   Sterne's celebrated metaphor ... hobby-horse   see note to 5.24.

22.37–38   splendid vanity of the manorial style   there is no specific architectural movement referred to here although the building of country houses expanded significantly after 1800. Abbotsford House itself might be said to be the best example of 'the splendid vanity of the manorial style' and Scott himself wrote that it 'is neither to be castle nor abbey (God forbid) but an old Scottish manor-house' (*Letters*, 7.111). James Macaulay places Abbotsford in its architectural context and states that it is the 'unsung prototype of Scots-Baronial architecture' with characteristics in keeping with 'the equivocal notion of a Scottish manor-house': *The Gothic Revival 1745–1845* (Glasgow and London, 1975), 227.

22.40   Sir Uvedale Price   Price (1747–1829) was a writer on the picturesque. He opposed the system of William Kent (1684–1748) and Lancelot Brown (1715–83), arguing in favour of natural and picturesque beauty, and endeavouring to show that the fashionable mode of laying out grounds was 'at variance with the principles of landscape-painting, and with the practice of all the most eminent masters'. Scott studied the works of Price when laying out his gardens at Abbotsford, and in his article on landscape gardening quotes Price's views on walking up and down stairs in the open air: 'however our ancestors may have been laughed at (and I was much diverted, though not at all convinced with the ridicule) for walking up and down stairs in the open air—the effect of all these objects is very striking' (Sir Uvedale Price, *Essays on the Picturesque*, 2 vols (London, 1798), 2.135: see *CLA*, 202), quoted by Scott in *Prose Works*, 21.84). In Quentin Durward (1823) Scott describes Price as the 'best qualified judge of our time, who thinks we have carried to an extreme our taste for simplicity, and that the neighbourhood of a stately mansion requires some more ornate embellishments than can be derived from the meagre accompaniments of grass and gravel' (*Quentin Durward*, ed. J. H. Alexander and G. A. M Wood, EEWN 15 (Edinburgh, 2001), 9).

23.2–4 a fashion … tarnished the essay 'On Modern Gardening' by Horace Walpole (1717–97) which expresses a taste for wildness was published in 1771 (see *CLA*, 234). In *Redgauntlet* (1824) Darsie Latimer writes to Alan Fairford: 'ever since Dodsley has described the Leasowes, and talked of Brown's imitations of nature, and Horace Walpole's late Essay on Gardening, you are all for simple nature—condemn walking up and down stairs in the open air, and declare for wood and wilderness' (*Redgauntlet*, ed. G. A. M. Wood with David Hewitt, EEWN 17 (Edinburgh, 1997), 59. Scott discusses the relative merits of Walpole and Price's ideas in his essay on landscape gardening: see previous note.

24.3 L.L.D. and A.S.S. *literally* doctor of laws and member of the Society of Antiquaries of Scotland (in the form Antiquarian Society of Scotland), but here pronouncing him 'learned doctor and ass'.

24.19 Suum cuique is our Roman justice *Titus Andronicus*, 1.1.280: 'Suum cuique is our Roman justice'. The Latin expression means 'to each his own', or 'give everyone his due'. See also Cicero, *De Officiis* (44 BC), Bk 1, section 15 (quoted by Scott in *Letters*, 9.136); and Ulpian (d. 228), *Digest*, 1.1.10. The opening sentence of Justinian's *Institutes* (529–33) is directly derived from Ulpian: 'Justice is the constant and perpetual desire to give each man his due right', and this became a maxim in those legal systems such as Scots law that were derived from the Roman. 'Suum Cuique' became the motto of the Faculty of Advocates when granted a coat of arms in 1856, but its first recorded use as the Faculty's motto was on the title page of the first *Catalogue of the Advocates Library* (1692).

24.27–29 mansion house of Trotcossey … monastic mortification see note to 1.1, and *The Antiquary*, note to 20.32.

24.31–32 a friend, who chooses to have his name concealed i.e. Scott himself.

24.35 a thing to dream of not to tell see Samuel Taylor Coleridge, 'Christabel' (written 1798–1800; published 1816), line 247: 'A sight to dream of, not to tell'.

25.2–3 halls themselves are haunted and the tenant bewitched while this reference may just be a bit of self-mockery, Scott could have had in mind an incident reported to Daniel Terry in a letter of 30 April 1818: 'The exposed state of my house has led to a mysterious disturbance. The night before last we were awaked by a violent noise, like drawing heavy boards along the new part of the house. I fancied something had fallen, and thought no more about it. . . . If there was no entrance but the key-hole, I should warrant myself against the ghosts' (Lockhart, 4.138–39). In a letter of 16 May he adds: 'I protest to you the noise resembled half-a-dozen men hard at work putting up boards and furniture, and nothing can be more certain than that there was nobody on the premises at the time. With a few additional touches, the story would figure in Glanville or Aubrey's Collection' (Lockhart, 4.143). It transpired that the disturbances occurred at the time of the death of George Bullock who assisted

Scott in designing and furnishing Abbotsford, two o'clock in the morning of 29 April 1818, a fact which greatly affected Scott (Lockhart, 4.140). See also note to 41.19–20.

25.4 ———— ———— Abbotsford House.

25.7 Lucian (1st century AD) writer of satiric diatribes in Greek, including 'To an Uneducated Book-Collector' (*CLA*, 203). Jonathan Oldbuck quotes Lucian in *The Antiquary*, 24.

25.9–10 to divide his speech into copartments this reference has not been identified. The term *copartments* denotes 'compartments'.

25.12–13 like the man in the play ... literally wanting words no specific play has been identified. The term *wanting* is used in the sense 'lacking', 'at a loss for' and Scott may simply imply an actor who has forgotten his lines.

25.19 magic lantern an optical instrument by means of which a magnified image of a picture on glass is thrown upon a white screen or wall in a darkened room. Its earliest use recorded in *OED* is 1696.

25.30–35 take a look from the balconies ... twenty or twenty-one years of age Scott bought the land for Abbotsford in 1811 for £4000. Shortly afterwards he wrote: 'The farm comprehends about a hundred acres, of which I shall keep fifty in pasture and tillage, and plant all the rest, which will be a very valuable little possession in a few years, as wood bears a high price among us' (*Letters*, 2.536–37). He added considerably to the estate in 1815, 1816, 1817, 1820, and 1824. By 1818 he claimed to have planted over one million trees. Abbotsford was therefore a much bigger estate than is implied here.

27.3 Antiquarienses a constructed Latin term, meaning 'people associated with antiquaries and antiquarian activities' but its somewhat pompous formation (the correct term would be 'Antiquarii') implies that those referred to make a great show of being experts in antiquarian lore, but are not genuine antiquarians.

27.5 labourer in the vineyard compare Matthew 9.37, 20.1–16; Luke 10.2.

27.7–8 Conundrum Castle in a letter to Lord Montagu of 8 June 1817 Scott writes of his building plans: 'We are attempting no castellated conundrums to rival those Lord Napier used to have executed in Sugar' (*Letters*, 4.464). In his *Journal* for 7 January 1828 he records: 'Mr. Stewart left us, amply provided with the history of Abbotsford and its contents. It is a kind of Conundrum Castle to be sure and I have great pleasure in it, for while it pleases a fantastic person in the stile and manner of its architecture and decoration it has all the comforts of a commodious habitation' (*The Journal of Sir Walter Scott*, ed. W. E. K. Anderson (Oxford, 1972), 411).

27.11 Ruthvenus Secundus *Latin* a second Ruthven.

27.16 elevation ... erected to the situation an *elevation* is a drawing of a building or other object made in projection on a vertical plane, as distinguished from a ground plan. The first use in *OED* is in 1731. In a letter of 12 November 1816 to Daniel Terry Scott writes: 'Mr. Blore has drawn me a very handsome elevation, both to the road and to the river' (*Letters*, 4.289). The phrase 'to the situation' means 'appropriate to the site'.

27.18–20 how his mansion will look from the outside ... display the gabions of its proprietor for an excellent discussion of the significance of both the exterior and interior of Abbotsford House see Clive Wainwright, *The Romantic Interior: The British Collector at Home 1750–1850* (New Haven and London, 1989), 147–207.

27.29 shew-house *OED* defines *show-house* as 'A house conspicuous and celebrated for architectural beauty, splendid furniture, or the like; esp. one which the public are at certain times admitted to be shown'. Its first recorded occurrence in this sense is dated 1806.

27.31   Doric verses   rustic verses, particularly referring to those written in (Scots) dialect.

28.1–11   Dialogue . . . and all is   this poetry is by Scott and is written in his own hand. A deleted section of the manuscript contains Edie Ochiltree's memorable words 'I mind the bigging o't' (*The Antiquary*, 30). It is not known what 'mop-moss' is, but the sense is that there is so much moss that it seems to have a *feu*, i.e. right of possession, on the house.

28.14   the builder   the anonymous friend of Jonathan Oldbuck, not the person doing the actual work.

28.14   anonymous   of unknown authorship, and so, in this context, in an unrecognised style. However it is possible that Scott meant to write 'anomalous', a term which would fit the context better.

28.16   Mr Atkinson's experience   William Atkinson (1773?–1839) was primarily responsible for the building of Abbotsford in 1816–24: see James C. Corson, *Notes and Index to Sir Herbert Grierson's Edition of 'Letters of Sir Walter Scott'* (Oxford, 1979), 358. In a letter to Daniel Terry of 28 December 1816 Scott writes: 'Mr. Atkinsons plans are very ingenious indeed & would promise in many respects better interior accommodation than those which with Blores assistance I have hammered out of Mr. Skenes original idea. The exterior of Mr. Blores plan I prefer as being less Gothic & more in the old fashioned Scotch stile which delighted in notch'd Gable ends & all manner of bartizans' (*Letters*, 4.333–34). (For Blore see note to 28.33–34.) Later in this letter Scott writes: 'You will easily conceive the extreme importance which I consider as attached to Mr Atkinsons advice' (336). In 1821 Scott was planning further work at Abbotsford and writes to William Laidlaw: 'I have got a very good plan from Atkinson for my addition, but I do not like the outside, which is modern Gothic, a style I hold to be equally false and foolish. Blore and I have been at work to *Scottify* it, by turning battlements into bartisans, and so on. I think we have struck out a picturesque, appropriate, and entirely new line of architecture.' (*Letters*, 6.323–24).

28.25   frittering blister   open blister, blister where the skin has broken.

28.27   cross-light   a situation where light comes from two directions, and where either beams cross each other or so illuminate a subject so as to eliminate shadow. This was thought to be aesthetically unpleasing. The dislike of a 'cross-light' may be related to the design of houses in 17th-century Scotland where rooms could go right through from front to back, thus allowing someone outside a clear view of the inside.

28.27   an awkward communion   i.e. an awkward communication or passage.

28.33–34   Mr Blore . . . gothic architecture   Edward Blore (1787–1879), an expert in gothic architecture, met Scott in 1816. He was one of several contributors to the final design of Abbotsford. He submitted a sketch for the new house of Abbotsford in a Gothic style, and was then invited to carry out designs for the exterior. In a letter of 12 November 1816 to Robert Surtees, Scott writes: 'I have had a visit from your draughtsman Mr. Blore, a modest and well bred young man, as well as an excellent artist' (*Letters*, 4.285–86). In a letter of the same date to Daniel Terry Scott writes of Blore: 'He is a very fine young man, modest, simple, and unaffected in his manners, as well as a most capital artist' (*Letters*, 4.289).

28.36   throw forward windows   construct projecting windows.

29.1–2 **in professional phrase, gave a picturesque effect**   see note to 22.40.

29.8 **some of the novels**   in the Introductory Epistle to *The Fortunes of Nigel* (1822) Captain Clutterbuck accuses the author of being 'of opinion with Bayes, —"What the devil does the plot signify, except to bring in fine things?"'. The Author of Waverley responds: 'Grant that I were so, and that I should write with sense and spirit a few scenes, unlaboured and loosely put together, but which had sufficient interest in them to amuse in one corner the pain of body; in another, to relieve anxiety of mind; in a third place, to unwrinkle a brow bent with the furrows of daily toil; in another, to fill the place of bad thoughts, or to suggest better; in yet another, to induce an idler to study the history of his country; in all, save where the perusal interrupted the discharge of serious duties, to furnish harmless amusement,—might not the author of such a work, however inartificially executed, plead for his errors and negligences the excuse of the slave ... "Am I to blame, O Athenians, who have given you one happy day?"' (*The Fortunes of Nigel*, ed. Frank Jordan, EEWN 13 (Edinburgh, 2004), 7). In *The Heart of Mid-Lothian* (1818) Jedidiah Cleishbotham similarly suggests that an extension to his house, comprising 'a second story with atticks' has been built on the proceeds of his novels (*The Heart of Mid-Lothian*, ed. David Hewitt and Alison Lumsden, EEWN 6 (Edinburgh, 2004), 3).

29.11–14 **Mr Dibdin's song ... Mr Mayor**   Charles Dibdin (1745–1814) was an actor, dramatist and songwriter. The precise reference has not been found but compare John O'Keefe (1747–1833), *Peeping Tom of Coventry: A Comic Opera* (1785), lines 154–57.

29.20 **to example**   as an example.

29.28–29 **entrance ... Linlithgow**   there was a castle and royal residence on this site from the time of David I (*c.* 1084–1153; reigned 1124–53). It was successively rebuilt and developed by the Stewart kings, and both James V and Mary Queen of Scots were born there. Scott describes the entrances to Linlithgow palace in *Provincial Antiquities and Picturesque Scenery of Scotland* (Edinburgh and London, 1819–26; *CLA*, 337): 'There were two main entrances to Linlithgow Palace. That from the south ascends rather steeply from the town, and passes through a striking Gothic archway, flanked by two round towers' (*Prose Works*, 7.395).

29.34–35 **panelling of the pews ... Dunfermline**   Dunfermline Abbey, founded in 1072, was ruinous by the time of the Reformation in 1560; a parish church was fitted out for reformed worship in the nave between 1564 and 1599. Following the collapse of the great tower in 1818 a new parish church was completed in 1821 on the site of the choir and transepts, and the panelling from the post-reformation building was given to Scott by the magistrates of Dunfermline in 1822: see *Letters*, 7.279.

29.35–36 **sepulchre ... Robert Bruce**   Robert I 'the Bruce' (1274–1329; reigned 1306–29), was crowned King of Scots in 1306 and fought English forces for Scotland's independence, culminating in his victory over the English at the Battle of Bannockburn (1314). A tomb believed to be that of Robert I was discovered at Dunfermline Abbey in 1818.

29.39–30.1 **painted glass ... Scott**   in a letter of 14 February 1823 to Lord Montagu Scott writes: 'I want a little sketch of your Lordships arms on the following accompt. You are to know that I have a sort of entrance gallery ... That the two windows may be in unison I intend to sport a little painted glass and as I think heraldry is always better than any other subject I intend the upper co[m]partment of each window which is to be divided by a transom shall have the shield supporters &c of one of the existing dignitaries of the Clan of Scott &

of course the Dukes arms & your Lordships will occupy these posts of distinction. The corresponding two will be Hardens & Thirlestanes, the only families now left who have a right to be regarded as chieftains and the lower compartments of each window will contain eight shields . . . of good gentlemen of the name . . . And so I will have my Bellenden windows.' (*Letters*, 7.334–35). The Duke was the 5th Duke of Buccleuch; Lord Montagu was his paternal uncle; and Bellenden is the old war-cry of Buccleuch.

30.2 Duke of Buccleuch Sir Walter Scott (d. *c.* 1469) was the first of the family to be designated 'of Buccleuch'. The modern dukedom was created in 1663 for James, Duke of Monmouth on his marriage to Anne, Countess of Buccleuch. Scott regarded the Duke of Buccleuch as his clan chief and Charles William Henry Scott (1772–1819), who succeeded as 4th Duke in 1812, was his friend and patron. *The Lay of the Last Minstrel* was dedicated to him.

30.4–8 that field Or . . . on the field Or terms of heraldry. *Or* is the colour gold, and the *field* is the ground or surface of the shield upon which all the emblems are placed. A *band* is a broad stripe, and *tincture* is the heraldic word for 'colour'. A *mullet* represents the rowel of a spur; a *crescent* is a quarter moon with the horns uppermost. *Azure* is a bright blue, taken to represent the colour of an eastern sky.

30.6 Murdeston family the history of the Scotts of Buccleuch commences with Sir Richard Scott of Rankilburn and Murdieston, who swore fealty to Edward I of England in 1296, and who acquired the lands and Barony of Murdieston in Lanark by his marriage with the heiress of Inglis of Murdieston. The lands of Murdieston passed out of the family when Sir Walter Scott (d. *c.* 1469), sixth laird of Murdieston and Buccleuch, exchanged them for the lands of Branxholm near Hawick in the Scottish Borders. See S. M. Scott, *Scott 1118–1923* (London, 1923).

30.6–7 Scotts of Harden the first laird of Harden, a house near Hawick in the Scottish Borders, was William Scott (d. 1561). Walter Scott the writer was descended from the 4th laird, Sir William Scott (d. 1655), and was his great-great-great-grandson.

30.12 Coat Armouris coats of arms.

30.12 men of name distinguished men, famous men.

30.13 Scottish Marches, in ye days of auld several Border families were responsible for administering the Scottish and English border (the *marches* were the several areas of the border) before the Union of the Crowns in 1603. See Thomas I. Rae, *The Administration of the Scottish Frontier 1513–1603* (Edinburgh, 1966).

30.15–16 number according to tradition is eighteen in 'Essay on Border Antiquities' Scott writes: 'A vague tradition asserts, that the number of Scottish Border clans was eighteen' (*Prose Works*, 7.49).

30.23 premit nox alta *Latin tag, literally* deep night conceals [them]. In classical literature there are several instance which combine 'nox' (night) with the verb 'premere' (to conceal, to press down upon), e.g. Horace, *Odes*, 1.4.16: 'iam te premet nox' (now night will conceal you, night, in this context representing the darkness of death); there are also several instances where 'alta' (deep) is associated with 'nox', but the 3 words are not found together in any classical source. However by the Renaissance it seems that the tag was established as a way of talking about matters lost in time.

30.24–25 estate of Rutherford of Hunthill near Jedburgh in Roxburghshire in the Scottish Borders. Scott's mother was Anne Rutherford, eldest daughter of John Rutherford, professor of medicine in the University of Edinburgh; his father was minister in Yarrow; his father in turn came from Jedburgh and was known as John Rutherford of Grundhousenook and seems to have been a son of a Rutherford of Hunthill. The Hunthill estate was sold towards the end of the 18th century. See *Letters*, 8.6–9, 58, 221–22, 233–34.

30.27–28 no likelihood ... canon of Strasburgh in many German bishoprics the canons were obliged to be of noble blood. To be a canon of Strasbourg, the principal city of Alsace, it was necessary to prove sixteen quarters of descent, i.e. that one had a long aristocratic pedigree: see note to 29.30–30.1, and Lockhart, 5.312–13.

31.4 pulpit and precentor's ... desk these too came from Dunfermline (see note to 29.34–35), where Ralph Erskine, brother of Ebenezer (see next note) was minister until 1733.

31.4–8 Ebenezer Erskine ... Burgher Seceders Ebenezer Erskine (1680–1754) and his followers broke from the established Church of Scotland (i.e. a church established by law) in 1733 over opposition to patronage, the right of certain landowners to choose the minister of a parish which had been re-introduced by the Patronage Act of 1712. The secession grew rapidly and in October 1744 was organised as an associate synod, containing the three presbyteries of Glasgow, Edinburgh and Dunfermline, but split in 1747 over the Burgher oath and to what extent this oath implied the recognition of the established Church. One of the resulting groups was known as Associated Synod of Non-Jurors or the Burgher Seceders. The term 'new licht' was applied to those who doubted Calvinist views on predestination, arguing for free-will, and tending towards a moral view of the Christian life. The Seceders eventually formed the United Secession Church, known as the United Presbyterian Church from 1847.

31.13 inter res sacros *Latin* among sacred objects, i.e. considered consecrated. The Church of Scotland does not consider ecclesiastical furniture as consecrated.

31.14 High Church of England High Churchmen place a great emphasis on the claim of authority, the Episcopate and the priesthood. They also tend to have a much wider conception of what are to be considered consecrated objects than is normally to be found in the Presbyterian Church of Scotland.

31.15–16 Jack ... Martin ... Peter i.e. John Calvin (1509–64), the theologian whose thought underpins the doctrines of many churches, including the Church of Scotland; Martin Luther (1483–1546) the German reformer and conceptual father of the Lutheran churches; and the Pope (successor to St Peter). The names are used satirically in sections 4 and 6 of *A Tale of a Tub* (1704) by Jonathan Swift whose works Scott edited in 19 vols (1814).

31.19–20 de ceteris *Latin* among other things.

31.20–21 the Antiquarian Society see note to 17.39–40.

31.21–23 John Knox ... mound in Edinburgh John Knox *c.* 1512–72, the prime mover in the Scottish Reformation. At the time when Scott was writing, Knox's pulpit was kept in the Royal Institution which was at the foot of the Mound in Edinburgh, where the Royal Scottish Academy is now situated. It later became part of the national collections: see James Grant, *Cassell's Old and New Edinburgh*, 3 vols (London, Paris and New York, 1883), 1.150.

31.27 al fresco *Italian* outside, in the open air. As the pulpit is in the entrance hall of Abbotsford Scott must have put his wine in the pulpit to keep it cool while they ate in the shade outside.

31.29–30 Bacchanalian chorus Bacchus was the Roman god of wine, his devotees were bacchanals; hence *Bacchanalian*, 'riotously drunken'.

31.30 a Jacobite rant a song or verse in favour of the Stewart dynasty who were deposed in 1688–89.

31.35 Kirk Synod of Dunfermline see note to 31.4. Scott probably means Kirk Session (the lowest of the church courts in the Presbyterian system of church government) rather than 'Kirk Synod', but may be referring to the Associate Synod into which the secession was organised from 1744 (see note to 31.4–8).

31.36–37 well known seat of repentance the 'cutty stool' on which offenders against chastity were forced to sit during the time of church service.

32.16 Mr John Smith of Darnick, builder 1782–1864, mason and builder of Darnick near Melrose in the Scottish Borders. Scott employed him to work on Abbotsford.

32.17–18 the Abbot's Seat in the cloister of Melrose although it cannot be shown to have been the abbot's seat, Scott refers to a single stall with an elaborate wall arcade on the west side of the processional archway from the cloister into the nave of the abbey. What remains of the cloister (which, unusually, is on the north side of the church) dates from the 15th century.

32.18–19 chimney or grate inserted under this ancient arch an illustration of this grate can be found in Mary Monica Maxwell Scott, *Abbotsford: The Personal Relics and Antiquarian Treasures of Sir Walter Scott* (London, 1893), vii.

32.20–21 James Sharp . . . after the Restoration James Sharp (1618–79) initially supported the Presbyterian form of church government, but after the restoration of the monarchy in 1660, and of episcopacy in 1661, he was created Archbishop of St Andrews and Primate of Scotland. He was murdered by extremist Covenanters on Magus Muir, 5 km from St Andrews, on 3 May 1679. The Covenanters, so-called because they supported the National Covenant of 1638 and the Solemn League and Covenant of 1643, refused to recognise Charles II as head of the church, a position they considered Christ's alone. The murder of Sharp is the event which gives rise to the action of Scott's novel *The Tale of Old Mortality* (1816).

32.21 revival of prelacy i.e. government of the church by bishops, restored in 1661 (see note above).

32.27–29 prelatist . . . different interpretation prelatists were supporters of a system of church government by bishops, as in the Scottish Episcopal Church ('the old Scottish church'). Presbyterians supported a system of church government by a hierarchy of courts (General Assembly, Synod, Presbytery, and Kirk Session). While the outward sign of their differences was the preferred mode of church government, the effective cause of the Covenanting wars lay in the differing views of the relations of church and state (see note to 32.20–21).

32.31 Fides dona superat *Latin* faith, or trustworthiness, triumphs over gifts. This sounds like a heraldic motto: no classical source has been found.

32.35 bronze pot of the largest size for an illustration of this pot see Mary Monica Maxwell Scott, *Abbotsford: The Personal Relics and Antiquarian Treasures of Sir Walter Scott* (London, 1893), vii, and Hugh Cheape, Trevor Cowie and Colin Wallace, 'Sir Walter Scott, The Abbotsford Collection and the National Museums of Scotland', in *Sir Walter Scott and Abbotsford: The Image and the Influence*, ed. Iain Gordon Brown (Edinburgh, 2003), 66.

32.36–37 domain of Riddell in Roxburghshire near Lilliesleaf, a village between Melrose and Hawick in the Scottish Borders.

33.8–9 sair up in Edinburgh highly priced in Edinburgh.

33.9 that gate that way.

33.11 gae off go [for], be sold.

33.15 Paris plaister plaster of Paris. In *The Antiquary*, 29, Oldbuck is having the sculpture on the stone which he has found at the Kaim of Kinprunes 'taken off with plaister of Paris'.

33.15–17   sculptured niches ... Melrose   although Scott does not describe taking plaster casts of niches when the entrance hall was being fitted out, he does describe the ornamenting of his first study in a letter to Daniel Terry of 12 November 1816: 'Besides these commodities, there is ... a study for myself, which we design to fit up with ornaments from Melrose Abbey. Bullock made several casts with his own hands—masks, and so forth, delightful for cornices, &c.' (*Letters*, 4.289–90).

33.18–19   feudal steel armour   tilt armour used for jousting. In a letter to Terry of 18 April 1819 Scott writes: ' I see Mr. Bullock (George's brother) advertises his museum for sale. I wonder if a good set of *real tilting* armour could be got cheap there. James Ballantyne got me one very handsome bright steel cuirassier of Queen Elizabeth's time, and two less perfect, for £20—dog cheap; they make a great figure in the armoury' (*Letters*, 5.364).

33.19–20   one of the gens de arm of the middle ages   a cavalier or mounted soldier, particularly one belonging to the royal guard.

33.23   the learned Dr Meyrick   Sir Samuel Rush Meyrick (1783–1848), the expert who was consulted on the arrangement of the armour in the Tower of London and Windsor Castle in 1826. At Scott's encouragement he wrote a book called *A Critical Inquiry into Antient Armour, as it existed in Europe, but particularly in England, from the Norman Conquest to the reign of King Charles II: with a Glossary of Military Terms of the Middle Ages*, 3 vols (London, 1824): *CLA*, 251. The peculiar shield referred to consists of a breast and shoulder plate attached to the breast plate of the armour.

33.30   Dr Meyrick's collection   Meyrick's home, Goodrich Court near Ross, Herefordshire, was specially designed by William Blore to house his extensive collection of arms and armour.

33.31–34   drawn sword ... knight's devotions   this sword is described in more detail by The Honble. Mrs Maxwell Scott in *Catalogue of the Armour and Antiquities at Abbotsford* (Edinburgh, 1888), 33.

33.36–37   took arms ... Bosworth   the Battle of Bosworth Field, 22 August 1485, was fought 19 km west of Leicester and 5 km south of Market Bosworth between the Yorkist Richard III and the Lancastrian contender for the crown, Henry Tudor, Earl of Richmond (later Henry VII, reigned 1485–1509). It effectively ended the Wars of the Roses and established the Tudor dynasty on the English throne.

33.39   John Cheney   a knight famed for his prodigious strength and for his loyalty to Henry Tudor. He features in *Polydori Vergilii Urbinatis Anglicae Historiae Libri Vigintiseptem* (1555: see *CLA*, 252), as 'a man of surpassing bravery'. There is an illustration of Cheney with a Welsh flag in Samuel Meyrick's *A Critical Inquiry into Antient Armour*, 3 vols (London, 1824), Vol. 2, plate 58, where Meyrick comments that Cheney was standard bearer to Henry VII on his arrival in London after the Battle of Bosworth Field (*CLA*, 251).

34.3   in sailors' phrase "to spin a tough yarn"   not a quotation but a colloquialism: the *OED* first records *yarn* in this sense in 1812; compare the second quotation under *nautical*, noun 2.

34.8–9   sword of the mountaineer ... both hands   Scott refers to the double-handed Scottish sword or claymore. The sword at Abbotsford is 1.98m in length and weighs over 3.6 kg.

34.9–10   gladius militis levis armaturæ   *Latin* the sword of a light-armed soldier. There is no specific classical source.

34.14–18   Scottish poet Barbour ... slain by him   in *The Bruce* (1375:

see *CLA*, 8), Book 7.205–32, John Barbour (?1320–95) gives an account of the king killing three men who had befriended him but tried to kill him while he was asleep.

34.18 rout of Dalry Battle of Dalry, 11 August 1306, at which Robert I was defeated by John, Lord of Lorn. Dalry is near the Perthshire and Argyle border.

34.22–23 tremendous blade of the Castle of Otranto in Horace Walpole's *The Castle of Otranto* (1764) large swords are described in Chapters 3 and 4 of the novel. In Ch. 3 a 'gigantic sword' is carried by 'the knight of the gigantic sabre', and in Ch. 4 Frederic tells a story in which a dying hermit instructs him to dig under a tree where he finds the 'enormous sabre'. Scott's edition of this novel was published in 1811 (see *CLA*, 63).

34.28–29 spoils from the immortal field of Waterloo Scott visited Waterloo in August 1815. He describes the sale of relics from the battle in *Paul's Letters to his Kinsfolk*: 'A more innocent source of profit has opened to many of the poor people about Waterloo, by the sale of such trinkets and arms as they collect daily from the field of battle; things of no intrinsic value, but upon which curiosity sets a daily increasing estimate' (*Prose Works*, 5.157).

34.30 cuirasses a *cuirass* is armour plating worn by a horse soldier reaching down to the waist and consisting of breast plates and back plates buckled or otherwise fastened together. In *Paul's Letters to his Kinsfolk* Scott describes having bought two cuirasses, that of a common soldier at six francs and a more splendid one for around twenty-four: see *Prose Works*, 5.158. An illustration of these cuirasses may be found in Mary Monica Maxwell Scott, *Abbotsford: The Personal Relics and Antiquarian Treasures of Sir Walter Scott* (London, 1893), Plate 13.

34.31–34 of the former metal … so much a pound Scott remarks on this activity as regards headpieces in *Paul's Letters to his Kinsfolk*: 'As for the casques, or head-pieces, which by the way are remarkably handsome, they are almost *introuvable*, for the peasants immediately sold them to be beat out for old copper, and the purchasers, needlessly afraid of their being reclaimed, destroyed them as fast as possible' (*Prose Works*, 5.158).

34.35–36 caps of the Polish lancers one of the French cuirasses at Abbotsford is a Polish lancer's headdress. A part of Napoleon's bodyguard was composed of a Polish squadron which followed him to Waterloo.

34.38 cum multis aliis quæ nunc me scribere longum est *Latin* with many others which it would tedious for me to write of at present. This is a tag without a specific classical source.

34.40–35.2 two of the few saints … St Peter and St Paul the north transept chapels in Melrose Abbey were dedicated to St Peter and St Paul. Their statues are in niches high up on the west wall of the transept. 'The exterior of the church was lavishly enriched with sculptural decoration, and although much of the statuary is missing, what has survived is still one of the most accomplished collections of medieval carving surviving in Scotland' (Marguerite Wood and J. S. Richardson, *Melrose Abbey* (Edinburgh, 1995), 8, 10).

35.2 vennel walls it is not clear what is meant, but as a *vennel* is a narrow passageway Scott may refer to the fact that there is a narrow passage within the walls of Melrose Abbey.

35.3 keys, his usual emblem St Peter is usually depicted holding the keys to heaven.

35.4 "that two handed engine" as Milton calls it John Milton, 'Lycidas' (1638), line 130. In the poem St Peter holds two large keys and refers to a 'two-handed engine' (two-handed sword), taken to be an instrument of judgment, at the entrance to heaven.

35.10–11   morass called Doorpool … Abbotsrule   Abbotrule is in the
Scottish Borders, 10 km E of Hawick and about 22 km from Abbotsford. The
estate of Abbotrule owned by Scott's one-time friend Charles Kerr was sold in
1818.

35.11   Robert Shortreed, Esquire   (1762–1829) a friend of Scott's who
accompanied him on his 'raids' into Liddesdale in search of antiquarian remains
and ballad material between 1792 and 1799. He was sheriff-substitute of Roxburghshire.

35.15–16   remains of the elk … museum at Edinburgh   the specific
animal referred to has not been identified. Natural history collections existed in
Edinburgh from the 17th century, and survived in the University of Edinburgh
until the mid-19th century when they were handed over to the government to
form the basis of the national collections. The National Museum of Antiquities
of Scotland was founded in 1780 by the Society of Antiquaries of Scotland and
had several locations in Edinburgh in the early 19th century. It was moved to the
Royal Institution at the foot of the Mound in Edinburgh's Princes Street in
1826. It also had natural history collections which were given to the Royal
Society of Edinburgh in 1828: see *The Wealth of A Nation in the National
Museums of Scotland*, ed. Jenni Calder (Edinburgh and Glasgow, 1989), 2–4.

35.19–20   Mr Humphrey Davy   (1778–1829) the eminent natural philosopher and chemist. His wife came from Kelso, was distantly related to Scott,
and maintained a correspondence with him.

35.25–35   wild cattle of this country … Wooler   the British white cattle
are descendants of domestic cattle introduced by the Romans which became
feral on their departure. At Drumlanrig, near Thornhill, Dumfriesshire (see
note to 42.7) the herd of British white cattle was removed to an unknown
destination about 1780. The estate and castle of Cumbernauld, NE of Glasgow,
was owned by the Fleming family until 1875: a herd of white cattle roamed wild
in a remnant of the ancient Caledonian Forest in the area until at least 1570 and
may have survived in the park as late as 1730. The Hamilton herd can still be
seen at Chatelherault Country Park, Hamilton, formerly owned by the Duke of
Hamilton. The purest herd still survives at Chillingham Castle, the seat of the
Earls of Tankerville, near Wooler, 24 km south of Berwick upon Tweed in
Northumberland. Scott alludes to these cattle in *The Bride of Lammermoor*, ed.
J. H. Alexander, EEWN 7a (Edinburgh and New York, 1995), 36–37; see also
note to 36.39–37.14. For more information see G. Kenneth Whitehead, *The
Ancient White Cattle of Britain and their Descendants* (London, 1953).

36.2   Babylon   the city, once the capital of the Chaldee Empire, which in the
Bible simultaneously represents exile, fabulous wealth and beauty, and confusion because of the number of languages to be heard there.

36.3   in point of   in respect of.

36.19   flirting corner   the phrase is possibly Scott's own coining.

36.20   octagon   the bay window in the library has six sides, with a further two
notional ones between it and the library.

36.28–30   great Burke … human understanding   Edmund Burke
(1729–97) was an eminent Whig politician, and man of letters. The precise
reference has not been identified although Scott repeats this *bon mot* on John
Locke's *Essay Concerning Human Understanding* (1690) in his article on 'Pitcairn's Criminal Trials' (*Prose Works* 21.216).

36.32–33   St Giles's … table   the custom has not been identified. St Giles
is the patron saint of cripples and outcasts and presumably some hospital for the
indigent named after St Giles was accustomed to retain its cutlery in this way.

36.36   a bibliomaniacal collection   see note to 16.11–12.

37.7–8 good double catalogue Scott's description of 'a double catalogue' conforms to *CLA*, and the working version on which it was based, compiled by George Huntly Gordon in the autumn of 1824: see Jane Millgate, ' "Litera scripta manet": George Huntly Gordon and the Abbotsford Library Catalogue', *The Library*, 20 (June, 1998), 118–25.

37.18–34 a gentleman ... gentleman I allude to Archibald Constable (1774–1827), Scott's principal publisher until 1826. Constable began a bookseller with a shop at the Cross, in the High St of Edinburgh, with a big trade in antiquarian and rare books, but gradually he reduced his business as a retailer of books to concentrate on publishing (the term 'bookselling' covers both roles). Scott tells the same story when musing over Constable's death in his *Journal*, 23 July 1827: *The Journal of Sir Walter Scott*, ed. W. E. K. Anderson (Oxford, 1972), 332.

38.12 seaboy upon the dizzy shroud not identified.

38.19–20 a late eminent literary character probably John Leyden (1775–1811) whom Lockhart describes as 'often balanced for hours on a ladder with a folio in his hand, like Dominie Sampson' (Lockhart, 1.323). In his essay on the life of John Leyden, first published in *The Edinburgh Annual Register*, 4 (1811) Scott commends Leyden both for his literary activities and his almost barbaric athletic prowess (*Prose Works* 4.156–57).

38.21 the unsteady footing of a spar not identified.

38.37–38 Talus in Spenser ... molde Edmund Spenser (*c.* 1552–99), *The Faerie Queene* (1589–96), 5.1.12 (*CLA*, 42, 187).

39.2–3 command my volumes ... Oberon's banquet Oberon in *Huon de Bordeaux* (see note to 70.33–36) claims that 'what meat or wine I wish for, I have it at once'. Later, he wishes his 'table and all that is thereon near to King Charlemagne's table' and 'He had no sooner said the words than by the will of God and the might of fairydom his table, with all that he had wished on it, was set just by King Charlemagne's table' (*Huon of Bordeaux: Done into English by Sir John Bourchier, Lord Berners: And Now Retold by Robert Steele* (London, 1895), 81 and 292). Scott possessed the 1516 edition of the romance in the original French (*CLA*, 121).

39.30–33 a young Hussar officer ... William Allan the painting is of Scott's eldest son, also named Walter, who joined the 18th Regiment of the Hussars in 1819, later transferring to the 15th Hussars in whose uniform he is seen in this portrait of 1822 by Sir William Allan (1782–1850). Allan painted many pictures of the interior of Abbotsford, and did several of the illustrations for Scott's novels.

40.7 Baldock's Edward Holmes Baldock (1777–1845), a London antiques dealer. Scott bought furniture from him via his friend Daniel Terry.

40.10–11 burnt the night after the Battle of Falkirk on 31 January 1746 the Duke of Cumberland and his army spent the night in Linlithgow Palace and whether by accident or design the castle was burnt to a ruin. Scott describes this in *The Provincial Antiquities of Scotland* (see note to 43.7–10): *Prose Works*, 7.394.

40.12–13 some paintings, chiefly relations of the family pictures in Abbotsford are not now in their original positions. Besides that of Scott's son (see note to 39.30–33) family portraits in Abbotsford in oils include Scott by Sir Henry Raeburn (1809), Lady Scott by James Saxon (1805); Scott's mother by Sir John Watson Gordon; Anne Scott by William Nicholson; Anne Scott by John Graham; and Sophia Scott by William Nicholson.

40.24 water-coloured portraits of members of the family although not all watercolours and not all in their original positions, these include: the

Scotts of Raeburn by Sir John Watson Gordon; Scott in his study by William Allan; Scott's cat Hinse of Hinsfeldt; Scott's dog Ginger by Sir Edwin Landseer; his friend, partner and printer James Ballantyne, his servant Tom Purdie, his gamekeeper John Swanston, his coachman Peter Mathieson. Some of these pictures were painted after Scott's death.

40.33–34 species of conservatory conservatories as parts of houses seem to have been introduced around the mid-18th century. In *Redgauntlet* (1824), which is set in 1765, Darsie Latimer writes: 'I have never before seen this very pleasing manner of uniting the comforts of an apartment with the beauties of a garden, and I wonder it is not more practised by the great': *Redgauntlet*, ed. G. A. M. Wood with David Hewitt, EEWN 17 (Edinburgh and New York, 1997), 53.13–16. In a letter of 28 December 1816 to Daniel Terry Scott writes: 'The Green-closet, for it cannot be term'd either a Green-house or Green-room, has not indeed room enough to swing a cat in but I am no botanist or florist & if it holds a few bow pots for Mrs. Scott through the season it will serve well enough. If I made more glass work I could have it in the garden for the purpose of a grapery—a solid luxury' (*Letters*, 4.335). The conservatory at Abbotsford was demolished during alterations in 1853–57: see Clive Wainwright, *The Romantic Interior: The British Collector at Home 1750–1850* (New Haven and London, 1989), 175.

40.38–40 in the words . . . forbidden to see Rev. Dr [T.] Lisle, 'The Power of Music. A Song. Imitated from the Spanish', lines 1–2, in *A Collection of Poems in Six Volumes by Several Hands*, [ed. Robert Dodsley], 6 vols (London, 1758: see *CLA*, 168), 6.166: 'When Orpheus went down to the regions below,/ Which men are forbidden to see,/ He tun'd up his lyre, as old histories shew,/ To set his Euridice free'. This is not a Scottish song. It was anthologised frequently in the 18th century; according to this collection it was set to music by 'Dr. Hayes', but a more famous setting is by William Boyce (1710–79).

41.19 my deceased friend Mr. Bullock George Bullock (d. 1818) was a house furnisher and designer in London. He had premises at 4 Tenterden Street, Hanover Square from at least 1814 onwards. For a full account of his life and work see *George Bullock: Cabinet-Maker* (London, 1988) and in particular the introduction by Clive Wainwright (13–39). On hearing of George Bullock's death Scott writes of his esteem for him in letters of 4 and 16 May 1818 to Daniel Terry: see *Letters*, 5.136–37, 147.

41.26–29 taste . . . meschinnerie this account of Bullock echoes the words of his obituary which states he 'carried taste, in design of furniture, to a higher pitch than it was ever carried before in this country': Clive Wainwright, 'George Bullock and his Circle', in *George Bullock: Cabinet-Maker* (London, 1988), 20. It seems likely that by *meschinnerie* Scott means 'mesquinerie', French for 'meanness', 'shabbiness'.

41.34 pyramidical form tapering downwards this correctly describes the defining characteristic of regency furniture: the legs of tables and chairs are very narrow and taper inwards as they approach the ground. Whether this indicates a 'false taste' is a matter of opinion, but in furnishing Abbotsford in the way he did in the period 1816–24 Scott was consciously rejecting prevalent fashion and in so doing helped to create the taste of the Victorian era.

41.37–38 Mr Bullock (who was bred an artist) George Bullock was originally trained as a sculptor and modeller and in 1810–11 was president of the newly founded Liverpool Academy: see 'George Bullock and his Circle', in *George Bullock: Cabinet-Maker* (London, 1988), 20.

42.7 Drumlanrig Castle near Thornhill in Dumfriesshire. Completed in 1689 on the site of the earlier castle of the Douglasses for William Douglas, 1st

Duke of Queensberry. Both castle and title were inherited by the Duke of Buccleuch in 1810, when, Lockhart writes, the parks and mountain slopes of Drumlanrig were almost denuded of trees (Lockhart, 3.180).

42.8 the late Duke of Queensberry William Douglas (1725–1810), 4th Duke of Queensberry from 1778.

42.27 Rokeby the home in N. Yorkshire of Scott's friend John B. S. Morritt (1771–1843). Scott often stopped there while travelling to London. Scott's poem *Rokeby* (1813) was his fourth verse romance.

43.1 woman-kind in his *Life* (first published 1772; *CLA*, 233) Anthony a Wood (1632–95), historian and antiquary, objects to a Warden of Merton who moved his family into College because most of them were 'woman-kind (which before were look'd upon, if resident in the College, a scandal & an Abomination thereunto)' (3 May 1661).

43.7–10 Several artists . . . Provincial Antiquities of Scotland topographical works in which subscribers were given a series of engravings accompanied by a historical description were popular with the wealthy in the early 19th century. Scott's prospectus for *Provincial Antiquities*, published in 1817, indicates that the traveller would consider it desirable to 'possess accurate, and at the same time graceful representations, of the scenes which he has viewed with interest' (William B. Todd and Ann Bowden, *Sir Walter Scott: a Bibliographical History* (New Castle, DE, 1998), 438). Artists including J. M. W. Turner, Alexander Nasmyth, Rev. John Thomson, A. W. Callcott, Edward Blore, H. W. Williams and J. C. Schetky, were invited to draw scenes for which Scott wrote the historical descriptions (*Prose Works*, 7.155–457). The work, in ten parts with 52 engravings appeared as *Provincial Antiquities and Picturesque Scenery of Scotland* (London, 1819–26), re-issued in 2 vols in 1826 (*CLA*, 337). An account is to be found in Gerald Finley, *Landscapes of Memory: Turner as Illustrator of Scott* (London, 1980), 49–68. Because the work was not profitable Scott refused payment for his work on *Provincial Antiquities*, and received instead some of the originals. Finley describes the Turner watercolours hanging 'at Abbotsford in a large oaken frame made from a tree on the Abbotsford estate' and adds that by 1886 these were in the possession of Ralph Brocklebank (66 and note).

43.34–35 will one day . . . seem to warrant the original design was to publish the *Provincial Antiquities* in twelve parts but owing to financial difficulties only ten appeared; in spite of Scott's hopes it was never profitable.

43.39 sunk story i.e. the basement.

44.7 amateur tourists tourists in pursuit of their interest in painting, sculpture and architecture.

44.14 animadversions of the fair authoress of Destiny Susan Ferrier (1782–1854) novelist, and a friend of Scott. Her novel *Destiny* (3 vols, Edinburgh, 1831) is a tale of domestic strife and an observation of Scottish society. Her 'animadversions' on looking through key-holes have not been located.

45.12–15 some peculiarity . . . Roxburghe sale the bibliophile John Ker (1740–1804), 3rd Duke of Roxburghe from 1755, had in his collection a copy of Valdarfer's edition of Boccaccio (1471). His father, the 2nd duke, had purchased it for 100 guineas. At the sale of the third duke's library it was sold for £2260. This led to the foundation of the Roxburghe Club. Scott describes the purchase of the book in his review of *Pitcairn's Criminal Trials* (*Prose Works*, 21.214–15).

45.22–23 the Roman Agricola or the Caledonian Galgacus Agricola (AD 40–93), Roman general and governor of Britain 78–84, defeated the Caledonians under Galgacus in AD 84. The site of the battle was (and still is) a subject of dispute: see *The Antiquary*, 28.21–26.

45.32   marked with a twice or even thrice repeated "R.,"   the Scottish historian and antiquary John Pinkerton (1758–1826) used the notation 'R— rare, RR, rarer, and RRR very rare' to indicate the rarity of his collections: see *The Antiquary*, 183.43–84.1 and note.

45.33   tell it not in Gath   proverbial: 2 Samuel 1.20, *ODEP*, 297.

45.34–35   like the man in the Arabian tale ... "open sesame"   see 'The Story of Ali Baba, and the forty Thieves destroyed by a Slave', in *Tales of the East*, ed. Henry Weber, 3 vols (Edinburgh, 1812), 1.402–14 (*CLA*, 43). The man who forgets the charm of 'open sesame' is Ali Baba's brother Cassim. He is thus stuck inside the robbers' treasure cave, and murdered by them on their return.

46.8   foresaid catalogue   i.e. *CLA*: see note to 37.7–8.

46.12–13   valuable and inexpensive reprints   a note to the 1842 edition of Thomas Frognall Dibdin's *Bibliomania; or Book-Madness; A Bibliographical Romance* (first published 1809: *CLA*, 247) states: 'The ANCIENT CHRONICLES of the history of our country are in a progressive state of being creditably reprinted, with a strict adherence to the old phraseology. Of these Chronicles, the following have already made their appearance: HOLINSHED, 1807, 4to., 6 vols.; HALL, 1809, 4to.; GRAFTON, 1809, 4to.; 2 vols.; FABIAN, 1811, 4to.' (337).

46.15   catalogues we have seen   Dibdin (see note above) gives extensive information on early catalogues of printed books.

46.16   black-letter   an old style of type, similar to Gothic, and used in the 15th and 16th centuries before Roman type became the norm.

46.18   curator of a library of considerable extent   Scott was appointed one of the curators of the Advocates' Library in June 1795.

46.26–27   principle of Don Quixote's collection ... native village   Don Quixote's native village was in La Mancha. He 'gave himself up to the reading of books of chivalry, with so much attachment and relish, that he almost forgot all the sports of the field, and even the management of his domestic affairs; and his curiosity and extravagant fondness herein arrived to that pitch, that he sold many acres of arable land to purchase books of knight-errantry, and carried home all he could lay hands on of that kind': Miguel de Cervantes Saavedra (1547–1616), *The Adventures of Don Quixote* (Part 1, 1605; Part 2, 1615), Part I, Ch. 1 (see *CLA*, 101). The term 'auto de fe' denotes an 'act of faith' particularly one related to the punishment of heresy. It is therefore, particularly appropriate for the fate of Don Quixote's library, which is burnt at the instruction of the barber and curate on the grounds that it is 'pernicious and heretical'. The housekeeper, we read, 'set fire to, and burnt, all the books that were in the yard, and in the house too; and some might have perished, that deserved to be treasured up in perpetual archives' (Part 1, Chapter 7).

46.28–33   admitted only to the extent of five or six pounds ... printers of Glasgow   Robert Foulis (1707–76) with his brother Andrew (1712–75), both educated at the University of Glasgow, began dealing in rare books in Glasgow around 1739. Shortly afterwards they began their own printing and publishing business, became printers to the University of Glasgow in 1743, and gained a reputation for high-quality printing, and for editions of Greek and Roman classics, including an edition of Homer (ed. James Moor and George Muirhead, 4 vols, Glasgow, 1756–58). However, their commitment to quality led to commercial failure, and Robert Foulis seems to have sold his collections in 1776. See David Murray, *Robert & Andrew Foulis and the Glasgow*

Press (Glasgow, 1913), and Philip Gaskell, *A Bibliography of the Foulis Press*, 2nd edn (Winchester, 1986).

46.34–39   Mr Lamb ... above prices   the poem of 'Flodden Field' was originally published in 1664. The edition of Robert Lambe (1712–95), vicar of Norham in Northumberland from 1747, is entitled: *An Exact And Circumstantial History of the Battle of Floddon. In Verse. Written about the time of Queen Elizabeth* (Berwick upon Tweed, 1774: *CLA*, 9). It contains a note (7) in which Lambe writes: 'If we estimate, by the price, the credit of the old chronicle of *Holinshed* printed 1586, we shall have no mean opinion of it; for his history is sold by the booksellers for L.6:16:6'. Henry Weber (1783–1818) assisted Scott in his researches and was his amanuensis 1804–13. He produced an edition of *The Battle of Flodden Field* (Edinburgh, 1805: *CLA*, 187) which was dedicated to Scott.

47.2–15   Mr Kemble ... House of Cavendish   John Philip Kemble (1757–1823), manager of Covent Garden Theatre, London. About 1820, owing to his impoverishment while working in theatre management, he was forced to sell his superb collection of plays to William Spencer Cavendish (1790–1858), 6th Duke of Devonshire from 1811. The Devonshire-Kemble collection was purchased by the Huntington Library, California, in 1914. The Devonshire seat is Chatsworth House, in Derbyshire.

47.17–21   Settle's Emperor of Morocco ... greatly envenomed   the dramatist Elkanah Settle (1648–1724) engaged in a series of disputes with John Dryden (1631–1700). Settle's play *The Empress of Morocco* was very popular when it first appeared, and it was published in 1673 with fine scenic illustrations (see *CLA*, 218). In *Lives of the English Poets* (1779–81) Johnson recounts the dispute between Dryden and Settle stating: 'Settle's is said to have been the first play embellished with sculptures [engravings]; those ornaments seem to have given poor Dryden great disturbance': Samuel Johnson, 'Dryden' (1781), in *Lives of the English Poets*, ed. George Birkbeck Hill, 3 vols (Oxford, 1905), 1.345 (see *CLA*, 42). Dryden, working with John Crowe and Thomas Shadwell, published a pamphlet attacking Settle (*Notes and Observations on the Empress of Morocco*, London, 1674), and also satirised Settle as Doeg in the second part of *Absolom and Achitophel* (1681).

47.21–22   Rev. Henry White of Litchfield   White (1761–1836) was sacrist of Lichfield Cathedral, was a cousin of Scott's friend Anna Seward, and collected ancient books and tracts.

47.33–35   cast of the Poet, Shakespeare ... Stratford-upon-Avon   before 1623 a monument with bust by London sculptor Gerard Johnson was erected. Lockhart observes: 'A cast from the monumental effigy at Stratford-upon-Avon—now in the library at Abbotsford—was the gift of Mr. George Bullock, long distinguished in London as a collector of curiosities' (Lockhart, 4.29n). In a letter to J. B. S. Morritt of 22 November 1816 Scott writes: ' One of our first occupations was to unpack Shakespeare and his superb pedestal, which is positively the most elegant and appropriate piece of furniture which I ever saw ... The figure came safe; and the more I look at it the more I feel that it must have resembled the Bard much more than any of the ordinary prints, unless it be that in the first folio edition, which has all the appearance of being taken from it. The forehead is more expanded, and has not a narrow, peaked, and priggish look inconsistent with the dignity of Shakespeare's character, and which strongly marks all the ordinary portraits, which seem to me more like Spenser than Shakespeare' (*Letters*, 4.295–96). After Scott's death the bust of Shakespeare was moved and replaced by Francis Chantrey's bust of Scott himself.

47.39–40   wood of the celebrated mulberry tree   the box is now situated in a display cabinet at Abbotsford and measures 9 by 6cm. The top of the lid is inscribed with Shakespeare's coat of arms and the words: 'wood/ Sharp/ Stratford/ on Avon'. The underside of the lid bears the words: 'Shakespear's wood/ Sharp/ Stratford on Avon'. A slip of paper inside the box carries the information given here in Scott's hand.

48.4   David Garrick (1717–79), actor.

48.4   Rob. Bensley Esqr   Robert Bensley (1742–1817), actor.

48.5   Mr Thornhill   not identified, although Scott entertained William Thornhill, Colonel in the 7th Hussars, in Abbotsford 6 October 1826, and received a letter dated 18 August 1828 from him.

48.7   remnant of the Jubilee   Shakespeare's jubilee was celebrated for three days 6–8 September 1769 at Stratford-upon-Avon under the direction of Garrick, Thomas Arne (1710–78), and James Boswell (1740–95).

48.7   arms of Shakespeare   Shakespeare's arms are given as 'a falcon rising Argent supporting with the dexter [right] claw a tilting-spear Or, steeled Argent'. The motto is 'Non sanz droict'. The arms are engraved on the top of the lid of the box.

48.15   complete collection of Congreve's original pieces   William Congreve (1670–1729), dramatist: see *CLA*, 221. Scott became aware of changes in the text in later editions of plays of the Restoration period when establishing the text for his edition of Dryden (see next note), and so saw the need to collect first editions.

48.15–16   those of Dryden   John Dryden (1631–1700). Scott edited Dryden's *Works* in 18 volumes in 1808 (*CLA*, 231).

48.17–22   original offences … repentance   Jeremy Collier (1650–1726), a non-juring bishop mainly remembered for his *Short View of the Immorality and Profaneness of the English Stage* (1698) in which Congreve and Vanbrugh were especially attacked (see *CLA*, 223).

48.19   editiones principes   *Latin* first editions.

48.28–29   L'Antiquité … Montfaucon   Bernard de Montfaucon (1655–1741), *L'antiquité expliquée*, 15 vols (Paris, 1719–24): *CLA*, 223. According to Lockhart (5.328) the set was presented to Scott by the King in January 1824. The French title means: 'Antiquity explained and presented in pictures by Dom Bernard de Montfaucon'.

48.33–34   King George the Fourth of happy memory   George IV (1762–1830; reigned 1820–30, but Regent from 1811). Scott was a long-standing admirer of George and arranged his visit to Scotland in 1822; the Magnum Opus edition of Scott's novels (1829–33) was dedicated to the King.

49.1   'Twas meant for merit though it fell on me   Edward Young (1681–1765), 'The Instalment' (1726), line 46. 'The Instalment' was addressed to Sir Robert Walpole on his being made Knight of the Garter.

49.3   Libri Classici cum Notis Variorum   *Latin* classic books with notes of variants. In the catalogue (*CLA*, 224–226) these appear as *Auctores Classici, Graeci et Latini*, 140 vols. They are described as 'editiones optimi' (the best editions) and were published in many different places in Europe between 1613 and 1813. This gift from Archibald Constable (see note to 37.18) arrived in Abbotsford on 5 January 1824 (*Letters*, 8.148).

49.7   by way of handseling the new library   the term 'handsel' is Scots and involves a gift to mark and celebrate a new undertaking or possession.

49.10–12   Lintot … ride to Oxford   Barnaby Bernard Lintot (1675–1736), the publisher of Alexander Pope (1688–1744). The anecdote appears in Pope's comic narrative written in a letter to Richard, Earl of Burlington, November 1716, where he recounts how, while travelling together to

Oxford on horseback, Lintot suggested they rest a while in a wood, and said: 'See here, what a mighty pretty *Horace* I have in my pocket? what if you amus'd your self in turning an Ode, till we mount again?' (*Alexander Pope: Selected Letters*, ed. by Howard Erskine-Hill (Oxford, 2000), 108). Horace is the Roman poet Quintus Horatius Flaccus (65–8 BC).

49.15–18 For long . . . Gothic rhime see Thomas Warton (1728–90), 'Verses on Sir Joshua Reynold's Painted Window at New College, Oxford' (1782), lines 7–10, in *The Poetical Works Of the Late Thomas Warton*, 2 vols (Oxford, 1802), 1.54: see *CLA*, 42.

49.20 my old friend Dr Adams Dr Alexander Adam (1741–1809), Scott's teacher and rector at the High School of Edinburgh. Scott was particularly influenced by his teaching of literature in Latin: see 'Memoirs', in *Scott on Himself*, ed. David Hewitt (Edinburgh, 1981), 23.

49.28 Ballads and Popular Poems see *CLA*, 159.

49.29–30 a line which may be thought peculiarly my own Scott published the first two volumes of *Minstrelsy of the Scottish Border*, a collection of mainly traditional ballads, together with four imitations, in 1802. It was reissued in 1803, together with a third volume, and together these constitute the 2nd edition. A further 3 editions followed in the next nine years.

49.31 first book i.e. in the sense that several volumes can constitute a single work.

49.31–32 an immense quantity of such gear in addition to the six volumes there is an 'immense quantity' of popular literature in this press in the library at Abbotsford.

49.32–33 six volumes of stall copies of popular ballads and tales these volumes contain many chapbooks (cheap, pamphlet-sized publications, usually containing popular narratives in prose or verse, which were sold by stall-holders and pedlars).

50.12–13 the very circumstance . . . insure their antiquity i.e. being printed in black-letter.

50.15–16 last century i.e. the 18th century.

50.20 Miller and Chapman Walter Chepman (*c.* 1473–*c.* 1528) and Androw Myllar (fl. 1503–08), Scotland's first printers. They were granted a patent by James IV in 1507. Both were burgesses of the city of Edinburgh; Chepman was a general merchant and Myllar a bookseller who had supplied books to the King for a number of years. Myllar had trained as a printer in France and brought over several skilled printers from the continent to work with him. Works printed by them include *The Flyting of Dunbar and Kennedy*, *The Gest of Robyn Hode*, and Bishop Elphinstone's *Breviarium Aberdonense*. Scott discusses Myllar and Chepman in 'Popular Poetry', in *Poetical Works*, 1.40–41.

50.20–21 down perhaps as low as perhaps as late as.

50.21 Watson James Watson (d. 1722). Watson's premises were at Craig's Close, opposite the Cross in the High Street of Edinburgh. He published *The History of the Art of Printing* in 1713 and a folio Bible in 1722. Scott discusses Watson and his publishing of a collection of ancient poetry in 'Popular Poetry', in *Poetical Works*, 1.41.

50.25–29 Wit and Mirth . . . new Set *CLA*, 159. Thomas D'Urfey (1653–1723) published *Wit and Mirth, or Pills to Purge Melancholy*, 6 vols, 1719–20.

50.28–29 announced as five volumes i.e. the catalogue of the sale announced five volumes; the sixth volume was stolen then returned and there are now 6 volumes in Scott's library at Abbotsford.

50.37 McLauchlan's Saleroom probably McLachlan and Stewart, booksellers, 62 South Bridge, Edinburgh.

51.1   Mr Blackwood winter & spring 1819   William Blackwood (1776–1834), Edinburgh publisher and founder of *Blackwood's Magazine*. A notice inside the copy at Abbotsford announces the sale as being on 4 and 6 March 1819.

51.20   mess of pottage . . . the birthright of Esau   see Genesis 25.29–34. Esau sells his birthright to his brother Jacob for a 'pottage of lentils . . . thus Esau despised his birthright'. Although the phrase 'mess of pottage' does not appear in the text of the story, several early Bibles (e.g. 1537, 1539 and the 1560 Geneva Bible) headed Ch. 25 'Esau selleth his birthright for a mess of potage'.

51.24–25   half-reputation . . . Augustan writers   as a dramatist D'Urfey (see note to 50.25–29) is frequently mentioned in the writings of his contemporaries. Since *Pills to Purge Melancholy* (1719–20) was published after the deaths of John Dryden (1631–1700), and Joseph Addison (1672–1719), editor of *The Spectator* 1711–12, it could not have been discussed by them, but in the debate generated by Addison's ballad criticism in *The Spectator* (see note to 52.28–34) D'Urfey is mentioned as one who liked, and had a collection of, popular poetry.

51.28–29   'Twas within a mile of Edinburgh Town   see '''Twas within a Furlong of Edinborough Town', in Thomas D'Urfey, *Wit and Mirth, or Pills to Purge Melancholy*, 6 vols (1719–20), 1.326–27.

51.35   tunes of the Beggar's Opera   *The Beggar's Opera* (1728), a play by John Gay (1685–1732) alternates dialogue and songs: *CLA*, 216.

52.2   John Bell's Ballads and Tales   see *CLA*, 32, 57 and 156. See also note 52.9–10 below.

52.9–10   his own little shop . . . anchorite's cell   John Bell (1783–1864) was a bookseller in Newcastle until *c.* 1816, when financial difficulties forced him to abandon bookselling; he became a surveyor and librarian to the Newcastle Antiquarian Society.

52.10   Patmos   a place of solitude and inspiration, named after the island in the Aegean where St John is supposed to have written Revelation (1.9).

52.12   Chevy Chase   one of the oldest of English ballads, 'Chevy Chase' probably dates in its earliest form from the 15th century. The poem was quoted with notes in *The Spectator*, nos 21 and 25 (1711) and is the first poem in Thomas Percy, *Reliques of Ancient English Poetry*, 3 vols (London, 1765), 1.1–17: see *CLA*, 172.

52.12   Magnus Apollo   *Latin* Great Apollo, i.e. the god whom he worshipped, or the great end which he sought. The traditional ballads are all anonymous; no authors have been identified, as all traditional ballads were transmitted orally, and texts were usually first written down long after composition.

52.14   Percy   the name of the family, which, in the later middle ages and in the sixteenth century, was the dominant power in Northumberland. It is a Percy who is the hero of 'Chevy Chase'.

52.15   of yore   of old, a long time ago.

52.16–19   Canny Newcastle . . . valuable as reprints   a song called 'Canny Newcassel' by Thomas Thompson, printed in North Shields, appears as number 36 (f. 8r) in Scott's own scrapbook collection 'Songs and so on' (*CLA*, 159) described above under the heading 'Ballads and Popular Poems' in the text at 49.28–50.23.

52.22   crypt   *properly* a chapel under the floor of the main church, sometimes used for burials, but here presumably used by Scott to suggest a secret space.

52.22–24   collection . . . Critical   Scott discusses this collection by Ambrose Philips (2nd edn, 3 vols (London, 1723–25): *CLA*, 171) in his essay on 'Evans's Old Ballads' first published in the *Quarterly Review*, May 1810 (*Prose Works*, 17.119–36). He suggests that the work cited here is one of the main sources for Evans's collection. It is now, he writes, 'extremely rare, and sells at a price very disproportionate to its size' (*Prose Works*, 17.122).

52.28–34   The public … panegyric   Addison's essay on 'The Ballad', published in two parts in *The Spectator*, attempts to establish a critical respectability for 'Chevy Chase' (no. 70, Monday 21 May 1711, and no. 74, Friday 25 May 1711, in Joseph Addison (1672–1719) and Sir Richard Steele (1672–1729), *The Spectator*, ed. Donald F. Bond, 5 vols (Oxford, 1965), 1.297–303, and 1.315–22). This provoked a negative response from William Wagstaffe (1685–1725) in his *A Comment upon the History of Tom Thumb* (London, 1711; *CLA*, 129) and John Dennis (1657–1734) in his *Remarks upon Cato, A Tragedy* (London, 1713). For other respondents see *The Spectator*, ed. Donald F. Bond, 1.322. Scott alludes to Addison's arguments in 'Popular Poetry', in *Poetical Works*, 1.22–23.

53.3   Bishop Percy   Thomas Percy 1729–1811, Bishop of Dromore from 1782. In 1765 he published his *Reliques of Ancient English Poetry* in 3 volumes (see *CLA*, 172). Scott writes: 'Bishop Percy, the venerable editor of the *Reliques of Ancient Poetry*, was, we believe, the first who turned the public attention upon these forgotten hordes of antiquarian treasure, by an Essay upon Metrical Romance, prefixed to the third volume of his work' (*Prose Works*, 17.18).

53.11–12   The Tea-table Miscellany … Allan Ramsay   Allan Ramsay (1684–1758) published *The Tea-Table Miscellany: or A Collection of Scots Songs* in 1724. It was frequently reprinted and by 1737 had expanded to 4 vols. Scott owned the 13th edition of 1762 (*CLA*, 171).

53.16–21   my Grandfather Robert Scott … forget   Robert Scott (1699–1775) of Sandyknowe, Roxburghshire, was Scott's paternal grandfather. Scott was sent to the farm (some 10 km E of Abbotsford) as a child for his health. His grandfather died when he was about four, and Scott commemorates him in the introduction to Canto 3 of *Marmion* (1808), and in his 'Memoirs' he recalls reciting 'Hardyknute' while at Sandyknowe (*Scott on Himself*, ed. David Hewitt (Edinburgh, 1981), 13–14). The ballad of 'Hardyknute', a tale of chivalry involving the wars between the Scots and the Norsemen, was written (although some traditional material may have been incorporated) by Elizabeth Halket, Lady Wardlaw (1677–1727), and published in 1719. It was included in Allan Ramsay's *The Ever-Green Being a Collection of Scots Poems*, 2 vols (Edinburgh, 1724), 2.247–64 (see *CLA*, 170), and in his *Tea-Table Miscellany* (see note above).

53.18   Automathes   John Kirby, *Automathes, or the Capacity and Extent of the Human Understanding, exemplified in the Extraordinary Case of Automathes* (London, 1745: *CLA*, 44).

53.19   Josephus's War of the Jews   Josephus, born *c*. AD 37, was a leader at the time of the revolt of the Jews in the reign of Nero. His *The History of the Jewish War* against the Romans, completed *c*. AD 75, was praised by contemporary Jewish and Roman communities and remains an important historical source (see *CLA*, 259).

53.22–30   Having spoken … decision   Scott discusses Ramsay's *Tea-Table Miscellany* in 'Popular Poetry'. He criticises Ramsay's editorial practice of 'writing new words to old tunes, without at the same time preserving the ancient verses' which led him to 'throw aside many originals, the preservation of which would have been much more interesting than any thing which has been substituted in their stead' (*Poetical Works*, 1.43).

128 EXPLANATORY NOTES

53.33–54.1 Scottish minstrelsy ... never published *CLA*, 172. Von Bergmann was a correspondent of Robert Jamieson (see note to 54.8). In *Illustrations of Northern Antiquities* (Edinburgh, 1814), 355, Jamieson writes: 'Of the coronets worn by the peasant girls in Livonia, Courland, Esthonia, Lithuania, &c., a curious assortment has been sent me by my learned and zealous friend, the Reverend Gustav Von Bergmann, pastor of Ruien, in Livonia'. *Livonia*, ruled by Russia but with German as the language of administration and education, was an area comprising of much of present-day Estonia and Latvia; the Duchy of Courland (1561–1795) was within present-day Latvia.

54.5 wrought off printed off.

54.8 Mr Robert Jamieson (*c.* 1780–1844), antiquary and ballad editor, editor of *Popular Ballads and Songs, from Tradition, Manuscript, and Scarce Editions, with Translations from Similar Pieces from the Ancient Danish Language, and A Few Originals by the Editor*, 2 vols (Edinburgh, 1806: *CLA*, 158). He acknowledged a debt to Scott and later worked with him and Henry Weber on *Illustrations of Northern Antiquities* (Edinburgh, 1814: *CLA*, 100).

54.10 Dr Bowring Sir John Bowring (1792–1872), traveller and linguist. Bowring visited Abbotsford in April, 1830 (see *Letters* 11.340). He published *Specimens of the Polish Poets* (1827), *Servian Popular Poetry* (1830), *Poetry of the Magyars* (1830), and *Cheskian Anthology* (1832): see *CLA*, 158 and 162.

54.18–19 Docti utriusque linguæ *Latin* the learned in both languages (i.e. Latin and Greek): see Horace (65–8 BC), *Odes*, 3.8.5: 'docte sermones utriusque linguae' (learned in the lore of both languages).

54.26 Joseph Ritson's publications Joseph Ritson (1752–1803), antiquary and the most exacting of ballad editors: see *CLA*, 174.

54.27–30 he suffered himself ... fire Sir Arthur Wardour and Jonathan Oldbuck allude to Ritson's quarrel with John Pinkerton on the origin of the Goths and Celts in *The Antiquary* (48) and Scott elaborates on Ritson's quarrels and disputes with his fellow collector Percy in 'Popular Poetry': 'It ought to be said, however, by one who knew him well, that this irritability of disposition was a constitutional and physical infirmity; and that Ritson's extreme attachment to the severity of truth, corresponded to the rigour of his criticisms upon the labours of others' (*Poetical Works*, 1.48–49). Ritson's biographer, Henry Alfred Burd, observes: 'Ritson's method of criticism was so invidiously personal and his beliefs and habits were so eccentric that attention was attracted primarily to his peculiarities, while his stable qualities were overlooked by the majority'. In September 1803 Ritson barricaded himself in his chambers and drove off all who approached him. He set fire to a mass of papers which included many unfinished manuscripts (Henry Alfred Burd, *Joseph Ritson: A Critical Biography* (Illinois, 1916), 9; 193).

55.23–30 Satans Invisible World Discovered ... Glasgow published Edinburgh, 1685 (*CLA*, 142). The author, George Sinclair (d. 1696) was successively professor of philosophy and mathematics at Glasgow University. His *Satans Invisible World Discovered* was one of the main sources for several of the stories in the Waverley Novels including 'Wandering Willie's Tale' in *Redgauntlet* (1824) and the hauntings in *Woodstock* (1826).

55.24 Saducees members of one of the three 'sects' into which the Jews were divided at the time of Christ. They denied the existence of angels and spirits.

55.28 Major Weir Major Thomas Weir (1600?–70), a Covenanting officer, noted for his zeal in the cause, who later commanded the Edinburgh City Guard. Late in life, he was struck with an illness, and upon his recovery confessed to crimes of bestiality, incest (with his sister), adultery, and wizardry.

He was found guilty of his crimes, and was strangled and burnt between Edinburgh and Leith. After his death his reputation as a wizard grew and he was thought to haunt his former house in the West Bow in Edinburgh.

55.32   Reverend Mr Glanville Joseph Glanvill (1636–80), educated at Oxford. He attacked scholastic philosophy in *The Vanity of Dogmatizing* (1661), and defended the belief in witchcraft in *Saducisimus Triumphatus* (1681), a defence which resulted from an attempt to find an empirical ground for a belief in the supernatural.

56.4–7   Much Ado About Nothing . . . reverence *Much Ado About Nothing*, 2.3.108–11.

56.10   an Oxford scholar in James Hogg, *The Private Memoirs and Confessions of A Justified Sinner* (1824) Robert Wringhim says: 'they had some crude conceptions that nothing was taught at Oxford but the *black arts*, which ridiculous idea prevailed all over the south of Scotland' (ed. P. D. Garside, Stirling / South Carolina Research Edition of the Collected Works of James Hogg 9 (Edinburgh, 2001), 159). In his note (247) P. D. Garside points out: 'One possible origin for the association might be Roger Bacon (1214–92), the Oxford scholar and Franciscan philosopher, who gained a reputation as a magician for his work in the experimental sciences'. Scott also implies a connection between Oxford and the black arts in *Guy Mannering* (1815): see *Guy Mannering*, ed. P. D. Garside, EEWN 2 (Edinburgh, 1999), 15.

56.20   printed by Reid in 1695 the first edition of Sinclair was actually published by John Reid in Edinburgh in 1685, and the copy at Abbotsford is the 1685 edition.

56.21   Mr David Laing (1793–1878) prolific editor and antiquary. From 1823 he was the secretary and a most energetic member of the Bannatyne Club. There is an inscription from him dated 21 March 1831 inside the board in the copy of Sinclair at Abbotsford. A note reads that Laing purchased the copy in February 1831, and another by Scott on the fly-leaf reads: 'This copy which Mr David Laing had from Mr Charles Kirkpatrick Sharpe in exchange for two drawings by Le Brun were given to me by my friend Mr David Laing. April 1832 Walter Scott'.

56.25   George Seaton, Earl of Winton and Tranent George Seton (1642–1704), 9th Lord Seton and 4th Earl of Winton.

56.26–27   Latin encomium . . . by Patricius Sinclarus a eulogy or a formal or high-flown expression of praise by Patrick Sinclair. This does not appear in all copies of *Satans Invisible World Discovered* (it is missing in the copy held in the National Library of Scotland: H.36.c.33), but it is present in the Abbotsford copy where it follows the Dedicatory Epistle and precedes the Preface to the Reader. It is entitled 'In Auctorem and Opus, Encomiasticon' (praise for the author and his work). Patrick Sinclair has not been identified, although the 1703 Latin thesis of a Patricius Sinclair is in the library of the Royal College of Physicians, Edinburgh.

56.28   the Cartesian Philosophy philosophy associated with the French philosopher René Descartes 1596–1650.

56.30   Carmen Steliteuticon *carmen* is Latin for a poem or song, and *steliteuticon* a rare Greek adjective meaning 'full of invective'; thus *Carmen Steliteuticon* is a poem full of invective.

56.35   his extensive coal mines the lands of the 4th Earl of Wintoun (see note to 56.25) included the coal-mining districts of Tranent in East Lothian and Niddry now on the east side of Edinburgh.

57.2   Kircher Anthanasius Kircher (1601–80), German Jesuit and physicist. Jonathan Oldbuck quotes Kircher in *The Antiquary* (98).

57.4 Dædalus legendary Athenian craftsman of great skill. He constructed the labyrinth at Crete for Minos and in an attempt to escape it after their imprisonment, Daedalus and his son Icarus made wings for themselves with wax and feathers. Icarus flew too near the sun and fell into the sea.

57.6 Hannibal (247–182 BC), Carthaginian general who led an assault against Rome during the second Punic war. He famously crossed the Alps with a herd of elephants.

57.7 Qui montes rupit aceto *Latin* who broke the mountains with vinegar: see Juvenal, *Satires*, 10.153: 'montem rupit aceto' (he splits apart the mountain with sour wine), describing in satiric terms Hannibal's procedure in forging a way through the Alps.

57.15 Archimedes (*c*. 287–212 BC), invented the compound pulley and the 'screw of Archimedes', an irrigation device.

57.18 Neip Tides tides occurring shortly after the first and third quarters of the moon, in which the high water level stands at its lowest point.

57.19 Portus ... ingens *Latin* a harbour sheltered from the winds, calm and spacious: Virgil (70–19 BC), *The Aeneid*, 3.570.

57.20–21 choice Coal ... New-haven the 4th Earl also built a new harbour at Cockenzie on the Firth of Forth, called Port Seton.

57.22–24 improving your coal for making of salt ... singular the main use for coal in the 17th century was for the making of salt from the sea. The area around the Firth of Forth was developed for this purpose from an early date, and the Earl of Winton owned large integrated ventures: see Baron F. Duckham, *A History of the Scottish Coal Industry 1700–1815* (Newton Abbot, 1970), 15. The Earl's father built twelve salt pans in Cockenzie, and in 1689 'a petition is presented to the Earl of Winton by Robert Ballenden, smith in Cockenzie, for payment for work done at the salt-pans in June 1686': see George Seton, *A History of the Family of Seton During Eight Centuries*, 2 vols (Edinburgh, 1896), 1.224, 244.

57.30 Te toti ... genti *Latin* to believe that you were born for the benefit of the whole race: see Lucan (AD 39–65), *Bellum Civile*, 2.283, where he describes Cato (Marcus Porcius Cato Uticensis, 95–46 BC).

57.37–38 fruitful Corn-fields ... Seton East Lothian has long been one of the most fertile regions of Scotland. One of George Seton's ancestors had been able to export 36 bolls of wheat (about 2¼ tons) to Bergen in spite of a perceived national shortage of corn: see George Seton, *A History of the Family of Seton During Eight Centuries*, 2 vols (Edinburgh, 1896), 1.225.

57.37 Ceres Italian deity representing the regenerative power of nature.

57.40 Casual and Land-Revenue casual revenue consists of payments from tenants and vassals in certain contingencies, and land-revenue is income from land.

58.4–5 famous of old ... Peace the family of Seton were long famed for their loyalty to the Stewart cause on account of which they took up arms on many occasions.

58.16–20 treatise upon hydrostatics *The Hydrostaticks* (Edinburgh, 1672: *CLA*, 121). This book deals with, among other things, the best way to drain coal seams.

58.17 winded up wound up.

58.18 a cock-and-a-bull story a long rambling story.

58.21–22 Alexander Agnew ... blasphemy Sinclair describes these events in *The Hydrostaticks*, 238–47, and places them in October 1654. He states that the events took place after Agnew had been denied alms by the weaver's family. He elaborates on the story in *Satans Invisible World Discovered* (Edinburgh, 1685), 76–77, where he describes Agnew responding to his judges in court that 'he knew no God but Salt, Meal, and Water'. A 'bold and sturdy beggar' was one considered to be able to earn his living, unlike someone old, sick or disabled.

58.31–32 Mr Constable see note to 37.18–34.

59.4–5 Bekker's Monde Enchanté *CLA*, 145: Balthasar Bekker, *Le Monde enchanté, ou, examen des communs sentimens touchant les Esprits, leur nature, leur pouvoir, leur administration, et leurs operations, &c*, 4 vols (Amsterdam, 1694). Scott also possessed a further volume which claims to refute Bekker (Amsterdam, 1699), and a one-volume English translation, *The World Bewitched* (London, 1695). The French reads: 'The enchanted world, or an examination of the views commonly held about spirits, their nature, their power, their organisation, and their operations'.

59.7 De La Lycanthropie *CLA*, 146. The French reads: 'On Lycanthropy, the transformation and ecstasy of sorcerers. The whole written by J. De Nyauld, doctor of medicine'. In *Demonology and Witchcraft*, 212, Scott describes lycanthropy as the idea that 'a human being had the power, by sorcery, of transforming himself into the shape of a wolf, and in that capacity, being seized with a species of fury, he rushed out, and made havoc among the flocks, slaying and wasting, like the animal whom he represented, far more than he could devour'.

59.10–13 The Discovery of Witches . . . 1647 *CLA*, 151.

59.14 the print prefixed see illustration. In *Demonology and Witchcraft*, 290, Scott writes: 'the broad vulgarity of which epithets shows what a flat imagination he brought to support his impudent fictions'.

59.14 Mathew Hopkins (d. 1647), a notorious witchfinder whose work brought about many hangings in the south-east of England. He himself was eventually hanged as a sorcerer. Scott discusses Hopkins at some length in *Demonology and Witchcraft* describing him as an 'impudent and cruel wretch' (253), and stating: 'A monster like Hopkins could only have existed during the confusion of civil dissension. He was, perhaps, a native of Manningtree, in Essex; at any rate, he resided there in the year 1644, when an epidemic outcry of witchcraft arose in that town. Upon this occasion he had made himself busy, and affecting more zeal and knowledge than other men, learned his trade of a witchfinder, as he pretends, from experiment. He was afterwards permitted to perform it as a legal profession, and moved from one place to another, with an assistant named Sterne, and a female' (255–56). In a note Scott writes that the pamphlet is 'a very rare tract, which was bought at Mr Lort's sale, by the celebrated collector Mr Bindley, and is now in the author's possession' (255).

59.22–23 Dr Grey's notes upon Hudibras *Hudibras*, a satiric poem by Samuel Butler, was originally published in three parts: 1663, 1664, 1680 (see *CLA* 182, 242). In his edition (first published in 2 vols, London, 1799), Zachary Grey identifies, and comments upon, many of Butler's satiric subjects, including Mathew Hopkins. Quoting from Francis Hutchinson's *Historical Essay concerning Witchcraft* (London, 1718), Grey says of Hopkins and his ducking of witches: 'some gentlemen, out of indignation at the barbarity, took him and tied his own thumbs and toes, as he used to tie others; and when he was put into the water, he himself swam as they[his victims] did' (*Hudibras*, ed. [Zachary Grey], 2nd edn, 3 vols (London, 1819), 2.169).

59.24 Pomponatius, his work upon enchantments Pet. Pomponatii, *De Naturalium Effectuum Causis* ([Basel, 1556]: *CLA*, 146). The Abbotsford copy has no date on the title page but the Prefatory Epistle is dated 1556; *Basileæ* is Basel.

59.26–30   The Certainty of the Worlds of Spirits . . . Infidels   *CLA*, 146.

59.30   Saduccees   see note to 55.24.

59.32   Glanville and Sinclair   see notes to 55.23–30 and 55.32.

59.33–34   worthy dissenting minister Richard Baxter   Baxter (1615–91) was a Presbyterian divine and a powerful preacher. He sided with Parliament during the Civil War, and after the restoration of the monarchy in 1660 he was fined and imprisoned for not conforming to the Church of England. His many writings include his autobiography *Reliquiae Baxterianae* (London, 1696: *CLA*, 29).

61. 2–4   Witches Apprehended . . . Witch or not   an anonymous work, printed for Edward Marchant (London, [1613]: *CLA*, 148).

61.5–6   new method of trying a witch is something akin to the old   Scott describes this process when writing of Matthew Hopkins's methods in *Demonology and Witchcraft*, 256: 'He also practised and stoutly defended the trial by swimming, when the suspected person was wrapt in a sheet, having the great toes and thumbs tied together, and so dragged through a pond or river. If she sank, it was received in favour of the accused; but if the body floated, (which must have occurred ten times for once, if it was placed with care on the surface of the water,) the accused was condemned, on the principle of King James, who, in treating of this mode of trial, lays down, that as witches have renounced their baptism, so it is just that the element through which the holy rite is enforced, should reject them; which is a figure of speech, and no argument'. The description is reminiscent of Madge Wildfire's treatment at the hands of the mob: see *The Heart of Mid-Lothian*, ed. David Hewitt and Alison Lumsden, EEWN 6 (Edinburgh, 2004), 362–64.

61.10   immense Dutch slops   full and often padded breeches of the late 16th and early 17th century.

61.12   persecution of the witches of New England   Scott writes at some length on the instances of witchcraft in New England and observes: 'If any thing were wanted to confirm the general proposition, that the epidemic terror of witchcraft increases and becomes general in proportion to the increase of prosecutions against witches, it would be sufficient to quote certain extraordinary occurrences in New England' (*Demonology and Witchcraft*, 274).

61.13–21   An Exact Narrative . . . London, 1709   according to the British Library catalogue the principal author was Jan Smagge (*CLA*, 148).

61.23–24   Sir Edward Coke . . . England   Sir Edward Coke (1552–1634). He was made chief justice of the Common Pleas in 1606 and of the King's Bench in 1613.

61.24–26   The Triall . . . wayes   *CLA*, 149.

61.26   John Cotta   (*c.* 1575–1650), author of a work on doctors and medicine (1612) as well as witches. The second edition of the witch book, *The Infallible True and Assured VVitch*, appeared in 1624.

61.28–37   Boy of Bilson . . . London, 1622   the author, given as R. B., was Richard Baddeley, and the preface of the copy at Abbotsford is signed 'Rye Baddeley' (*CLA*, 149). The Boy of Bilson (William Perry) pretended to be possessed. Scott refers to him in a Magnum note to *The Fortunes of Nigel*, citing this case as one of a number of impostures personally investigated by James VI and I (Magnum, 27.322–23). No information has been found concerning the relationship of the work or the boy to notes on Shakespeare.

63.3–4   This collection . . . Ashmole and Lilly   *Lives of those Eminent Antiquaries, Elias Ashmole, Esq. And Mr William Lilly; written by themselves, &c.* (London, 1774: *CLA*, 149). Elias Ashmole (1617–92) was a writer and editor of

antiquarian and Rosicrucian works, and William Lilly (1602–81) a noted astrologer who published yearly almanacs and pamphlets of prophesy. In *Demonology
and Witchcraft*, 347–48, Scott comments: 'From what we learn of his own
history, Lilly himself, a low-born ignorant man, with some gloomy shades of
fanaticism in his temperament, was sufficiently fitted to dupe others, and perhaps cheated himself, merely by perusing, at an advanced period of life, some of
the astrological tracts devised by men of less cunning, though perhaps more
pretence to science, than he himself might boast. Yet the public still continued to
swallow these gross impositions, though coming from such unworthy authority
... Lilly was a prudent person, contriving with some address to shift the sails of
his prophetic bark, so as to suit the current of the time, and the gale of fortune.'
63.9–12   a bargain of astrological books ... interest   Lilly first turned
his attention to astrology in 1632 after a friend introduced him to Arise Evans,
an astrologer living in Gunpowder Alley. He bought books on the subject
belonging to William Bedwell, read them day and night, and within six or seven
weeks was a fairly accomplished astrologer. In *Demonology and Witchcraft*, 345,
Scott calls astrology 'the road most flattering to human vanity, while ... at the
same time most seductive to human credulity'.
63.18–20   Lord Henry Howard ... Northampton   Henry Howard
(1540–1614) was created Earl of Northampton in 1604.
63.20–29   A defensative ... 1583   *CLA*, 149. In a Magnum note to *The
Fortunes of Nigel* (26.239), Scott writes: 'Lord Henry Howard was the second
son of the poetical Earl of Surrey, and possessed considerable parts and learning.
He wrote, in the year 1583, a book called, "A Defensative [something which
protects] against the Poison of supposed Prophecies." He gained the favour of
Queen Elizabeth, by having, he says, directed his battery against a sect of
prophets and pretended soothsayers, whom he accounted *infesti regibus* [*Latin*
those dangerous to monarchs], as he expresses it.' The Latin phrase *De futuris
contingentibus* means 'concerning future occurrences'.
63.30–34   adherent of James the Sixth's claim ... Scottish monarch
Howard, along with Robert Cecil (1563?–1612), created 1st Earl of Salisbury
in 1605, conducted a long secret correspondence with James VI of Scotland
designed to ensure the latter's smooth succession to the English throne after
Elizabeth's death. James succeeded in 1603.
63.39–64.2   supposed prophesies ... cause of Queen Mary   Scott refers
to the prophecies that were continuously circulated among Catholics during the
20-year imprisonment of Mary Queen of Scots in England. Mary was a Catholic
and until her execution in 1587 was next in line to the English throne. The
prophecies and plots which repeatedly put Mary forward as heir to the English
throne strengthened the position of her Protestant son, James VI.
63.39   Froissart   Jean Froissart (1337?–c. 1410), French chronicler who
travelled widely, lived in England for a period, and also visited Flanders, Scotland, Italy and Belgium. His *Chroniques* is a brilliant account of the chivalric
exploits of the nobles of England and France 1325–1400, but also reports the
suppression of the Jacquerie, the peasants of northern France who rebelled in
1357–58. Scott, who frequently draws on his work in the Waverley Novels,
owned the *Chroniques* in the edition of J. A. Buchon, Vols 10–25, in *Collection de
Chroniques Nationales Françaises*, 47 vols (Paris, 1824–28: *CLA*, 50), the translation of 1523–25 by Lord Berners in an edition ed. E. V. Utterson, 2 vols
(London, 1812: *CLA*, 29), and the translation by Thomas Johnes, 4 vols
(Hafod, 1803–05: *CLA*, 28). His comment on prophecies in England in the
14th century comes from either Bk 1 or Bk 4 of the *Chroniques*.
64.4–6   suited to the taste of James ... inversions of speech   the

appeal that Howard's pedantic style would have had for James VI and I is evident to all readers of *The Fortunes of Nigel* (1822).

64.12–23   noble author was ... promotion   after James's accession Howard was created Earl of Northampton (1604) and Lord Privy Seal (1608).

64.15–16   Reverend Mr Cotton Mather   (1663–1728), a puritanical Presbyterian minister in Boston, Massachusetts. He played a prominent part in the Salem witchcraft trials of 1692. In *Demonology and Witchcraft*, 83, Scott describes Mather as 'an honest and devout, but sufficiently credulous man'. For the tracts see *CLA*, 150.

64.23   twelfth class of Granger's engraved British portraits   Rev. J[ames] Granger, *A Biographical History of England from Egbert the Great to the Revolution Consisting of Characters Disposed in different classes and Adapted to a Methodical Catalogue of Engraved British Heads*, 2nd edn, 4 vols (London, 1775); Scott possessed the 4th edn, 4 vols (London, 1805: *CLA*, 235). The quotation is taken from 'Plan of the Catalogue of Engraved British Portraits', on un-numbered pages before the prefatory material of Vol. 1.

64.32–39   A General and Rare ... Birmingham, 1742   see *CLA*, 127 and 154. This book furnished Scott with materials for *The Pirate* (1822). For more information see the notes to *The Pirate*, ed. Mark Weinstein and Alison Lumsden, EEWN 12 (Edinburgh, 2001).

65.4–16   A Compleat History ... London, 1719   *CLA*, 131.

65.17–24   Sir Richard Steele ... Englishman, No.48   Richard Steele (1672–1729), dramatist and journalist, founded the political paper *The Englishman* (1713–14), as well as working on *The Spectator* and *The Tatler*. Scott has copied this passage from *The Englishman* onto the fly-leaf of his copy of Smith's *Compleat History* at Abbotsford.

65.28–29   first edition ... printed for Markhew   *The History of the Lives, of the Most Noted Highwaymen ...* (London, 1714), was published by J. Morphew and A. Dodd. No bookseller of the name *Markhew* was operating in Britain in 1714.

65.30–39   Ausfürliche ... diverse cruelties   *CLA*, 149. This book, published in Frankfurt and Leipzig in 1727, is edited by Dr John Benjamin Weissenbruch, an assessor of the criminal tribunal. Scott himself had a long-standing interest in gypsies and wrote a number of articles on them for *Blackwood's Magazine* (rather than the *Quarterly*). These included 'Notes Concerning the Scottish Gypsies' which appeared in *Blackwood's* in April, May and September 1817 (1.43–58, 154–61, 615–20). John Hoyland's study, *A Historical Survey of the Customs, Habits, & Present State of The Gypsies; Designed to Develope the Origin of this Singular People, and to Promote the Amelioration of their Condition*, was published at York in 1816. Scott had responded to Hoyland's request to Scottish sheriffs for information and his articles refer to the book, and his letter appears in Hoyland's book at 93–96. Scott wrote a further article which appeared as 'On the Gypsies of Hesse-Darmstadt in Germany' (*Blackwood's Magazine* (2.409–14). He does not refer to Hoyland's book in this article, but does specifically mention this German study and states (409): 'The volume from which I collected the information which I now transmit to you, fell into my hands at the sale of foreign books made last month by Mr John Ballantyne'. He continues: 'The work is a quarto, the German title of which may be translated, "A circumstantial Account of the famous Egyptian Bands of Thieves, Robbers, and Murderers, whose Leaders were executed at Giessen, by Cord, and Sword, and Wheel, on the 14th and 15th November 1726"'.

65.33   wheel   mode of execution whereby criminals were tied to a wheel and their limbs broken with an iron bar.

66.1–6 A Recantation... London, 1628 *CLA*, 127.
66.6–7 John Clavell... "stand to a true man" Clavell (1603–42), a highwayman, was condemned to death and then pardoned in 1627. The poem (London, 1628) is a metrical autobiography which offers to: 'stand and deliver to your observation Right serious thoughts...'. The passage quoted appears on pages 12–13 of this volume. The phrase 'stand to a true man' comes from *1 Henry IV*, 1.2.105–06.
66.9–10 Anthony Wood mentions... gallantly for the king Anthony a Wood (1632–95), antiquary and historian. Jonathan Oldbuck borrows a phrase from Wood in *The Antiquary*, 20.
66.10–11 but weary fa the waefu wuddy a curse upon the woeful hangman's rope: Robert Burns, 'Love and Liberty—A Cantata' (written 1785; first published 1799), line 86.
66.26 The rolling stone... moss proverbial: *ODEP*, 682.
67.7 Daniel Defoe... Chalmers Defoe (1660?–1731) was a novelist and journalist: see *CLA*, 125–26. The controversy on the subject of which works can be attributed to Defoe continues into modern times with P. N. Furbank and W. R. Owens providing one of the more recent contributions to the debate in their study *Defoe De-attributions: A Critique of J. R. Moore's 'Checklist'* (London and Rio Grande, 1994). George Chalmers (1742–1825), who produced the first comprehensive bibliography of Defoe in 1790 as an appendix to a new edition of his *Life of Daniel De Foe*, attributed 128 works to him.
67.16–18 Topsell's History... 1658 *CLA*, 122. The chief claim to fame of Edward Topsell (d. 1638), divine and author, is as the compiler of two elaborate manuals of zoology, which were drawn mainly from the works of Conrad Gesner.
67.20–24 Burton's Anatomy... 1676 *CLA*, 123. Robert Burton (1577–1640) published the first edition of his book in 1621.
67.25 The Voyages and Adventures... Travels London, 1663: *CLA*, 123.
67.27–29 William Godwin... credibility William Godwin, 1756–1836. *St Leon* was published in 1799, one of a series of novels designed to broadcast his philosophical and anarchical political views. In his copy at Abbotsford Scott has inscribed on the fly-leaf: ' "Ferdinand Mendez Pinto was but a Type of the first magnitude." Love for Love.' The quotation comes from Congreve's *Love for Love* (1695), 2.1.236. Godwin's motto reads: 'Ferdinand Mendez Pinto was but a type of thee thou liar of the first magnitude'.
67.30–31 The Divine Weekes and Works of Du Bartas, translated by Sylvester *CLA*, 123. Guillame de Saluste du Bartas (1544–90), French poet and soldier. Josuah Sylvester (1563–1618) was a poet; his translations of parts of the *Divine Weekes* appeared 1584–99 and were published as *Du Bartas his Devine Weekes and Workes* in 1605–06.
67.32 Sylva Sylvarum of Lord Bacon Francis Bacon (1561–1626), *Sylva Sylvarum... whereunto is newly added the History naturall and Experimentall of Life and Death*, 6th edn (London 1651): *CLA*, 229. The first edition appeared in 1627.
67.33–34 Thomas Heywood's... Angels (1574–1641), prolific dramatist, and author of *Nine Books of Women* (*CLA*, 123), and *The Hierarchie of the blessed Angels* (*CLA*, 123).
67.35 Reginald Scott's... London, 1665 *CLA*, 123. The first edition of this work by Reginald Scott (1538?–99) was published in 1584. In a note to *The Antiquary* (Magnum, 5.314) Scott writes: 'A great deal of stuff to the same purpose with that placed in the mouth of the German adept, may be found in

Reginald Scot's Discovery of Witchcraft . . . the work of Reginald Scot is a compilation of the absurd and superstitious ideas concerning witches so generally entertained at the time, and the pretended conclusion is a serious treatise on the various means of conjuring astral spirits'.

69.3 Dalilahs of the collector's imagination Delilah was a Philistine who attracted Samson and distracted him from serving his own people and God: see Judges Chs 14–16. Metaphorically the term denotes any temptation. John Dryden refers to ranting passages in his earlier plays as 'those Dalilahs of the theatre' in his Dedication to *The Spanish Friar* (1681): *The Works of John Dryden*, ed. Walter Scott, 18 vols (Edinburgh, 1808), 6.377. Scott used the phrase of his childhood love of ballads in his 'Memoirs' (*Scott on Himself*, ed. David Hewitt (Edinburgh, 1981), 28), and of Abbotsford in *Letters*, 5.60. In his article on 'Pitcairn's Criminal Trials' Scott describes rare books as the 'Dalilahs of their [bibliomaniacs'] imagination' (*Prose Works*, 21.206).

69.11 3 Tom, in Folios i.e. 3 volumes, with the sheets of paper comprising the book being folded once to produce 2 leaves, 4 pages.

69.11 History of Lancelot du Lac *CLA*, 122. Scott discusses this work in 'An Essay on Romance' (1824), stating: 'It is in the prose folios of *Lancelot du Lac*, *Perceforest*, and others, that antiquaries find recorded the most exact accounts of fights, tournaments, feasts, and other magnificent displays of chivalric splendour; and as they descend into more minute description than the historians of the time thought worthy of their pains, they are a mine from which the painful student may extract much valuable information' (*Prose Works*, 6.185–86). The French reads: 'newly published in Paris, 1533. Sold in Paris in Rue St Jacques by Philippe le Noir, one of the two accredited bookbinders of the University of Paris at the sign of the White Rose and Crown'.

69.17 de Bure Guillaume-François De Bure, *Bibliographie Instructive: ou Traité de la connoissance des livres rares et singuliers* [literally, Instructive Bibliography, or a treatise of information about rare and unusual books], 7 vols (Paris, 1763–69: *CLA*, 39). On the missing leaf Scott must have been continuing the discussion of Arthurian romances which he began with *Lancelot du Lac*.

69.21–24 La Tres . . . dieu. &c. *CLA*, 122. The title means: 'The very delightful, mellifluous, and very pleasing history of the most noble victorious and most excellent king Perceforest, king of Great Britain, and founder of the Noble Palace and of the Temple of the supreme God'. In the romance the *Noble Palais* is both the name of an order of chivalry and of a place. Scott discusses this work in 'An Essay on Romance' (1824) suggesting that it 'may serve to show that modern authors were not the first who invented the popular mode of introducing their works to the world as the contents of a newly-discovered manuscript' (*Prose Works*, 6.179). The copy at Abbotsford has 1531 written in ink on the title page.

69.27–34 Le Premier Livre . . . 1552 *CLA*, 122. The French reads: 'the First Book of the Chronicle of the very valiant and redoubtable Lord Flores of Greece, known as the Knight of Swans, second son of Esplandian, emperor of Constantinople. A story not previously heard, but an excellent one and most highly recommended. Put into French by the Lord of Essars, Nicolas de Herberay, an artillery commissioner in ordinary. In Paris, for Jan Longis, bookseller, whose shop is in the Palais, in the gallery which takes one to the Chancery'. For Nicolas de Herberay see note to 70.18.

70.5–6 like the shipwrecked sailors . . . immense gulph see Virgil (70–19 BC), *The Aeneid*, 1.118: 'apparent rari nantes in gurgite vasto' (the crew can be seen here and there, swimming in the vast ocean).

70.6–8 demanded with Audrey . . . a true thing or no see *As You Like It*, 3.3.15.

EXPLANATORY NOTES   137

70.13–14   Flores of Greece ... Bellianis of Greece   see 69.27–32. Both
Flores of Greece and Bellianis of Greece provide continuations of the Spanish
romance *Amadis de Gaul*. Scott elaborates on the relationship between these
romances in 'An Essay on Romance' (*Prose Works*, 6.196–99), and in his 1803
review in *The Edinburgh Review*, of Robert Southey's and William Stewart Rose's
versions of *Amadis de Gaul* (*Prose Works*, 18.1–43).

70.14–16   famous ... Don Quixote's library   the examination of Don
Quixote's library by the curate and barber takes place in Part 1, Ch. 6 of Miguel
de Cervantes Saavedra (1547–1616), *The Adventures of Don Quixote* (Part 1,
1605; Part 2, 1615); see *CLA* 101. Here, the barber claims to have found 'the
renowned Don Belianis'. Although the barber and curate order that all books
that are 'of the lineage of Amadis' should be burnt in the yard the work is spared
from the fire (see note to 46.26) and the priest suggests that the barber removes
it to his own house.

70.17   called into review   subjected to examination.

70.18   Nicolas de Herberay   Nicholas Herberay des Essarts (died *c.* 1552),
French translator of *Amadis de Gaul* from its Spanish original. His translation
contributed to the development of idealistic romance in France.

70.21–23   French romance ... Mr Utterson   *CLA*, 276. Edward V. Utterson (1776–1856), literary antiquary and one of the original members of the
Roxburghe Club. *Cheuelere Assigne or the 'Knight of the Swan'* was published for
the Roxburghe Club in 1820. Utterson describes the history of the poem in his
introduction and says that it is 'the story of the Knight of the Swan and his
descendants, though a strange tissue of romance and historical truth, down to
the capture of Jerusalem, in the eleventh century, by the Christians under the
guidance of Godfrey of Bouillon'. The text of Utterson's edition is taken from
the Cotton Manuscripts in the British Library.

70.30–33   Les prouesses ... Petit   *CLA*, 121. The French reads: 'The
feats and marvellous deeds of the noble Huon of Bordeaux, peer of France,
duke of Guyenne'. A woodblock at the end of this book bears the name 'Jehan
Petit'. It is listed in the Abbotsford catalogue as published in Paris, 1516. Scott
writes extensively about this poem in 'An Essay on Romance' (*Prose Works*,
6.182).

70.33–36   foundation of the very gay ... excellent original   *Huon de
Bordeaux* formed the basis of the vast fairy-tale *Oberon* by Cristoph Martin
Wieland (1733–1813): *CLA*, 52. Wieland's work was translated from German
into English by William Sotheby as *Oberon, A Poem*, 2 vols (London, 1798).

71.2   fratricide Cain   Cain murdered his brother Abel: see Genesis 4.8.

71.2   Rabbinical fiction   fiction characterised by its similarity to the writings of the Rabbis, the chief Jewish authorities on matters of law and doctrine.

71.4–5   belonged to the celebrated Roxburghe collection   Scott has
written on the fly-leaf of the copy at Abbotsford 'From the Roxburghe Collection' (*CLA*, 121).

71.6–7   Rabelais ... original edition by Du Chat   Jacob Le Duchat
(1658–1735) produced an annotated version of François Rabelais (*c.* 1494–1553),
Oeuvres, 6 vols (Paris, 1732). Scott owned a revised edition, 3 vols (Paris, 1741:
CLA, 122). Rabelais's *Le Grant roy de Gargantua*, and *Les Horribles et espouvant-
ables faictz et prouesses du très renommé Pantagruel* were both originally published
in Lyon in 1525.

71.8–9   Scottish edition ... broad Scottish   Sir Thomas Urquhart
(1611–60), of Cromarty, whose translation of the first two books of Rabelais's
Gargantua and Pantagruel romances was first published in 1653: *The Lives,
Heroick Deeds, and Sayings of Gargantua and his Sonne Pantagruel*, and *The*

Heroick Deeds and Sayings of the good Pantagruel (London, 1653). A third book was published in 1693, and all three, together with Pierre Motteux's translation of Books 4 and 5, appeared again in 1694. Scott possessed an 1807 edition of the revised version of Urquhart and Motteux's translation, *The Works of Francis Rabelais . . . Now carefully revised, and compared throughout with the late new edition of M. Le du Chat*, ed. John Ozell, 4 vols (London, 1784): see *CLA*, 121. Urquhart's translation is not in 'broad Scottish', but in English, at times plain English but at others a fantastical language well adapted to accommodate both the extravagance and the earthiness of the original French.

71.18–21   Yseult . . . love   Sir Tristrem was one of the earliest romances in English and was probably drawn from earlier French sources. There are several versions of the story: in one Tristram, son of Roland is slain by King Mark of Cornwall as he sits harping before Yseult; in another he dies in despair believing Yseult has abandoned him as he lies wounded from a poisoned arrow. Yseult, his lover, and in some versions wife, was the daughter of the Duke of Brittany. It is not clear which particular book Scott was about to discuss, but there are two manuscript copies of versions of the Sir Tristrem story in the same press, one transcribed and with notes by George Ellis: see *CLA*, 103–04. Scott himself edited the version in the Auchinleck manuscript (in the National Library of Scotland): *Sir Tristrem*, ed. Walter Scott (Edinburgh, 1804). He ascribed the poem to Thomas [Learmonth] of Ercildoun, but the manuscript is now considered to be of northern English origin.

GLOSSARY

This selective glossary defines single words, but proper names and phrases are treated in the Explanatory Notes. It covers Scots and archaic words, and occurrences of words in senses that are not familiar in modern English. For each word, or each distinguishable sense, up to four occurrences are noted; when a word occurs five times or more only the first instance is given, followed by 'etc.' Because words often need to be explained in their contexts, at times the reader is referred to the appropriate Explanatory Note.

accession act of joining 14.14
accoutre equip 13.27
affability openness of manner 57.42
afflatus for 14.36 see note
airn-cap *Scots* iron cap, helmet 3.3
amateur for 44.7 see note
amulet something worn as a charm to prevent evil or mischief 6.6
anchorite hermit 52.10
anes *Scots* once 28.10
anglice in English 17.5
anonymous for 28.14 see note
antiquarienses for 27.3 see note
apropos as regard to 42.2
ardelio busybody or meddler 3.4
armouris for 30.12 see note
artist professional architect or designer 28.13, 29.3; craftsman 28.26
assoilzie acquit from a charge 15.8
athorter *Scots* athwart, across in various directions 10.1
attaint accuse, make charges against 12.30
auld *Scots* old 3.2, 3.6, 28.3, 30.13
Bacchanalian for 31.29 see note
bairn child 10.4
band *heraldry* see note to 30.4–8
bannet bonnet 9.37
bargain contend, make wagers 15.28
bibliomaniac someone afflicted with a mania for collecting books, avid book collector 45.29, 50.33
bibliomaniacal suffering from a mania for book collecting 16.12, 36.37

bident sheep or other animal whose two rows of teeth are complete, used for sacrifice 8.21
bizarrerie the bizarre as a principle in design or decoration 29.6
black-lead blacking for iron cooking-pots, fire grates etc. 32.39
black-letter an old style of type, similar to Gothic 46.16 (see note), 50.16, 50.19, 69.26
blazon proclaim, make public, trumpet 7.23, 22.23
blazonry collection of heraldic devices 30.30
bookpresses book-cupboards, book-cases 36.23
bookselling publishing 37.19
born borne 9.17
borne held liable for 15.17
boutgate round-about way or course 57.3
broun brown 9.36
buckie *Scots* whelk 8.22, 9.20
buffet-stool for 9.40 see note
buffoon comic actor, 'man whose profession is to make sport by low jests' [Johnson] 7.13
burges for 14.28, 14.29 see note to 14.28–30
cabin small room 8.15 etc.
cabinet case for the safe custody of valuable items 8.4
candor openness of mind 58.1
canons rules for judging *or* the list of books comprising the genre 70.30

cant pet phrase, phrase used as the 'secret' language of some group 5.35

canting-dictionary dictionary of thieves' slang 65.11

career charge of a cavalryman during battle or tournament 33.27

caup *Scots* wooden bowl for carrying food 10.3

cautelous cautious 66.3

censor person who keeps the roll of members or persons attending a meeting 17.11

centaur for 7.10 and 8.11 see note to 7.10

centurae *Latin* waist bands or girdles 9.4

chimæra for 7.10 and 9.12 see note to 7.10

close closed, apart 8.15

cloud diversify with patches of colouring of uncertain outline 41.14

coal-sink mine-shaft 57.16

colosse colossus, vast structure 7.15

compleat complete 65.4

condiddle filch, purloin 50.35

condiddler thief 51.1, 51.6

consideration importance 17.13

contortized contortioned, twisted 9.8 (see note)

contrare *adjective* adverse, unfavourable 11.27; *noun* contrary 12.21, 12.32

copartment compartment 25.9, 70.5

copperplate engraving 43.9

coug *Scots* cog, wooden vessel or tub made of staves 10.3

cozen cheat 67.2

crescent *heraldry* see note to 30.4–8

crisp curly 9.9

cross-light lights coming from different directions 28.27 (see note)

crypt for 52.22 see note

cuirasse armour worn by a horse soldier reaching down to the waist 34.30 (see note)

curious skilfully made or executed 9.7

cuts woodcuts 65.15

damp noxious gas in a coal-mine 57.9

deal plank of pine or fir 32.5

decore adorn, embellish 9.6

dedicate solemnly commit 13.20

defensative something that defends, a defence 63.20, 63.38

deperdition destruction by wasting away 27.10

derogate work adversely to 12.7

disappoint fail to comply with, frustrate 21.2

dispend spend, expend 11.41

dissenting declining to worship in the established church 59.33

dogmata dogma, principles, opinions held as truth 19.13

Doric for 27.31 see note

dub *Scots* small stagnant pool of water 8.34

easy comfortable, reasonably prosperous 17.20

elevation for 27.16 see note

enchiridion handbook, manual, concise treatise used for guide or reference 58.7

encomium eulogy, formal expression of praise 56.26 (see note)

ensign sign 9.21

escutcheon shield on which a coat of arms is painted 30.10, 30.12, 41.9

esquire gentleman owning land 30.3

even evening 13.36

excursive discursive 16.38

exhalation meteor 22.14

extrinsic lying outside, not relevant to 56.3

fa *Scots* fall 66.11 (see note)

fanning fan-tracery; a feature of gothic architecture consisting of vaulting composed of pendant semi-cones covered with foliated panel-work 28.7

field *heraldry* see note to 30.4–8

folio for 67.17 etc. see note to 69.11

foot-pad person on foot who robs travellers 65.5

fouth *Scots* plenty, abundance 3.2

fowse fosse, ditch 7.16

freak for 22.8 see note

fritter for 28.25 see note

frized curled 9.9

front forehead 9.17

fuer for 28.6 see note

gabion for 1.3 etc. see note to 1.3

gae go 33.11 (see note)

gaes dyke in a coal-seam 57.5

gambade for 22.8 see note

gate way 33.9
gaudie for 9.22 see note
glaxe *Scots* glaik, child's toy or puzzle sometimes of notched wood 9.32
guardareilly for 10. 5 see note
guildrie for 14.30 see note to 14.28–30
gull hoax 56.6
gulph gulf, the deep 70.6
hald *Scots* hold, supply 3.4
halt limp 20.37
handsel *Scots* celebrate a new undertaking or possession with a gift 49.7 (see note)
hap chance 11.29
harthorn horn of a hart 9.16
hauld *Scots* hold keep, fortified tower 28.4
hobby-horse for 5.24 etc. see note to 5.23–24
humorist fantastic or whimsical person, person addicted to fancies 5.29
humorist humorous talker, actor or writer 64.21
hydrostatics study of the pressures etc. exerted by liquids 58.16
imp child of the devil, one of those with whom witches were supposed to be familiar 59.17
incontinent immediately 15.28
infest trouble, attack 12.33
inspire infuse [some thought or feeling into someone] 5.30
interesting that concerns, is important to 21.35
interlocutor speaker 21.8
intrust entrust 23.8
jacket *Scots* coat of mail 3.3
jannet early variety of apple 9.38 (see note)
judicialles *astrology* determination of the future from the position of the stars 63.24
kail a form of cabbage 33.11
ken know 11.35
knapsea close-fitting metal headpiece worn under a bonnet 9.18
lap enfold 20.27
lapster *Scots* lobster 9.20
level shaft used to drain water from a mine 57.5
list listen to 49.17
lucubration study, particularly

nocturnal study 22.19
march for 30.13 see note
matchlock musket in which the powder is lighted by a slow-burning rope match 19.21
maugre in spite of 12.3
meander *of a river etc.* wandering 57.
meschinnerie for 41.29 see note to 41.26–29
mess dish 51.50 (see note)
mine underground passageway 57.5
mold plan, pattern 28.7
molde stuff, earth regarded as the material of the human 38.38
moliminous massive, weighty 57.16
mop-moss moss 28.5 (see note)
morceau *French* bit, extract 58.14
morter mortar, basin in which food or medicines can be ground 10.2
mortification *Scots law* disposal of property for religious or charitable purposes 24.29
mullet *heraldry* see note to 30.4–8
native for 11.39, 11.40, 11.40 see note to 11.39
neip for 57.18 see note
nook corner 9.31
offend be annoyed, be displeased 10.24
oppose set up in contrast or counterpoise 14.5
or *heraldry* see note to 30.4–8
palmated having the form of an open hand or palm 35.22
panthera *Latin* panther 9.13
parritch-pat *Scots* porridge pot 3.6
partan *Scots* crab 9.20
patrocination action of supporting, maintaining or patronising 58.7
paynted illustrated 63.22
philomath student of astrology 63.1
pinch pinch of snuff 19.32
pithy vigorous, strong 51.11
plaister plaster 33.15
pleadge toast, drink in honour of 15.30
pottage thick vegetable soup 51.50 (see note)
precentor person appointed by a kirk session to lead unaccompanied praise in church 31.4
preen *Scots* pin 17.5
prelacy government of the church by

bishops 32.21

prelatist supporter of a system of church government by bishops 32.27 (see note to 32.27–29)

preses person who presides at a meeting, president 17.11

press cupboard 30.40, 31.3; bookcase with doors or grills 48.10 etc.

pretend present or assert [themselves] 70.2

prithee pray thee 15.20

proceed can be argued 17.28

prodigy extraordinary happening 59.38

proem introductory discourse, preface, or preamble 5.1

prognostic symptom on which a medical outcome is forecast 67.21

prophecie prophesy 14.33

propine offer, present 8.23, 9.25

purtray portray 8.27

quality standing 17.19

quha *Scots* who 30.12

quod quoth, said 15.9, 15.12

rabbinical for 71.2 see note

rampier rampart 57.16

rant *Scots* song 31.30

reader person appointed to read the prayers and lessons in church in the absence of an ordained minister 31.4

receipt recipe 1.11

recherché *French* rare, much sought after 70.28

reft stolen 12.37

registrate recorded 7.24

regulation *here* rules laid down in a will or trust deed 21.2

relics surviving memorials of a people 54.11

rencontre meeting 71.1

robin early variety of pear 9.38 (see note)

rousty *Scots* rusty 3.3

ruling principal, one which surpasses others 20.31

running extending (a mine working) 57.4

sair sore, very 33.8

satyr companion of Bacchus, part man part beast 9.10

sault-backet *Scots* small wooden box for holding salt water, kept near the

fire 3.6

scutcheon escutcheon, shield on which a coat of arms is painted 30.10, 30.15

sexangular for 9.40 see note

shew-house for 27.29 see note

shop-lift shoplifter 65.5

shroud set of ropes from the head of a mast, part of the permanent rigging of a sailing ship 38.12

singularity distinction due to some distinguishing feature 7.17

sith since 12.40

slops padded breeches 61.10 (see note)

soulter swelter 66.34

spar collective term for masts, yards, booms etc. of a sailing ship 38.27

spell engage in study or contemplation 49.18

sphinge for 7.10 see note

stale *Scots, of ale* that has stood for a long time, clear and ready for drinking 9.2

stay is sustained 10.29

strait narrow passage 34.12

strangular *jocular* suitable for strangling or throttling 9.39

stucco fine plaster 41.8

suburban having the inferior status and narrowness of view thought to characterise inhabitants of suburbs 52.27

supplied filled 49.26

swat sweated 8.37

tacket *Scots* hob-nail for boots 3.4

tap *Scots* spinning top 10.4 (see note)

tapster person who draws beer in a public house 9.20

teaze worry, irritate 28.28

tenor character, nature 32.28

testator one who makes his will or testament 21.32

threnodie song of lamentation 6.17

tincture *heraldry* see note to 30.4–8

tine lose 15.11

toil *verb* subject to toil, weary, fatigue 41.23

tom *French* volume 69.11

totum for 10.4 see note

towmont *Scots* twelve months, a year 3.5

traducer person who belittles or defames 12.42

traite trait 70.4

traiteur one who keeps an eating house or who otherwise supplies meals, particularly in France and Italy 25.36

trump trumpet 10.6

turkass pair of smith's pincers or forceps 9.33

vaudeville light popular song, especially a stage song, commonly of a satirical or topical nature 52.4

vennell narrow passageway for pedestrians 35.2

wad *Scots* would 3.4

waefu *Scots* woeful 66.11

weary *Scots* for 66.11 see note

wuddy *Scots* hangman's rope 66.11

ye the 30.12, 30.13

youthead youth 10.25

yron iron 38.38

zany *contemptuous* attendant, follower, comic performer who attends a clown 7.13